"A fast-paced, foul-mouthed thriller, the story of a man clinging to his humanity in a city that sold its own a long time ago."
—*Christopher Ruocchio, internationally best-selling author of The Sun Eater*

"Batman as the detective he's meant to be."
—*Joshua Walker, author of The Song of the Sleepers*

"Payne's debut novel is legally un-putdownable."
—*Scott Palmer, author of The Last Ballad*

"An action movie in book form."
—*A.J. Calvin, author of The Caein Legacy*

"So addictive, it should honestly be criminal."
—*Esmay Rosalyne, Grimdark Magazine*

"Fun and fast-paced from the start. If you're looking for super charged, cyberpunk crime-thriller, you should give this a go!"
—*Matt Pitmann, FanFiAddict*

"Core cyberpunk. A cross between The Dresden Files and Blade Runner."
—*Benjamin Hills, Benjamin's Bookclub*

Cover art by Katerina Belikova (@ninjajo_art on Instagram)

ISBN 979-8-9908126-0-4 (ebook)

ISBN 979-8-9908126-1-1 (paperback)

ISBN 979-8-9908126-2-8 (hardback)

To my Dad.

"I'll get you two of them."

Content Warning

I want to ensure that as many people as possible can read and enjoy my book. If you are sensitive to the below content, please be mindful of these and other potential triggers.

This story contains graphic depictions of violence, dismemberment, body horror, drug use, and frequent profanity.

FALLING
INTO OBLIVION

TENDRILS OF CHROME

BOOK 1

AARON M. PAYNE

1

Pursuit

Rain pours over a sea of umbrellas as I run down a people-infested street, weaving and dodging through the crowd. The cacophony drowns out the sounds of the relentless street ads vying for my attention. Gasping, my lungs feel as if they are about to burst, but I cannot stop. Not now that answers are so close. Not now that I'm so close to getting paid.

The suspect is within sight, frantically speeding ahead, shoving whoever is in his way. I see myself sprinting in the reflection of the building next to me, my faux-leather coat flapping. Sweat burns in the corners of my eyes. Both feet squelch every hurried step I take.

What a waste of 2000 creds. Fucking shoes are supposed to be weather adaptive. I don't care how long it takes on the 1-800-BULLSHIT customer support line. I'm getting my money back.

Growling, I clench my jaw while trying to push my legs faster through the press of bodies clogging the pavement of Nox City. Pushing forward and closing the gap, the lights of street vendors and stores blur past my vision. Cars furiously honk while a zip train barrels above, screeching through the city on an elevated railway.

Hologram advertisements dance and pulsate above autonomous vehicles designed to promote the latest thing you need to buy. Grime coats the walkway and street, trash collecting in growing piles.

Heart thumping, I spot an opening in the crowd a few feet away where I can finally make a move to bring down my target.

Just a little further... almost... almost... NOW!

I jump toward the suspect, reaching as far as I can, trying to grab anything off him. My hand clutches something thin and doesn't let go as I roll onto the waterlogged concrete. The suspect does not lose momentum while approaching the next wave of people with a wire trailing off his jacket. A sharp tug pulls at my grip before the wire pops off with a snap, ending the red neon glow emitting from an embossed logo on the back of his jacket. A circle wrapped around a downward-pointing triangle with circuits in the middle, spreading like the veins of a tree to form the shape of the letter "X." The logo of a modi shop franchise named RootX performing "legal" cybernetic body modifications at several locations across the city. A logo I'm all too familiar with.

The suspect stops and turns, giving me a snarled look. His modified eyes glow a deep purple around each iris, casting an ominous light across his sharp features. Like most Nox City inhabitants, his mouth and nose are covered behind a translucent filtration mask that removes the sting from breathing the noxious air that grips the city. A mop of bright green hair is slicked back, revealing a receding hairline. Under his jacket, a white shirt sticks to his thin, pale body while a silver-plated necklace traces down his neck, ending on a bush of wet chest hair. Tall skyscrapers loom above in the gradually darkening sky as he yells, "Fuck me! Took me fucking three years to get this jacket, and you go and fuck it up the same week I get it!"

Groaning, I stand and shout through the rain, "Mirk, let's make this easy for both of us! We both know you loaded defective modies on that poor kid. He's brain-dead now! Also, it's just a stupid jacket!"

Swirling gray clouds continue to pour sheets of rain. Water seeps into every fiber of my clothes. I inch my cold, wet hand toward my belt, where my Z4 hand cannon rests.

"I didn't do shit!" Mirk roars back. "Those modies came from a clean supplier. All legal! So, you can back the fuck off! Why the hell am I explaining this to you, you plebo pig?" Mirk turns toward a new wave of incoming bodies, his legs in motion again. "I didn't do shit!"

Sighing, I rip my Z4 out of its holster, thumbing the dial to the tracker-bolt setting. With a tracker set, I shouldn't have to worry about running through this wretched crowd anymore. An image forms in my mind, a location pin flickering on my map, giving me precise directions. I can't afford to botch my aim if I want to keep my promise to Zinny. With a quick glance, I double-check the holographic display on the side of the silver barrel. A couple of dials too far would incinerate Mirk and those around him.

It would be hard to explain why I'm bringing my perp back to the station in a plastic bag.

Holding my breath, I aim and squeeze the trigger. The display counts down from four to three as a bolt launches out of the barrel, speeding toward Mirk. Just before he disappears into the incoming crowd, the bolt launches the tip of the round and sticks a tracker beacon to the back of his jacket.

Holstering my Z4, I speak to no one in particular. "Why do they always have to run?"

It does make the job more interesting, though.

With the tracker set, I make a fist with my left hand and turn it inwards to display my holo grid above my wrist. I tap the display until I open the tracking app to get a readout on Mirk's location. The corners of my mouth twist into a frown, irritation making my eyes twitch while reading the screen. *ERROR! Unable to recall tracker TRK5467899103 due to error code 117.*

"Shit..."

I take a deep breath of filtered Nox City air and let out a long sigh. Technology not wanting to play nice for me again. It always has to be something. Echoes of malfunctioning tech play across my mind.

I'm sorry, Raena. It's looking like I'll be late for dinner... again. She always tells me she understands with a half-smile, but I know she is disappointed. I'm not happy about it either, but no bonus is coming my way without closing this case. Unease ignites in my gut, glancing at the notification of an unread message on my display. I chew on my lip, knowing who it's from. Somebody looking for a debt to be paid, and they're not the only ones. I swipe the notification away, sidelining my worry for now.

A glimmer of hope blooms in my chest while staring at the time on my holo grid. 5:34 p.m., perfect. I still have plenty of time to read that book to Zinny.

2

Tracker

Technology seems to never work when I need it the most.

Pulling up the tracker app again, tendrils of annoyance creep across my face. I should be seeing a readout on Mirk's location overlayed on a map, but instead, Error 117 flashes in my face as if to mock me. My eyes continue reading the error, hoping it will fix itself, but it doesn't. I click the refresh button. Same error. I click the refresh button again. Same error.

My eyes roll back while droplets of rain trail down my forehead. There's no getting around it. I'm going to need to call for help if I want to close this case anytime soon.

Moisture clinging to every inch of my body, I finally decide to escape the endless rain and start walking toward somewhere that has cover, preferably a spot with indoor seating, so I can take off this vexing mask. My feet slosh with every step, only further reminding me of my wasted money. Slowly, I shuffle my way through the crowd toward food joints I can see in the distance. I inhale deep draws of breath while pushing out steady streams of air through my parted lips. My racing adrenaline starts to subside.

People from all walks of life stumble, wander, hobble, or walk with determination around me in a chaotic symphony. Continuing to put one foot in front of the other, noise and color envelop me.

A grunt escapes my lips and a spasm of pain shoots up my leg as something clunks against my knee. A battered transport droid releases a modulated wail, rolling back from my leg. I shake my head and rub my knee, staring toward the tarnished chrome droid wobbling back into the maw of humanity.

"Goddamn droids," I mutter. Well, that's probably going to bruise, and Raena is not going to be happy about it.

With a deep inhale, I wince, pulling my hand from my knee, and begin moving again. Staring ahead, I try to peer over the hundreds of umbrellas to see if I am getting any closer to the food joints. Narrowing my eyes, I spot an orange flashing-neon symbol of a cup of steaming coffee.

Dropping my gaze below the surface of the wall of canopies, I glance at the press of bodies passing by. Bloodshot eyes, nervous lip-licking, hunched shoulders, fidgeting hands, incoherent mumbling, and pleading sobs surround me. Within the second of locking eyes in the ebb and flow of traffic, I catch a mix of emotions from the people who are not transfixed on their Infinity devices.

I wonder what they see behind my eyes.

My nose scrunches from hints of rancid odors permeating my mask. Shaking my head, I know it's not from just people. Trash collection looks to be an afterthought in this section of the city with mounds of discarded waste gathering in random piles and nauseating green-brown liquids oozing from them.

My face contorts with revulsion while staring at a pile of tattered bags, entrails of rot spilling into the street. I flick my eyes toward the towering buildings that stand like steel monoliths. My scowl deepens while tracing the walkways and paths connecting the skyscrapers, creating a separate world up high.

"Veridian," I say, my voice coming out as a snarl.

Images flicker in my mind of enormous homes, immaculate shopping centers, state-of-the-art healthcare facilities, and pampered, perfect little families resting on top of piles of credits. I glare at the skyscrapers and lavish cars flying to and from the various buildings. Taking a deep breath, I envision greenery being used as decoration. A longing bitterness wells within me thinking of seeing colorful flowers, or even a tree, a *real* tree.

I stare back at the pile of trash to the right of me. The closest thing to a tree down here is a hologram version being used in an advertisement. Other than that, the stacks of trash bags could resemble a tree if I squint hard enough.

The people around me seem oblivious to this trash-filled reality, with the majority focusing on their heads-up display or holo grid, sucked into the world of Infinity. A "utopia" where problems don't exist. A virtual and augmented paradise.

It doesn't matter where you are. If people are involved, there will be problems.

I tighten my jaw, tugging at my soaked black T-shirt, rain continuing to pour on my already sodden clothes. A crack of thunder booms as if confirming that the rain is not going to stop anytime soon.

As I step through a holographic ad of a young female with angled, sleek black hair and glowing pink eyes, I wince from seemingly non-existent speakers. "One tablet is all you need," blares in a seductive voice while she holds a sparkling translucent pill between two fingers, placing it on her outstretched tongue. She swallows the pill and offers a gentle smile. The ad flickers to a smiling family embracing while laughing. "Ask your doctor about Senervamene today. Sicarius Pharmaceuticals, we're here for you now and for the you of tomorrow."

I scoff, knowing the ad is bullshit. Just another corporation wanting to take my credits. Too bad for them, I don't have any modies installed. No need to get a script for a monthly pill to keep the damn implants functional. I try to swallow my annoyance, the sound of the looping ad fading behind me.

Finally approaching the entrance of a food joint, I glance at a flashing neon sign declaring its name, "Grubbies." The sliding door opens as I step forward, allowing me to pass through an enclosed breezeway to a second entrance. With the door behind me hissing shut, I make my way to a seat in one of the remaining empty booths, where a holographic menu materializes above the table. Reaching behind my right ear, I unclasp my mask, which comes loose with a quick pop as the air-tight seal releases. The smell of burnt bread and frying oil seeps into my nostrils. I tap around the menu and order a coffee, two creams, and two sugars. Caffeine. An essential in my life.

We're all addicted to something, right?

A second later, a white-marred tubular droid on three wheels pops out of an opening that I assume leads to the kitchen. A screen on top of the droid displays, *"Proceeding to table 4,"* with a tray balanced on two outstretched arms. On the tray is a cup of steaming coffee with two packets of synthetic sugar, two packets of powdered cream, and a plastic stirring stick on the side. While grabbing the tray, the screen flickers to *"Customer, for 18.99, would you like to try our new SynaBLT Burrito? Made with 5% real juicy meat."* A white tortilla sparkles and flashes on the screen. I roll my eyes and click *"No."*

"Thank you, customer. Have a grubby day." The screen flashes a thumbs-up icon and emits a high-pitched chime. A second later, it rolls back to where it came from, waiting to serve the next order.

What the hell does "have a grubby day" mean?

Setting the tray on the table, a sense of unease trickles up my spine. I can't shake the feeling that eyes are studying me. My heart rate quickens and I become hyper-aware of my surroundings. Slowly, I raise my gaze. The glint of something reflective stands out in the corner of my vision. My eyes flick to the source and narrow.

Blue shades in the shape of an elongated triangle hug the narrow face of a woman sitting in the corner. Her arms are crossed and a look of disgust curls her red lips down. She steps out of the booth and rises to her full height.

Recognition sets in my mind. My hands clench into fists.

"Fuck me," I mutter.

Memories start flooding into my brain as if the wall of a dam suddenly collapsed.

Vanya steps closer, her skin-tight leggings squeaking with each step. She stops adjacent to my table and turns in my direction. Her hand moves to her shades and plucks them off the bridge of her nose, resting the frames on top of her dark brown hair. Her glowing white irises bore into me.

"Sol," she says with disdain. "So, after all these years, you're still plebo." She shakes her head and sighs. "When are you going to wake up? You can be so much more." She raises her palm and a hologram sparks to life, depicting a shimmering ball of flames.

Modifications...

"I'm fine," I bark. "I'm not putting that shit in my body."

A sad chuckle escapes her. "Still the same boy." Her fist closes and the hologram winks out. "You're never going to change, are you, Sol?"

I try to swallow my building annoyance. Staring up at her, I see the youthful girl I used to be friends with behind her smug expression. There was a time I thought she was going to be my future, but I was young and naive.

"Just leave me be," I say, averting my eyes.

"Whatever," she snaps. "You're the one that fucked it up, remember?" She leans forward and raises her brows.

I don't say a word and grind my teeth. I grab my cup of coffee which feels heavy in my hand.

"I shouldn't have bothered. You'll always be a burnout." She storms off toward the exit, clipping a mask around her face and placing her shades back over her eyes.

My mind starts swirling. Mirk getting away. Wanting to head home to my family. Vanya's words. *Burnout.* I'm not a fucking burnout just because I don't want modies installed. Call me plebo all you want. I don't give a fuck. She doesn't know jack shit about me. What has it been? Twelve or thirteen years since I last saw her? It doesn't even matter anymore. She's out of my life and has been for a long time.

My vision blurs. I can't help but think about what she's been up to since our last conversation. My face twists at the memory. I picture the exchange of words thrown back and forth. I try to shake it from my mind. There are more important things to worry about.

Taking a deep breath, I look around. The place is filled with people. Glowing eyes, flickering body decorators, chrome teeth, and facial holographic projections surround me. Is this the *change* that Vanya wants? It seems ridiculous to have modifications purely in the hopes of altering your appearance. Here and in Infinity, people spending thousands of creds to appear as something they are not. I roll my eyes at the thought of spending my hard-earned money to have useless implants installed into my bones. What's even more confusing is thinking of spending credits on my Infinity profile avatar. It doesn't make sense to me. It's not real. All it is, is just pixels online, that's it, nothing else.

Infinity... It's just another way to hide from the truth of our trash-filled reality.

People are addicted to the online world. I envision thousands, maybe millions in this city strapping a headset on, logging in to their profiles, and slumping back into their chairs, effectively making them warm, breathing meat sacks. As if nothing else existed outside, their eyes and minds are in Infinity while their bodies rot away.

I glance at the holo grid device strapped around my wrist and frown. Even the NCPD is wrapped around Infinity's finger. This piece of plastic is my only way to communicate, pull files, access internal databases, process reports, and run background checks.

Scanning the joint, I notice a plump, elderly man with his neck arched back and his head resting against the cushion of the booth. Blotches of ketchup stain his oversized white shirt. His mouth is open. If it weren't for the feeds and screens bouncing all over his mask, I would have thought he was dead. I smack my lips in disgust, seeing the reverse of an explicit video playing on his display. The corners of his mouth rise into a smile. I glance away and shake my head. Another lowlife using their filtration mask as an Infinity heads-up display. Instead of seeing filth and ads in the real world, he can see windows into the web along with filth, ads, plus whatever smut he's watching now.

Sighing, I think back to the last time I placed an Infinity rig over my face. I understand there are benefits to it, but I don't like being in such a vulnerable state. My body slumped and my mind somewhere else entirely. Sometimes, though, if the case requires it, I will suck it up and enter the "utopia" of Infinity.

I sip my coffee, which is still too hot to drink. I'm relieved that touch, smell, and taste cannot be simulated in Infinity, but it's only a matter of time. Will people leave their homes anymore? With Nox City as it is, I can't blame them if they don't, but they gotta eat, right?

Setting the cup back down, I stare at the holo grid strapped to my left wrist and frown. The holo grid is the most common implant people receive, but even that I am reluctant to put in my body, opting for the external version. It must have been a dead giveaway to Vanya. Sure, there are benefits to having a device implanted into my arm, but I worry.

Technology doesn't always work. Technology is not always secure. Technology is created by somebody with profits in mind. Technology can fuck you up, implanted or not.

Just a couple of months ago, I was dealing with people being slaughtered in their sleep because the *Algorithm* selected them.

The NCPD found all these bodies with a nice little note left by the killer. *"Congratulations. You have been chosen by the Algorithm."*

It wasn't some almighty computer program instructing which people should die. Turns out it was just some soulless asshole who worked at a company installing home security systems. The fucker had complete control over the home without any resistance or warning to the residents. After a couple of button taps, he strolled right in and gutted whoever was inside. Time and time again.

I clench one fist and rub the back of my neck with my other hand.

Why put some overpriced tech in my body that has the risk of it being defective? Something that has the risk of being compromised? Something that will make me reliant on a drug just to keep my body from rejecting it. It doesn't make sense to me, but looking around this lousy diner, it must make sense to thousands of others.

I mean, look at my current case. Benji Davis is brain-dead because of a slimy bastard installing faulty modies.

Burnout... Fuck off, Vanya.

I push out a long, steady breath of air and relax my shoulders. Lifting my wrist, I bring up the display on my holo grid. I navigate different menus until I get to a screen displaying a person named Tommy Coleson. I have two options: call or message. My finger hesitates above the call button.

Coleson is young, but he's one of the most gifted technical agents I know. It still surprises me how fast he can break down network security barriers. He puts everyone on his team to shame and makes cyber investigation look like child's play. He is unmatched in the field. I sigh, knowing I need to borrow his skills again.

My finger finally descends, tapping the call button, and a ringing chime sounds. Waiting to see if Coleson picks up, I briefly overhear the conversation in the booth in front of me.

A twenty-something kid with spiked blonde hair streaked with blue is talking while chewing a mouthful of food. "You try out that"—*smack smack*—"that new shit yet? Fuckin ginchy stuff man, like nothing I have tried before."

From across the table, a guy with a slim face and sunken, glowing yellow eyes responds, "Nah man, heard there was something fresh coming out, but... what's that shit called again?"

"They're calling it something like—"

My focus shifts as my call is answered. Coleson materializes above my wrist as a four-inch-tall hologram. A deep scowl is plastered on his face, and leering green eyes are visible under a Nox City Police Department cap.

"Harkones? What do you need now? Want to take more credit for your heroic deeds?" Coleson says while talking fast. His mouth morphs into several angry emotions all at once.

After an anxious breath, I respond, "Coleson, I'm sorry I didn't tell the lieutenant you gave me the tip to catch Wendigo. I had a lot thrown at me, and I mean that literally! Electrified knives. Did you forget that? Did you hear the *ELECTRIC* part?"

"A *tip*? A *TIP*? You know that I did more than that, and it doesn't change the fact that after you caught him, you didn't tell the lieutenant that I was the one who found out where he was hiding. I spent days tracking this guy down, and you stroll back into the station with everyone treating you like some investigative prophet."

"I'm sorry! I had a lot of things going on at home, and it must have slipped my mind. If you remember, I booked him and headed home straight after. Coleson, I will let her know when I get back, okay?"

Coleson shakes his head. "Too fucking late, man. You had your chance."

Pinching the bridge of my nose, I take a deep breath. I respond to Coleson, trying to sound as apologetic as possible. I could call another technical agent, but it would take longer to get what I need.

"Coleson, you know how much I value your work. No one else in your division can surf Infinity like you." I offer an apologetic smile. "I need your help with something."

After a long pause, Coleson appears to consider my words as his lowered brows rise, no longer glaring. He runs his tongue along his teeth and sighs. "Fine. You owe me, though, and I'm not going to let you forget it. Now, what do you need?"

My shoulders relax and I push out a sharp breath of relief. "I was in a foot chase trying to catch the suspect of that Benji Davis case—"

"Is that the kid that had his brain fried from those bad modies? Damn, what a grody way to go," Coleson interrupts.

Nodding, my mouth forms into a flat line. "That's the one. I was inches away from nabbing a suspect, but..." I sigh. "He slipped through my fingers. I shot off a tracker that I know landed somewhere on him."

"What's the problem then?" Coleson asks, palms raised while shrugging.

"Error code 117. The tracker landed but I'm not getting any data from it. You able to do anything with that?"

Coleson smacks his lips and crosses his arms. "I should be able to. What's the tracker unit number?"

I swipe back to the tracker app on my holo grid and slowly read off the ID, emphasizing each character.

"Give me a few minutes and I'll reach back out." The call ends before I could say another word, bringing me back to the home screen.

"Okay..." Well, that could have gone worse. Hopefully, he'll call back soon with some good news. Or any news, for that matter. Would love to wrap this up and start heading home. I promised Zinny I would read her that new book she was so excited about.

I take a sip of coffee that finally isn't burning my tongue off and scrunch my face at the sour taste. Something doesn't sit right with the coffee, like it's been burnt two times over, but I'll take whatever I can get. After a couple more sips, I slump further into the booth, exhausted. I stretch my toes and roll my ankles around, trying to get comfort back to my wet feet. Leaning my back against the soft red rubber of the booth, I close my eyes and try to shut off my brain.

What feels like seconds later, my wrist vibrates, making me jolt back up. Glancing at the display, I see that Coleson is calling me back. I tap the answer button, unsure how long my eyes were closed.

Coleson appears above my wrist again, nodding and squinting. "You should be good now. Had to debug the error and reinstate the connection back to the servers, but you should be able to track his path." He looks to the left while leaning closer to a screen that is not visible to me.

"I also checked the last known location of the tracker and sent it over," Coleson says with annoyance etched across his features, brows furrowed and mouth forming into a frown.

A chime sounds on my holo grid a few seconds later, with a message containing the address.

"Looks like he's about ten blocks north of your location at an establishment called... Descent." Coleson squints even harder and purses his lips. "Hmm, this is odd..."

My eyes narrow as I wait for him to continue. Snapping my fingers, I ask, "What is it?"

As if he forgot he was talking to me, he continues. "Oh right, it looks like the tracker is about two hundred feet below ground level."

"Two hundred feet... below ground level? Are you sure?" I ask.

"That's what I'm seeing. So... there you go, have fun with that."

I glance at the address on my display and nod. "Thanks, Coleson, I really do owe you one."

"Yes, you do, and you can start with a pizza and a Diet Zuke. Also, when this is over, don't forget who is helping you... again!" While shaking his head, Coleson flickers out, ending the call.

I down the remaining coffee in my cup, which is now lukewarm, and stand from the booth with a grunt. Walking toward the exit, I clasp my mask back over my face. The airtight seal re-establishes with a soft whoosh. Green lights on each side of the mask come to life, the filtration system kicking on.

Time to descend into the unknown.

3

En Route

Dancing light from countless advertisements streaks my vision as my cruiser zooms toward the address Coleson sent me. About forty stories off the ground, I stare at nothing in particular, my vision blurring. I run my hand through my damp brown hair and chew on my lip. Even with the thunder rumbling outside, it's ominously quiet in the cabin of the sound-absent cruiser. My brain shifts between work and home. An image of Raena and Zinny flashes across my mind, both smiling, suddenly morphing into disappointment. Their heads lower, looking at the ground.

Raena and Zinny. The last thing I want to do is disappoint them, but this is my job. I know it pulls me away, but the money is there. As long as I keep closing cases, we should be able to scrape by, and Zinny won't be kicked out of her school. I'm a couple of months... actually maybe a few months behind on making payments to her academy, but I'll get caught up. My face twists into a frown, knowing I'm also behind on making my loan payments.

Last month was terrible for my wallet, covering low-level cases that took longer than they should to close out. Hopefully, catching Mirk doesn't prove to be the same. QuikCred Loans was my last resort, but I needed to give Zinny's school something. I don't want to dig my hole any deeper. The last thing I need is one of their Torquemen coming after me to collect payment. Once I close this case, the attached bonus should buy some time.

Finances... The last thing I want to think about, but it always slithers into my mind, a continual worry. My detective base salary is shit without racking in the extra lumps of credits. What level is this case again? A level three?

Slowly, I pull my display up and scan over the Benji Davis file again. A sigh escapes my lips, looking at the case level. Just as I thought, level three. The bonus won't be substantial compared to a level five or six, but it should do. I don't remember the last time I've seen anything come close to a level ten. When that happens, something fucked is going on.

Flicking the screen over, I scroll through an endless list of active cases being worked by other detectives, my brows rising. Seeing all the crime taking place in this city never ceases to amaze me. For one thing, these criminals always have light to work by. As the sun descends, neon remains.

My brain shifts, thinking back to when I told Raena that I had been accepted into the NCPD academy. It feels like it was so long ago. I was so eager, so happy, and so full of determination. I remember running inside her apartment and picking her up to tell her the news. She was so excited for me, and I was excited, too. We were smiling and embracing. I told her that this would be the start of our future. It was a great moment.

The corners of my mouth curl up until I remember that it *was* a start. A start to getting deeper into this hellhole of a city. I always knew Nox City wasn't some magical place of bliss and perfection, but seeing violence, blood, death every day for years on end, my excitement has turned sour.

Becoming a detective a couple of years ago was a highlight, though. I enjoy getting deeper into a single case rather than reacting to the countless phone calls made to the station.

After six years as a cop and two years as a detective, I'm still running on this hamster wheel, with a cookie of a bonus held on a string ahead of me. I need to make money for my family, which means I need to catch the lawbreakers. The pay, though, is not consistent. The faster I close cases, the more credits I earn.

I stare again at the Benji Davis case level and let out a frustrated sigh. Why is this taking so long? I shouldn't have let him slip away into that crowd. A sliver of relief enters my mind, knowing I have a new lead to Mirk's location. I bite my lip while rolling my neck. Hopefully, the grimy bastard didn't notice the tracker.

Reading through my case notes, Mirk stands out as the prime suspect—the only suspect, for that matter, due to the overwhelming amount of evidence already stacked against him. Mirk, a modifier, installs modies into Benji one day before the kid becomes catatonic. I think it's a safe bet to say that Mirk has something to do with it, even though he claims he didn't do anything.

The hardest part of this case should be catching him and taking him back to the station. There are a few variables that add to the level-three assessment, mainly coming from his association with RootX and potentially having illegal or dangerous implants not recorded in his self-identification record.

The heads-up display on the front windshield indicates that we are about three minutes away from our destination. I pull up

Mirk's spec sheet again on my holo grid and skim through it one more time to see if anything stands out.

Mirk Spurcus
  Age: 27
  Height: 5ft 5in
  Weight: 154lbs
  Occupation: Modifier at RootX
  Time in Occupation: 3 years
  Recorded Implants: 4
  Criminal Record: Misdemeanors: 3, Felonies: 1

My eyes move left to right, slowly scrolling down the display. I don't see anything alarming that I should note, but I raise my eyebrows when reading "Felony." I tap on the *"Criminal Record"* icon, which takes me to a new screen showing his offense's timeline.

Scrolling down, I start reading off each recorded crime. "Aggravated battery, disorderly conduct, drug possession, and"—I chuckle, reading the last offense—"resisting arrest." Yep, that sounds about right. This all seems in line with the man I tried to catch today, but what strikes me as odd is that his criminal history is from offenses taking place five years ago or even further back.

I guess at some point, old habits come back to the surface. No matter the person, you can't take the crime out of the criminal. Mirk's words echo in my brain, "I didn't do shit." Is there any truth to it?

"No," I mutter, shaking my head. There is no way. There is too much evidence pointing directly at him. We even have a video recording of him installing the modifications on Benji. Plus, he ran when confronted, really fast, by the way.

A blue light illuminates the cruiser cabin, slowly increasing in brightness, and then dims, indicating that we are about to land. A speaker in the cabin confirms this by announcing in a toneless modulated voice, "Prepare for arrival, landing in thirty seconds, thank you."

Through the window, I peer to the ground, which is quickly rising to meet me. The vehicle starts rounding a corner and I spot where it will land. These damn machines have a mind of their own. Hopefully, it doesn't come back to bite us in the ass in the future.

With a metallic clunk, the cruiser lands on top of an above-ground parking lot that is a two-minute walk to Descent. A long whoosh emits from the cruiser, the propulsion units whirring down. Before stepping out, I glance at Mirk's spec sheet and open his implant history.

Eyes narrowing, I read each modification, Optic illumination. "Okay..." Achilles tendon fortification. "Mm-hmm, so that explains how he was able to run so fast." Phalanx transplantation. "Huh," I say, tilting my head. I think that has something to do with hands, but I am not sure. Embedded Holo Network Interface. "Nothing unusual about this one." My eyes lower to the external version wrapped around my wrist.

While standing and ducking so as not to hit my head on the roof of the cruiser, I reach down to double-check that my weapons are still attached to my body. My fingers rest on the familiar grips on both sides of my belt.

Unholstering my Zephyr-400, I wrap one hand around the pistol grip and the other around the foregrip, bringing the hand cannon up to eye level. I stare down the hologram scope, tracing my gaze along the silver body of the barrel. Using my thumb, I flick the dial on the first grip, cycling through the four settings. The holographic display on the side flashes through text that reads PUSH, BLST, TRKR, and SHLD.

I shudder, remembering the last time I used the BLST setting at max charge only a couple of weeks ago. A shockwave of blue energy jerking my arm back and bursting from the barrel. The blast ripped through the air toward a thug aiming an LMG in my direction, tearing through him and disintegrating the upper half of his body. I can swear I still remember him screaming after the fact, but... that's not possible without a head.

Grimacing, I stare at the weapon and holster the bulky pistol back to my side. My fingers move from the cannon, brushing my belt and feeling two metal disks attached to the faux-leather fabric.

"Damn..." I spit out. I wish I could have used one of these EWEBs on Mirk earlier. Just wasn't enough room. Possibly, I could have used my hyper coil, but in that crowd? I can envision it now: people shrieking and scrambling after seeing the coil unfurl, pulsing with electricity. It would have created more chaos.

Satisfied that both weapons are still attached, I rub my hands together and smack my lips. Pressing on a circular red button on the side wall of the cruiser, the single door on the left opens, pointing toward the smog-filled sky. With my mask now clasped around my face, I take a deep breath and exhale, ready for whatever comes next.

4

Descent

Walking toward the tracker's location, the sound of the city hums in my ears until a cacophony of horns blares out. Turning my head, something races past me. A silver Musokie hurtles down the road, its sleek lines catching with nearby light as it zig-zags in and out of traffic. I shake my head in annoyance, seeing the two-door sports car recklessly careen down the street.

Ledoma. Of course, I would see flashy sleazebags like that in this section of the city.

A deep, throaty horn sound reverberates through my bones, making me wince. I turn toward the source. A man in a neon-orange jacket is shaking his fist in the air, hanging outside the window of a waste disposal truck.

"I almost fucking ran into you, you fucking prick!" the man screams. "My boss would have had my ass!"

The man shouts something else that is incoherent, slips back into the van, and starts punching at the steering wheel of his truck. His rage-filled eyes snap in my direction.

"What the fuck you looking at? You one of these Ledoma fuckers? Rich asshole? Huh?"

There is no use in arguing with people who are this fired up. I shake my head, inching my hand into my jacket, ready to reveal my badge if he escalates further.

"Fuck you and your clean streets!" The truck makes a whirring noise as it moves forward, the man gripping the wheel with tight fists. A corroded metal arm, jetting from the side of the truck, is clamped around a stuffed trash bag. As the truck speeds forward, garbage spews out onto the road.

Laughing, I shake my head and continue walking. People shoulder past me, but it's noticeably less crowded and feels cleaner, even with the waste-truck incident. The people around me are wearing suits and heels compared to the ragged crowd from when I was chasing Mirk. Their chins are high, and they talk on their Infinity devices, making deals, laughing, and discussing what's for dinner. I feel out of place with my worn clothes, stinking of mildew.

My nostrils flare as I sniff through my mask, staring at the bleached concrete. The sidewalk looks like it was scrubbed recently, with stains barely visible. Enormous towers loom, plunging into the smog-filled clouds above, flashing from random bursts of lightning.

Instead of the shoebox-sized apartment I have now, moving the family to this side of the city wouldn't be so bad. I smack my lips and push out a puff of air, knowing it's not feasible now. I'm behind as it is. Having the family in a safer section of the city would be nice, though.

The rain has finally lightened up, now just a soft drizzle. Dark clouds still linger, threatening to pummel the city once again. My wrist vibrates from an incoming call. Bringing it up, Coleson's ID is on the display, which is a surprise as I did not expect to hear from him again, especially so soon.

Answering the call, Coleson's appearance forms above my wrist. A solemn line is spread across his face with one eyebrow arched. "I know I basically said go fuck off, but..." he pauses and smacks his lips. "I couldn't help myself. This mystery place intrigued me, so I did a bit of digging."

"Oh, great," I say, curious. "So, you must have found something, right?"

He waves his hands in the air and leans back in his chair. "It looks like Descent is an exclusive nightclub with seven levels."

I place my hand on my chin and tilt my head. "Seven levels? Seven levels of what?"

Coleson squints his eyes and his head moves closer to the screen. *"Descent is an experience where virtue is absent and you can be your true self.* I found this online, deep within a forum talking about the nightlife in Nox City."

I bark out a laugh and grimace. "I still don't know what this place is. Anything else?"

"I found a webpage for it. Only had two red lines of text, though." He takes a deep breath. *"Descend Into Seven Levels of Sin,"* he says, emphasizing each word. "Then, there's the address. So based on that, this place must involve the seven deadly sins."

Warring senses of both disappointment and curiosity fill me. "Really, the seven deadly sins?" I scoff. "Sounds like a gimmick to get more people through the doors. Strange that we haven't had any cases related to this place, at least that I know of."

"That changes today, it looks like," Coleson says with a joyless grin. "Now, you owe me a little more."

Grinning, I shake my head. "Great. Thanks, Coleson. Good timing, too, because I think I'm here. I'll let you know what I find." The call flickers out and I drop my hand to rest on the grip of my hyper coil.

Taking a deep breath, I walk up to a two-story building with a black metallic door gleaming from ambient light. Above the door, a single debossed word is visible on the white surface of the building as if it's been hand-pressed into the structure: *DESCENT*. I sigh, not seeing anything exceptional. It's as if I'm only seeing the tip of an iceberg and I wonder what is beneath the surface.

Approaching the building, I start walking the perimeter, checking for signs of anything that helps identify what's inside.

My wrist starts vibrating again. I pull up the incoming call and click the answer button, thinking it's Coleson calling me back with more information.

"Is this Mr. S Harkones?" A heavy-sounding voice rings from my holo grid's speakers.

I stare down at the caller ID and wince. Shit, I knew they were hounding me but twice in one day? I don't have much time.

Clearing my throat, my mouth opens to respond but I'm cut off as he continues. "This is Edwardo Pruevo from Eligere Academy. I'm calling about your outstanding balance of 34,032 credits for your child, Zinny Harkones. Failure to pay will result in your child being expunged from the curriculum."

I smack my lips and rub at a temple.

"Yes, I understand. I'll get the payment sent over soon. Just give me a day or so."

"You have forty-eight hours to issue payment. Additional fees will be applied to your account. This is your last warning."

"I said I'll send it over!" I yell through clenched teeth.

"Have a good day, Mr. Harkones." The call flickers out.

"Fuck!" I curse.

The muscles in my jaw start twitching. I draw a deep breath through my nose and push out a steady breath of air, trying to calm myself. All I have to do is close out this case and I should have enough to pay some of the balance. I can't let Zinny be ripped out of her schooling. Eligere is the only way she will have opportunities in this city. The only way she'll grow and advance above the filth down here on the ground. She deserves more.

A trickle of worry creeps up my spine, thinking I won't have enough. That Zinny will be left to the underfunded and outdated free public schooling open on the web. Public school offered by Nox City as a courtesy. A courtesy that can go and fuck off. It's just schooling that leads to dead-end jobs, and that's if you're lucky. Lucrative careers will always be out of reach without *"quality education."* Education behind a paywall.

My mind splinters thinking of Zinny's schooling while assessing what could be behind the walls of this building. I chew on my lip and shake my head, focusing on what's in front of me. One thing at a time. First thing is just getting in this facade of a building.

I walk the perimeter and stand back in front of the single gleaming door, then cross my arms and sigh, unsure how to get in. I'm not seeing any handholds or buttons to get inside. I don't even see any cameras attached to the building.

"I guess I should just knock?" I murmur.

My clenched hand is about to knock, but inches before it makes impact, the door makes a sudden deep whirring noise and begins turning inwards. I glance to my sides to see if anyone else is seeing this, but no one is around. Peering through the doorway, I only see a dim room with a single recessed light illuminating another door a few feet ahead. Stepping inside the narrow room, a sense of danger fills me. The metal door clunks shut behind me with a sharp hiss of air. What feels like minutes later, the second door clicks and opens into the unknown. Focusing through the widening doorway, a single source of blue light shines in the middle of the structure.

Gritting my teeth, I take my first step into Descent and let out a short gasp at the scene below.

Holy... shit.

Standing on a solid metal bridge, I peer over the railing into a seemingly endless circular cavern. In the middle of this hollow structure is a double-helix glass and steel staircase at least ten feet wide. Inside the double helix is a pillar of blue neon that stretches the height of this underground structure. My jaw hangs open, and the hairs on my arms stand on end, never seeing anything quite like it before.

What the hell kind of place is this? I know people like to party and escape, but damn, this place seems excessive.

Exuding colors from each level assault my eyes. Consistent rhythmic thumping from competing music pounds from within the cavern. Examining the staircase again, the spiraling steps lead to different building levels, seven to be exact. From my vantage point, I can peer into the two closest levels, with the additional floors extending beyond my sight. Each floor is dark but has a different color spinning and twirling from within. A mass of silhouettes undulate within the first two levels. Above each floor, I make out bright words around the circumference of the levels. I squint and focus on every word my sight can reach—*greed, pride, wrath, envy.*

All these people, all this money being poured into a club? A club focused on sin, of all things. Money that could have gone toward cleaning up this city, but no, let's build a massive club honoring evil. I scoff, thinking of how this cavern stretches down into the earth, inching closer to the fires of hell.

I don't know how much the gimmick of sin plays into each level, but that is not my immediate concern. Scanning each floor, I struggle to imagine how massive this structure is. With the amount of people I see below, finding Mirk would be like searching for a needle in a haystack. Thank god, I have a map pointing to the needle's location.

Steadying myself, I let out a heavy breath and check my surroundings. The bridge only leads straight ahead. Staring across the walkway, I make out a circular booth-like structure with a woman standing behind a dimly lit counter. Two bulky guys loom while sitting on stools on each side of the booth's exterior wall.

I brush sweat off my brow with the back of my hand and start walking toward the center of the cavern. Strapping my mask to my belt, the distant sound of thumping music begins to wrap around me, the acoustics of the cavern amplifying the different layers of noise. Approaching the booth, I make out the appearance of the woman behind the counter. A single warm white strip of light on the left side bounces off the woman's dark complexion and contrasts with her glowing blue eyes. The two bouncers stare off to the side of the bridge, not moving an inch, making me question if they are human. It looks like their eyes are closed, which strikes me as odd.

"Welcome to Descent," the woman says in a raspy, melodic voice. "What level of sin will you visit today?"

She turns one palm up. Bold text materializes a few inches above her hand, displaying each floor of sin. I scan the list, seeing that the bottom level is attached to the sin of *lust*, the floor closest to hell itself.

"Keep in mind that, for you to descend, you must raise pay-men—"

She stops as I reach into my jacket and pull out my detective's badge, flipping it toward the counter. The bouncers' eyes snap open, revealing red-glowing irises. They both stand, towering over me.

"Hold on, boys. Everything is fine," the woman says while stretching her palms out. "Again, officer, what level do you want to visit today?"

My eyes scan for any sign of aggression from the bouncers. With my hand resting on my Z4, I speak as clearly as possible. "Ma'am, I'm not here for a visit. I have reason to believe a suspect is hiding out in this... building... or club... whatever it is."

The woman's mouth draws into a flat line. "I see... well, you are welcome to search the premises. Descent is a club like no other, catering to our primal desires and fantasies. If you should stop during your search to *enjoy yourself*, I'm sure it will convince you to come back again."

My face contorts to revulsion. "Great, sure thing," I say. There won't be next time unless I am here with more officers to ensure nothing suspicious is going on. I move toward the staircase and pause, gesturing ahead of me. "Is this the *only* way to get up and down?"

She narrows her eyes, scanning me over. "Yes, it's the only way. Now, please enjoy your time and try not to scare away our guests; it would be... sacrilegious."

I chuckle as her voice makes me think she is holding something back. Still grinning, I shake my head and walk past one of the bouncers. His glowing red eyes follow me like laser-guided missiles locked on target. With a deep breath, I take my first step of many down the spiraling stairway toward the deadly sin of lust.

Mirk, you better still be here.

5

Rhythm

The rhythm of electronic music thrums in my skull each step down
the staircase, inching me further away from heaven.

Thump... Thump Thump... Thump.

I shoulder through droves of people coming and going to live
out their primal *fantasies*. Whatever that means.

Through a spectrum of flashing lights, I take in people of all
colors, all races, all having varying levels of modifications, and all
appearing to be drunk or under the influence of something. My
feet move in repetition: step, descend, step, descend. Staring down
the staircase, I notice gleaming white eyes under the black hood of
a jacket focused in my direction. Blue light of the neon pillar in the
middle of the staircase bathes half of his presence. He appears to
be a man of average build and height and walks toward me up the
stairs. His hands seem to fiddle with something in his coat pockets,
not breaking eye contact with me. A sadistic smile spreads across
his face. Narrowing my eyes, a sense of unease fills me. My hands
reach to rest on my weapons.

Thump... Thump Thump... Thump.

I lift my chin and speak clearly. "Sir, do we have a problem?" With my right hand still resting on my Z4, I pull the left side of my jacket out, revealing my NCPD badge.

The strange smile plastered across his face does not falter. "Problem? No, Officer. We have no problem here," he says in a high, scratchy voice.

"What are you fiddling with in your pocket?" I ask with a short nod toward his jacket. Behind the hooded man, red lights are beaming and bouncing in all directions from the floor of Wrath.

"I wanted to see if you would be interested in experiencing something new. Something like you have never felt before." The man pulls something out of his jacket. Whatever it is, it's concealed within a closed hand. I spot a glimmer of white plastic as he shrugs. "What do you say? You up for a trial of—"

I cut him off. "What makes you think asking an officer of the law if he is interested in drugs is a good idea? I suggest you keep walking or I'll have you detained and in a cell before you can say another word."

My nostrils flare while grinding my jaw. I don't have time for this bullshit. Whatever this guy has, it can wait.

He turns his palms up and gives a quick nod. "Whatever you say, Officer. Have a good day now." Placing both of his hands back in his jacket, he continues his ascent to the higher levels of sin, maintaining a deviant smile.

Thump... Thump Thump... Thump.

I shake my head, trying to swallow my annoyance. Focusing my eyes on the floor of wrath, I make out a raging crowd before a stage with two large holograms of people fist-fighting. Below the holograms, two people are fighting. They appear like small children compared to the immense projections. Fists and blood fly in sync, making me realize this is a live display for the entire crowd to spectate. The crowd roars in satisfaction every time a fist connects with flesh. Excitement radiates over the mass of people, seeing a bloody spectacle.

Interested, I study the fight. I enjoy a suspenseful brawl, even though it's usually humanoid droids doing the fighting. Smacking my lips, I tear my eyes from the scene. No time for this now.

Continuing my descent, I pause my next step and gaze up the staircase. Damn, this is going to be hell to have to walk back up.

Shoving that thought away, I focus on what I need to do: apprehend Mirk and bring him back to the station. Then I can collect my bonus and finally head home.

Vibrations from the music pulsate through my bones with each step. Halfway to the seventh floor, I'm passing the level of Envy that oozes green. I raise my hand closer to my face and pull up my holo grid to call Coleson and check in. I know he's already done more than enough, but he may have gathered more information about this place. Clicking the call button, a text window materializes on my display. *"Error, unable to connect the call at this time."* My face twists into a frown, staring at the screen. It was as if the call didn't even attempt to connect, with the error popping up so fast.

Goddamn technology not working. What is it with today? Do I have something in my body that just messes with tech? Another reason why I am not having any lowlife modifier like Mirk install implants into me. No telling when it will fuck up, leaving me in a spot just like Benji, a warm husk.

Tapping the call button again, I am met with the same result. Even my messages are not able to be sent, resulting in a similar error. My tracker app still appears to be online and functional, thank god. I just can't send messages or make video calls. I can only assume something is blocking the signal or not allowing the connection to be made. A pang of worry travels down my spine.

I am alone. If anything were to go wrong, I cannot call for help. I take a deep breath. Should I head back up and request backup? Maybe Coleson has some information that could help me. Resolve suddenly floods through me. No... I am almost there. I can handle the little bastard.

Thump... Thump Thump... Thump.

Breathing heavily, I finally stand at the entrance of the final floor, Lust. I slowly lift my head and gaze up toward the ceiling, flicking my eyes from floor to floor. My brows rise in astonishment at the immensity of the tubular cavern stretching toward the surface above me. Deep in the belly of sin, I stare up to the kingdom of heaven.

It's too bad there is just another level of sin outside this structure— Nox City. Years of bloody and violent crime scenes flash across my mind.

Studying the floor before me, blue bounces and dances in all directions. Blue is an odd choice. Being so far away from the gods above, I would expect to find fiery red colors writhing throughout the level.

Scanning ahead of me, I make out two main stages on the left and right sides of the floor. Large holographic projections of male and female faces flash across the stage in sync with the music, producing an almost psychedelic effect.

Stepping onto the floor, I am greeted by a female in lingerie who leaves little to the imagination. Her face and hair shapeshift as she glides over to me, rapidly changing her features. One moment, she has short dark hair with a dark complexion, and the next, sleek purple waves of hair spiral over porcelain-white shoulders. Her slender hand reaches for my shoulders. Oval nails glide across the fabric of my shirt and continue down. An overpowering scent of lilac drifts into my nose.

"Come here. I can be anything you want me to be," says the woman.

A ghostly effect follows her movements, with the digital image trailing with a small degree of delay. It's difficult to see her true self with the holographic projection system overlaying her organic features. She moves to reach for my hand. I pull away, revealing my badge.

"Ma'am, you can move along now," I say.

Her projection overlay snaps to a single angular face with platinum blonde hair. Her eyelashes bat in my direction, and her large purple eyes sparkle. "Oh, an officer. Are you sure you don't want to have a good time?" she says. "Is it my face? What's your type?"

Sighing, my brows furrow. "Ma'am, I will state again. Please be on your way."

She moves her hands into a playful stance of surrender while slowly stepping away. "I'm sorry, Officer. Lock me up if you need to." She moves away toward new arrivals, her hips swaying and hair flickering to different colors and styles.

Staring ahead, women and men dance overhead on raised transparent stages across the floor. Under each stage, a circular bar stretches around and highlights faintly glowing bottles of various alcohols. A mass of people crowd around each bar, trying to get drinks or gaze above, mesmerized by the twirling flesh on display.

I sigh, taking in my surroundings. Bass pounding, lights whirling, alcohol spilling, and the smell of musk and perfume fills every pocket of air. Descent is something I've never seen in all my years living in Nox City. I have to give credit to Mirk. A wise choice for the little bastard to hide out.

Glancing at my wrist, I grin. A topical map is visible on my display with a little red dot flashing, indicating the tracker's location. Next to the map, a red arrow points in the direction I need to go. My feet move through the crowd, which is full of intoxicated people laughing and flirting, skin inches apart.

Twenty feet... Nineteen feet... Eighteen feet... I rest my hand on the grip of my holstered Z4. Nearing the tracker, anticipation tingles at my fingertips, traveling up my arm and into my beating heart. I step between more people, gawking and drooling over the dancers above, watching for anything suspicious. Whiffs from all the overpowering scents congeal, making me scrunch my nose as I slip through the crowd.

Now, only six feet ahead of me, the red arrow points directly ahead at a door. My eyes dart from my wrist toward my destination. Taking a deep breath, I step toward the door and hesitate, taking notice of a rotating projection. Thick gray stick figures of a man and woman hovering above a single word: *Restroom.*

Thump... Thump Thump... Thump.

6

Push

My mind starts racing, thinking of all the scenarios that could unfold. Could he still be here? Did he find the tracker and dump it? Am I walking into a trap? Or is he in the process of using the restroom for its intended purpose?

A snort escapes me, envisioning myself pointing my Z4 at Mirk while he's on the shitter. That would be new.

I grit my teeth and place my left hand on the door, ready to push it open. With my right hand, I reach toward my hand cannon and unholster it, thumbing the dial to the PUSH setting.

With a shove, the door swings open. Holding my Z4 out in front of me with both hands, I scan around the dimly lit room, checking each corner, ruling out any potential threats.

Left wall, glass mirror, and large black sink... clear. Straight ahead, a dark wall with metallic hand dryers... clear. I step inside and dart my eyes to the right wall filled with closed-door stalls. Taking short, steady breaths, I don't see any threats in the room. It appears that I am alone.

Ducking my head, I glance at the bottom of each stall, checking if any limbs are sticking out. Nope, nope, no, no. Along with the thumping bass outside the room, my pulse pounds in my head. I move down the row, pushing open each stall door. Nothing...

Of course he's not here. My eyes roll back while my lips form into a thin line.

I pull open my tracker app again, indicating I'm within two feet of the beacon. Turning in a circle around the room, the red arrow points at a trashcan in the left corner.

With a frustrated sigh, I step toward the trashcan and peer in. Unsure of its contents, I holster my Z4 and tip the can over, pouring everything onto the floor. I squat with my hand on my chin, scanning the spilled trash. My eyes sweep over tubes, bottles, food wrappers, plastic bags, triangular white pieces of plastic, and other random crap.

Holding my breath, my eyes halt on a small object. Walking over the trash, I purse my lips and slowly shake my head. About the size of a small coin, I pick up the circular black device and hold it up between my thumb and index finger. Twisting it in my grip, I stare at the tracker with a deep frown.

"Where the hell did you go?" I roar through gritted teeth.

This is only supposed to be a level-three case, but I am not catching any breaks here. What should I do now? Should I just call it a day and head home? Maybe tomorrow I'll have more luck.

"NO!" I yell, snapping out of it. With the tracker in my hands, I know Mirk was here, so... I should stick around a little longer and see if I can find anything that points to where Mirk went. Plus, with Eligere breathing down my neck, I need this bonus yesterday.

Pocketing the tracker, I walk over to the sink and place both hands on the ledge, leaning close to the mirror. Staring back is a disheveled man who looks like he's seen better days. My damp brown hair is a mess, stubble on my neck needs to be shaved, and bags under my eyes that a single night of rest won't fix. I stare deeper into my organic green eyes, trying to will strength back into me.

The distant rhythmic thumping from music beyond the door reverberates through the floor. I wave my hand over the spout on the sink and run my fingers through the cool water that starts to pour down. Splashing the water against my face, a sense of revitalization washes over me. After taking in a long breath and exhaling, I bend down to cup more water—

Involuntarily, my head whips up a few inches and slams the black stone countertop with a hard crack. Pain shoots through my skull. I tumble onto the ground, dazed and confused, and blood starts to trickle down my nose. A quiver of fear rushes through me as someone towers over me. The figure appears to be constructed of black and silver metal. A human-like face with glowing orange eyes looks to be stitched onto the front of its metallic skull. The figure holds a massive hammer in its grip, with the block end resting on the floor. An Ogre...

Oh god, not one of these bastards. This is a case where cybernetic modifications have gone too far. I don't know if you can still call this thing human, with it being more machine than organic.

A high-pitched maniacal laugh sounds from behind the Ogre. About half the height of this metallic brute, a bald woman with pale skin and protruding telescopic eyes steps into view. An iridescent bodysuit of sleek fabric clings to her thin body under a long black jacket that trails along the floor.

She tilts her head, a smile forming. Something with multiple legs crawls up her jacket and perches on her shoulder. Silver pincers clink together below the red glow of beady eyes. Curving over its head, a razor-sharp stinger gleams off the light in the restroom. Seeing the Ogre, and the creature's resemblance to a scorpion, recognition floods my brain.

Pandemon. What the hell does this gang want with me? Whoever labeled this case is going to hear from me after today.

"Hello, love. Sorry to rain on your parade, but we need to chat." She points at the metal figure above me. "Bronk, would you be a darling and bag him up?"

Bronk glances back at the woman and shrugs.

"Hmph. I think we can handle this here," Bronk protests in a low, modulated voice, lifting his hammer and gripping it in both hands.

"Honey, please do as you are told and restrain him. We have business to discuss. You can have fun after." The woman chuckles again while the metal creature on her shoulder utters a high-pitched screech that echoes in the room, making me wince.

Bronk places the hammer back on the ground with a metallic thunk and reaches behind his back for something I assume will be used to bag me up.

The restroom door swings open. A man who looks to be in his late twenties stumbles in, almost falling over. Halfway into the room, he notices us. An expression of horror forms across his intoxicated face, eyes darting between the Ogre and the woman's shoulder. He raises both hands.

"Hey man, I'm cool. I'm cool," he sputters, tripping backward. The woman nods in the man's direction. In a blur of motion, the scorpion leaps off her shoulder with inhuman speed and knifes the pleading man in the throat. An arc of blood spews out like a geyser across the floor and splatters the large mirror. He collapses to the ground, eyes twitching. A chill courses through my veins.

She scoffs, staring at the pooling blood. The scorpion skitters back to her shoulder, crimson beads trailing down its stinger. She snaps her head in Bronk's direction. "Hurry up!" she screams in a feral voice while pointing at me. Bronk's head swivels, his glowering eyes focusing on me.

As if staring at a solar eclipse, darkness falls across my face as his hand descends toward me, blotting out the light behind him.

Through clenched teeth, I scream, "Fuck this!" I reach for my Z4, unholstering it and pointing it in the Ogre's face. His orange eyes widen in surprise as he lunges to grip his hammer. Too late.

My finger slams the trigger back with the holographic display indicating a maximum charge by a full green bar. A heartbeat later, an electronic whirring emits from the cannon and releases a concussive blast, jarring my hand backward from the recoil. A force of kinetic energy smashes into the metal giant, throwing him back with such force it sounds like thunder when he makes impact with the wall behind him. Fragments from the wall splinter off, leaving a crater indention as he falls to the ground.

The woman looks at Bronk in surprise and darts her telescopic eyes back to me. An insidious grin spreads across her face. She lifts her hand, pointing at me, and screams. The creature's blood-chilling eyes snap from the woman to me as it lunges off her shoulder, letting out an electronic shrill. It lands on the ground and charges toward me, each leg clicking the ground in rapid succession.

I raise my cannon and notice the charge indicator blinking red, the percentage quickly rising to show when the PUSH setting will be ready to fire again. Twenty-five percent. Fuck fuck fuck fuck… Heart racing, I thumb the dial to the BLST setting. Too late.

The metal beast crashes into me, knocking the breath out of my lungs and making me drop my Z4 to the floor. Its stinger twitches in the air above me. I look up in horror. It feels as if time slows as the stinger descends to my chest. Searing, white-hot pain races through me, originating from the stinger's impact below my collarbone. The sound of my anguished scream rushes into my ears.

The scorpion hops off my body with a clink and sprints back to the woman. My limbs go numb. Like a stone sculpture, I'm frozen and unable to move. My gaze darts around the room, searching for anything I can use to escape the situation.

Realization sets in. Panic courses through me. No one is coming to help.

The woman starts laughing again while shaking her head. "Now that was fun! Bronk, darling, get your ass back up and bag him. It's time to talk."

The metallic beast of a man reaches out, slapping the floor with a clunk. The Ogre creaks back up to a standing position. He rolls his head from side to side. "I should have expected that," he grumbles.

Bronk walks back to me and kicks my Z4 across the room. He grunts, his imposing face peering down at me as if I were an insect. I don't feel anything as he moves me into position. A large black bag is in his hands.

Like lightning, an image of Zinny's smile streaks through my mind, flashing to a time when I was holding Raena close. Rapidly breathing, the bag zips over my head. A powerful blow plows into the side of my face. All is black.

7

Ascent

A wide grin spreads across my face. I slowly tiptoe around my apartment. Anticipation builds. Soft giggles sound from across the room. Turning my head, the curtains stir. I lick my lips, hold my breath, and step closer to the panel of fabric. My hand inches out, grabbing hold of the curtain. In a sudden motion, I pull back the fabric, revealing a young girl holding one hand in front of her mouth and twinkling eyes going wide.

"Boo! Got you, honey!" I say with a laugh.

"Daddy! How did you find me so fast?"

I chuckle and point to her pink socks sticking out beyond the curtain in full view of the living room. We both burst out into laughter. I am happy, and all is right.

Another sinister laugh rips me from my dream-like state and snaps me back to reality.

Where am I?

I question if my eyes are open. I see nothing. Frantic, my heart jumps in my throat. I rapidly blink. The events of today hit me like a zip train all at once. Chasing Mirk, descending the nightclub, finding the tracker, and... *Pandemon.*

Oh shit...

A wave of confusion washes over me. Why am I still alive? Why did Pandemon go through so much trouble to get to me?

A dull pain throbs in my chest. I take breaths through my nose, feeling my body bounce. Straining to move, I realize I still don't have any sensation in my arms or legs. With each bob of my head, I'm confident that I'm being carried by Bronk or somebody else while walking through Descent. My ears pick up fading music from the club, so I know we have not gone too far since our encounter in the restroom. I hear ragged mechanical wheezing coming from whoever is holding me. If this is Bronk, there is a sliver of humanity left, gasping to survive.

Zinny and Reana materialize in my thoughts. Moisture wells in my eyes. I need to be there to protect them, to provide for them. Zinny's small smile flashes in my mind, igniting my resolve. I'm getting home.

What reason could Pandemon have to abduct me? Could this be related to Mirk? They are keeping me alive for a reason. I haven't dealt with any Pandemon cases in years.

The scorpion's screech sounds from somewhere nearby, piercing my brain as if its stinger was stabbing into one of my eardrums.

A memory sparks in the recesses of my mind: my first year as an NCPD officer. I arrived at an active crime scene, blood and bodies everywhere. Limbs twisted and torn apart. A deep guttural roar sounded in the distance. A fleeting glimpse of something inhuman, something large, scaling a building and moving out of sight. My breath caught seeing something soar through the air, a metal-plated beast with the features of a wingless dragon. It landed on the ground, sending tremors through the earth. Riot teams arrived on sight, charging toward the bloodless creature. My skin crawled, staying back and keeping pedestrians away from the carnage.

I remember almost dropping off my badge that night, thinking it wasn't worth it. I did not sign up to mess with gangs using animal droids to do their insidious bidding. That night, all officers who helped with the scene received an extra payment. I did not tell Reana what I saw.

Since then, I've only had a few cases involving Pandemon. Memories of a vicious artificial wolf howling at night and the rapid scuttering of a metal spider loop in my mind. An old scar on my inner thigh suddenly sparks with a trickle of pain, a nagging reminder of fighting off the gang's creatures. I try to shake the thought and take a deep breath.

Plunging into the unknown, ideas rapidly bounce in my brain, trying to figure out what is happening. It seems like we make a sharp turn. Pain erupts in my skull as my head smacks against something hard. Through clenched teeth, I groan, unable to move or defend myself.

The dreaded woman's voice sounds from just outside the bag. "Sunshine, would you please shut the hell up until we get outside to the van?"

An agonized grunt escapes my mouth, and I lose what breath I have remaining as something slams into my ribs. Wheezing from the impact, my brain throbs. Whoever is carrying me resumes walking.

The sound of my captor's footsteps change. It sounds like we stepped onto a platform of a different material. A louder echo rings out compared to the solid ground we were just on. The metal scorpion's legs make a hollow clink with each step.

I wince as the woman speaks in her high-pitched, shrill voice. "Come on! Click the button!"

"Yes, Sabine."

Without warning, gravity pulls me down, my limbs crashing to the floor. Growling, heat slithers up my face. I'm unable to move, call for backup, or do anything.

The floor shudders when something mechanical starts clicking, leading to a deep whirring noise. I think that we are moving... moving... upward.

Of course, the woman at the front counter was giving me complete bullshit. I knew the staircase was not the only means to move up and down the club. Damn, why does everyone want to mess with me today? Do I have something on my forehead that says, *"Hey fuck with me!"*?

The elevator hums in my ears. My helpless body vibrates from the elevator's ascent. A chime dings, indicating that we have arrived somewhere above. Bronk picks me up and tosses my limp body over his shoulder as if he were picking up a small child. We continue walking and my head starts to bob up and down.

Still within the darkness of the bag, I'm not sure where we are. A whoosh of air sounds as if a door just opened.

An air-tight door... we must be going outside. Panic runs down my numb spine.

My heart starts hammering against my chest. I strain to move while growling. It takes considerable effort to speak.

"Hey!" I croak. "Mask!"

With a chuckle, Sabine responds. "You'll be fine, honey. Only a little further, and it might do you some good to get some fresh Nox City air."

My chest expands, sucking in one last, deep breath. The sound of the city rushes into my ears.

Do I scream? Does anyone know I was kidnapped? What the hell does this gang want with me?

Clenching my gut, my abs are straining while trying to hold in filtered oxygen, but slowly, I release small puffs of air until I'm depleted. My head is still bobbing. I try to hold out as long as possible, but the need for air overtakes me. As if pouring fire down my throat, the polluted air of Nox City burns within my lungs. I feel as if I'm drowning in the depths of a deep sea with no lights guiding me to salvation. I'm in agony and all I hear is laughter. Not the laughter of my daughter that brings me joy, but laughter that stokes the burning fire already in my gut.

My body is weightless for a second before abruptly crashing to the ground. Gasping in pain, I realize that I can breathe again without fire running down my throat. I hear something slam shut behind me. Something unzips. Blinding light assaults my eyes. Quickly blinking, my pupils re-adjust to the newfound illumination behind the glowing eyes staring at me.

With a grin, Sabine's gaze drills into me. "Detective, I'm going to talk now, and it's up to you if you will listen. Dear, I recommend that you perk your ears."

Looking past the woman, I see the rear doors of what I think is a large cargo van. Bright light strips run along the ceiling, illuminating rows of storage racks filled with white plastic boxes on both interior walls. I don't see any text or stickers indicating the contents of the boxes.

They have kept me alive until now, so they must want something I have. What that is, I have no idea, but there is only one way to find out.

Sweat dripping down my forehead, I take a deep breath and steel myself, staring back at Sabine. "I'm listening. Now, what do you want?"

Sabine lets out a wretched laugh while the scorpion on her shoulder screeches, making me wince. Bronk stands behind Sabine, his head ducked so as not to hit the ceiling, his grip around the shaft of his massive hammer. My eyes widen slightly, feeling a tickling sensation at my fingertips. With a slight, almost imperceptible smirk, a sense of hope blooms in my chest.

I will do more than just listen.

8

Coil

Trying not to draw any attention to my limbs regaining sensation, I remain fixed to the floor. Licking my lips, the taste of salt lingers on my tongue. My eyes snap between the Ogre and Sabine, thinking of my options and trying to piece together my next move. The city buzzes with life beyond the walls of the cargo van.

I picture myself walking with Raena and Zinny down the street to one of our favorite food joints. An electronic shriek shatters the image. My vision trails toward the woman's shoulders, the corners of my mouth twisting into a frown.

"Since you know my name and you know that I'm with the NCPD," I say in an authoritative voice, "you must know this isn't going to end well for you two, right?"

Sabine snickers while shaking her head. "Detective, this is the only reason we're keeping you alive... for now. The boss wanted us to deliver you a message before we escalate further. So, sweetheart, I would listen well." The scorpion clicks its pincers together, its stinger twitching in the air while moving shoulder to shoulder. "You will stop pursuing your current investigation, this chase that you are on," she says, leaning closer to my face.

I stare at her as if she lost her mind. Stop pursuing this case? Why? What does Mirk have to do with this? This is not what I was expecting to hear. Unsure of how to respond, I mirror the question back to her. "Stop pursuing this case?"

"Your search ends here and now. After our talk, if you decide to intervene, I will visit you at home. And from the ring on your finger, it looks like you have a family. Any kids? My friend here would love to play with them." The metal creature screeches as if on command.

Something snaps at the mention of my family. My pulse beats faster. Heat rushes up my neck and into my face. "You will not touch my family!" I roar through gritted teeth. "I'll kill both of you!"

Sabine lets out a detestable laugh that only enrages me further. "Darling, you are in no position to make threats. So, what do you say? Will you drop the case and make sure no one picks it up in your tracks? The boss will be most pleased if no one interrupts our little operation, especially cogs like you in the NCPD."

As she glances back to Bronk, I test my fingers again. I can curl them, but it's not enough to stand a chance against the two and the metal creature. I must buy more time and keep her talking. One thing that strikes me as odd is that they haven't mentioned Mirk's name once. Is he even involved?

"What does Mirk have to do with this?"

Sabine's eyes zoom back into her face as she tilts her head. Her grin flattens. "Mirk? Who is or what is a *Mirk?*"

What? Is she toying with me? What does she mean, who is Mirk? This is the only case I have been working on the past few days.

"Mirk... my suspect," I say. "The guy I'm trying to track down." I chuckle. "Do you even have the right detective?" They have the wrong person. I know it's still not ideal that any detective or anyone in the force be in this particular situation, but I can't help but laugh at the absurdity of it all.

Sabine glances at Bronk, who responds with a grunt. His grip tightens on the end of his hammer. Twisting her gaze back at me, she walks in my direction and settles in front of me in a squatting position. Her face is inches from mine. She reaches out one cold hand and grasps my chin, tilting my face up to her murderous gaze. A smile starts to widen on her face, with her head twisting to an angle. Her face is so close to mine that I smell her rancid breath.

"So, Detective Harkones, you are *not* searching for Oblivion?"

I stare down at her tubular eyes, bouncing from pupil to pupil as my brows narrow in confusion. Oblivion? What is that?

My eyes harden as I respond. "I have no idea what you are talking about."

She rises back into a standing position with her hands on her hips and starts laughing.

I'm missing something. I do not have all the puzzle pieces, but neither do they.

"I guess we have a misunderstanding, and I know you don't want to cause further harm to an officer of the Nox City Police Depart—"

A kick from Sabine slams into my gut, making me exhale in pain. I hear a whoosh of air as a second kick crashes into my stomach. The foot slams with such force it feels like my innards are going shoot out of my throat. I continue to lay sprawled on the floor of the van, gasping.

While laughing, she looks at Bronk. "This fool has no idea, at least for now. I think it's best to keep it that way."

Bronk grunts. "It seems that he has no knowledge of Oblivion," he says in a deep, modulated voice. "I think the boss will be happy if we keep it so."

The woman bends down and tilts her head to be parallel with mine. The edges of her lips curl. "It seems that our information was off. I guess we don't need you after all." She stands to her full height and starts shaking her head. An instant later, Sabine nods toward the scorpion on her shoulder. The creature's beady red eyes dart in my direction, and it leaps off her shoulder with a shriek. Landing on the van's metal floor, each of its eight legs clink together in harmony. Drawing closer, a hollow ping sounds with each step.

"We'll also pay a visit to your family afterward, just to make sure the message is clear." Sabine continues smiling.

Fiery rage burns hotter in my chest. I strain to move. My hands can make a fist, but that's not enough. The metal creature's stinger twitches in the air as it crawls up my feet and onto my legs. My veins begin to bulge with how hard I'm straining to move.

I wince from each of the scorpion's legs digging into my skin. Sabine nods.

My left hand clenches in a tight fist, reaching toward the grip of my hyper coil. The tips of my fingers just brush the end of the grip, unable to fully grasp it. The scorpion is now on my chest, its stinger above me, ready to strike a fatal blow.

I'm sorry, Raena. I'm sorry, Zinny.

I grind my teeth and tense my face, expecting the stinger to pierce my skull and drop me into an eternal dream. Still reaching for my hyper coil, I notice a blinking green light indicating I have a message. With a slight tilt of my wrist, I make out two bold words. "STAY LOW!"

An ear-splitting screech echoes in the van as the creature's tail curls toward my face.

A loud pop sounds from outside the van that resembles a high-caliber gunshot. Sabine gasps before one of her telescopic eyes shatters into a thousand pieces, throwing glass across the van. The scorpion's tail stops centimeters away from making impact. The woman crumples to the floor, blood oozing out of the extended scope of her left eye. My eyes go wide, seeing the creature screech as if in pain, stumbling back toward the pooling blood of the woman.

The van starts to tremble as a cacophony of bullets rain hellfire inside. The boxes on the side walls blast open and fall on the floor, spewing its contents in every direction. Beams of city light streak through holes peppered across the van.

Bronk turns toward the incoming rain of bullets and turns his arm inwards to shield his face. Using his other hand, he swings his massive hammer in an underhand arc that smashes into the van's back doors, tearing them off their hinges. The doors fly through the air. A black NCPD drone hovers outside through the smashed doorway and darts left and right to dodge the careening doors. The drone remains unfazed and continues firing off rounds of bullets toward Bronk.

Anticipation courses through my veins and tingles at my fingertips. Coleson must be piloting the drone and be the one who sent the message. Damn it all, I really do owe him after this.

Bouncing my sight from the gaping hole in the back of the van to Bronk, something jets out of his chest armor, reaching up to cover his mouth and nose. My brows furrow in confusion until recognition hits me like a slap across the face.

My cheeks puff out while pulling in a deep breath of air, hoping I'm not too late. The van bounces when Bronk jumps out the doorway and hits the ground with a thump. With one arm in front of his face, he runs toward the drone that is still sending a stream of bullets. The drone zig-zags in motion with a hologram above it, which displays NCPD in bold yellow letters. Jumping higher than I thought possible, Bronk flies through the air, holding his hammer arched behind him. Bullets collide with and bounce off the layer of metal acting as skin. The steel block of the hammer descends on the drone, smashing it with a hard crunch. The hunk of NCPD metal plummets toward the ground, making rapid clicking noises. What's left of the drone explodes on impact, sending its internal components flying in every direction.

Staring at the plume of dust, a shiver emanates from my core. My heart falls deeper, and a sense of dread washes over me. I slowly release puffs of air and strain to move. A metallic scraping sounds out as if something was being dragged on the road. Glowing orange eyes materialize through the smoke of the destroyed drone. Bronk steps into full view, dragging his hammer behind him.

You have to be shitting me. Please let this be a dream.

The metal scorpion is still screeching near the woman as Bronk steps back into the van. In a low, deep voice, he grunts. "You're full of surprises." He nods in the direction of Sabine's sprawled body. "It will be interesting to see what the boss makes of this."

With a clunk, he sets the hammer down next to him and steps in my direction. I'm running out of air and will have to take a breath soon. The ethereal glow of his eyes grows more prominent as he nears, descending above me. His raspy breathing struggles more than before, with his head inches above mine. Metallic hands reach toward my neck. Cold fingers graze the sides of my skin. I let out a frustrated scream, releasing what air I have left. Taking in a breath, agony burns down my lungs.

Just a little further... I'm so close... so close... GOT IT! The grip is now in my palm. Growling, I jerk my hand upward, wrapping the coil around the neck of the Ogre.

His glowing eyes narrow, unsure what slithered around his neck while glancing at my hand. Recognition sets in and his eyes widen.

I slam my thumb into the dial, kindling the weapon. The hyper coil thrums to life as electricity pulsates through each vertebra, emitting a blue glow that bounces in the van. Bronk jerks to end me, but it's too late. The coil is already in motion.

Bronk's eyes start to bulge as the coil tightens around his neck. He spits out coarse choking sounds, his hands reaching to unwrap the coil. The coil only constricts more.

He lets out one last gasp before the sound of a wet pop rings out, ending with a thump next to my ear. I look up to where Bronk's head should be, noticing it's no longer there. Blood flows from the remaining stump. I glance to my left and see Bronk's face staring back, an expression of disbelief stuck across his features. The metal body crashes to the side of me.

My lungs are screaming for clean air. I snap my hands to grab my mask off my belt and quickly strap it on. The green lights of the mask flicker to life. I lean my head back, take a deep breath, and exhale.

My skin crawls from the adrenaline coursing through my veins, mixing with the lingering effects of the scorpion's artificial venom.

I should be dead right now, but my racing heart confirms I'm still alive. How the hell did I get mixed up with these psychos? Gulping air, my eyes flick to the mockery of a creature above the pool of blood.

Using one of the storage racks as leverage, I slowly pull myself up and wince from the effort. My body feels heavy, as if I were wearing a weighted vest. The scorpion is still hissing in distress as I approach. Thumbing the dial of my hyper coil, it straightens to a rod still glowing blue with the electrical current coursing through it. Raising the rod as high as possible without hitting the ceiling, I slam it down on the scorpion, thumbing the dial to wrap around its metal body and constrict. I almost feel a pang of sympathy as it screeches before being severed in two, both sides clinking to the van floor.

Stepping outside, my wrist vibrates from an incoming call. With a soft whine, I deactivate my hyper coil and set it back on my belt. Clicking the answer button, Coleson appears above my wrist with an astonished look, his eyebrows raised and mouth open.

"Holy... shit!" Coleson exclaims. "What the hell did you get yourself into, Harkones? And how the fuck are you still alive?"

I shake my head, peering at the carnage of the vehicle, and sigh. "What toppings do you like on your pizza? Because I'm buying you two of them."

Coleson bursts out laughing, slapping the desk in front of him. "I think that is more than fair. Just another favor on the already growing pile. That huge metal guy scared the shit out of me when he flew through the air. His hammer made me jump in my seat."

Stepping back toward the van, the contents of the boxes are scattered everywhere in the vehicle and on the ground outside the blasted doorway.

I take a deep breath and lick my lips, my hands shaking. "I'm not sure what this was all about just yet but I'm glad you were here to help... again." My eyes linger on the scattered contents. I don't see anything that sticks out to me as I scan the technical gear, ammunition, guns, and other random piles of cargo.

What was all that talk about Oblivion? They seemed confident I was searching for it, whatever it is.

Squatting closer to the ground, something triangular and white catches my eye amidst the wreckage. Picking it up and holding it between my thumb and index finger, I examine it, unsure of what I'm looking at. It's wholly scuffed up from the warzone we were in, but I see an inner ring on one side of the device. I think it's a device, but I'm still unsure.

Twisting it to examine the back, I squint, staring at a solid white surface devoid of any markings besides three silver dots near each of the three rounded corners.

"You might want to go ahead and place that order for me and tack on some wings because I have more news." Coleson's brows rise, and a wide grin spreads across his face. "I know where Mirk is, and he's not far."

I pocket the device and look down toward Coleson with concern etched across my face. "What would I do without you?"

"Based on today, it looks like you would most likely be dead."

My eyes roll. "Can you have a clean-up crew check this van and catalog everything they find?"

"Yeah, sure thing."

"Great." I stretch my back out and rub at my temples. "Before we meet up with our friend Mirk, I need to pay a little visit to Descent. Hopefully, they have a lost and found."

Deep in thought, I walk toward Descent to retrieve my Z4. Shaking my head, I pray I did not just ignite a war with Pandemon.

I do not need anything else pushing this investigation out further. Level-three case my ass.

9

Zorgossie

The smell of freshly cooked ramen mixed with the pungent odor of urine drifts through my mask into my nose as I meander through the sprawling labyrinth of Zorgossie. I make my way through the slum, full of shops, bars, pop-up food joints, and adult entertainment. Scanning the cluttered streets, I glance at people indulging themselves inside janky-looking transparent dividers that barely keep filtered air within a small perimeter around each establishment. Neon signs and advertisements compete for space amidst the hundreds of shops demanding my attention. A cacophony of voices echo and bounce off the graffitied transparent walls that overlap with the hum of neon weighing on me like a blanket of static. Through the maelstrom of people and color, my eyes dart back and forth, searching. Mirk is somewhere within this chaos.

It's getting late. I know Raena will be putting Zinny to bed within a couple of hours or so. I already missed dinner, but I still have time. I made a promise.

Determined to end this soon, I place one foot in front of the other, hoping to find and catch Mirk once and for all.

"You sure you saw Mirk head into this mess?" I ask Coleson while twisting to avoid walking into people aimlessly wandering through the narrow makeshift streets.

"Uh-huh, absolutely," Coleson says while raising one pointer finger in the air. "When I lost contact with you at Descent, I spun up a drone and had it monitor the area around the club, looking for anything... suspicious. I got an alert a few minutes later saying there was a ninety-nine percent facial recognition match."

Damn. He must have slipped by me while I walked down the stairs. Or, he could have used a different means to move about the club... like possibly an elevator. I grimace at the thought of the elevator again.

"That's when I had the drone tail him from above," Coleson continues. "I followed him to Zorgossie when I saw that your holo grid came back online." With a snort, Coleson starts to chuckle. "Glad I had the drone double back to you, too. I was thinking of just keeping on his tail, but uh... looks like you needed help."

"I'm just happy he didn't vanish completely after dumping that tracker we had on him. Do you have any surveillan—"

Something tugs at my jacket, catching me off guard and spiking my adrenaline. I sharply turn my head toward whatever is pulling me, with one hand resting on the grip of my Z4. The wrinkly hand of a wiry, tattooed woman in tattered clothes is clenching my brown jacket.

"You got any spare creds?" she spits out in a gruff voice. Saliva sputters from her mouth, slapping against the inside of her transparent mask beneath gray puffed-out hair that looks like she was just electrocuted a few moments ago. Mania bounces in her bloodshot eyes.

"Ma'am, please take your hand off my coat."

"I didn't ask you about your goddamn coat!" she continues, with more spit flying out that starts to drip down her mask and chin. "Do you have any creds? I'm hungry!"

Another example of the homeless in Nox City. Usually, they will tell you precisely what is on their mind in a very abrasive tone while on whatever drugs they can get their hands on.

With a sigh, I shake my head while pulling out my badge and flashing it in her direction. "If you're hungry, there are facilities I can direct you towar—"

"I ain't asking for no goddamn facility, you fucking pig! Ah, fuck off!" She putters away toward more people.

I shrug and turn up my palms, unsure of what just happened. She is one person among what feels like millions in this city, desperate and willing to do anything to get their next fix.

The volume on my earpiece spikes. "Harkones!" Coleson screams out. "We got a sighting! Just eighty feet east of your location. Putting a pin on your device now."

A chime rings on my grid. I raise my hand inwards to pull up the map view, indicating where to go. I sprint. A kaleidoscope of color streams past my eyes as I run up and down the streets of Zorgossie, following wherever my arrow hologram is pointing.

I'm running for Mirk... again. This time, it's going to end differently. He is not getting away.

Now ten feet away, I slow down to catch my breath and calm my anticipation while leaning my hand against a nearby store wall. Staring ahead, the red pointer faces an establishment named Zorgasbord.

63

I let out a slight chuckle. This is the place from which Zorgossie got its unofficial name. Zorg, the owner, he's a nice guy, and damn, he can make some good food. My mouth salivates, thinking of the selection of home-cooked food winding through his shop on a conveyor belt.

From my position, I narrow my eyes, trying to peer into Zorgasbord, searching for Mirk. I unholster my Z4 and conceal it in one hand behind my jacket. My feet start walking closer to the storefront.

"Coleson, you got eyes on this place? I want to make sure he does not slip away." I say, speaking toward the mic in my earpiece.

"Yep, I'm tapped into every available camera near Zorgossie. Got the alert for Mirk just minutes ago so he should still be there."

"Good. I'm about to head in now. Keep tabs on this place in case he does something unexpected."

"You got it," Coleson says, giving me a thumbs up before his appearance flickers out.

I take in a deep breath and walk toward the entrance. A line of people are waiting to get in, licking their lips. Scanning the store through the marred and graffitied walls, people are sitting in every available seat. Food is rapidly coming out of a little shoe-box-sized hole in the wall leading to the back of the shop. Steaming soup, sandwiches, sushi, and things I have never seen before snake throughout the room.

A high-pitched feminine voice breaks my focus. "Hey! What the hell do you think you are doing?"

I turn my head and see a young woman standing at the front of the line. Glowing pink heart-shaped holograms hover in front of her pale cheeks. Her mouth forms into a scowl below her brightly lit green eyes. Behind her, a large bald man with a head resembling a bowling ball rests a gleaming hand on one of the woman's shoulders.

"What the fuck you doing, man?" he says in a deep, irritated voice. "We're next in line, and don't think for a second you're jumping ahead of us." With broad shoulders, he moves his hands and pounds one fist into his palm, making a metallic clinking sound.

How many times do I have to flash this badge? I might as well just tattoo NCPD on my forehead.

Sighing, I glance back into the restaurant, checking for sudden movements or if anyone is paying attention. I holster my Z4 and reach into my jacket, flashing my badge... again. "Sir, please, I'm here on police business," I say in a hushed voice. "I'm not here to eat or cut your place in line... so please remain calm."

The woman's face tenses. Her heart holograms suddenly morph into red flickering fires on each cheek. "He's fucking lying!" she spits out. "You can buy a fancy badge anywhere on the web. Doesn't mean shit! Fuck him up, Gerx!"

Gerx, the big man, steps in front of the woman and lifts his chin, red eyes glaring down at me. "My woman thinks you're lying, so... that means I think you're lying too." He moves closer in my direction while the people back in the line stare and start yelling curses.

So much for being inconspicuous.

Blue and pink neon from nearby signs reflect off the chrome surface of his balled fist as it starts careening toward my face. I hear a whoosh of his fist passing by while ducking under his haymaker. Lunging, I unclip my hyper coil and jab the grip end into the man's wide gut. Clenching at his stomach, he lets out a sharp grunt. Not wasting another moment, I follow with an uppercut, smashing into his hunched-over chin, knocking him to the ground.

The woman raises a single hand to cover her mouth. A gasp escapes her lips, fire holograms flickering to blue teardrops. She backs up, mouth agape, while moving her hands in a terrified stance of surrender. The crowd behind is silent and in shock, unsure what to do next.

In the corner of my eye, something rises inside the restaurant. My focus shifts, frantically searching for Mirk. A thousand eyes seem to be staring into my soul as every head in the store turns toward the commotion outside. I come to a halt on a set of deep-purple-glowing eyes that stand out in the mix of blinking gazes. Recognition floods through my brain as I know who these eyes belong to.

Mirk bolts to a standing position, knocking over the chair he was sitting in while holding chopsticks with a sushi roll clenched. Through the transparent walls of Zorgasbord, I can see his mouth form the words, *"Oh shit!"*

Pain explodes in my gut, making me release a breath. My eyes shift outside where Gerx is on his feet, winding up for another blow. Through clenched teeth, I activate the coil and whip it around his arm, slamming the dial up. It crackles with energy and starts to constrict around his meaty arm. A heartbeat later, he unleashes an agonizing scream. People scramble and wail while running in every direction away from the store.

I release the coil off of his arm, knowing that a bit further on the dial, his arm would sever and slap against the ground. Still screaming, he collapses to his knees, his other hand holding his pained arm. The teardrop-hologram woman rushes to comfort Gerx, real tears streaming down her face.

"Stay down!" I scream, searching for Mirk again. Through a back door, I catch a glimpse of a RootX logo before the door closes. He's going out the back!

Quickly tapping at my wrist display, I call for Coleson. He immediately answers, brows furrowing. "What the hell is going on there? I leave you alone for two secon—"

Interrupting Coleson, I spit out, "Do you have eyes on this place or not? He just ran out of the back of the store. You better be tailing him!" Before he can respond, I'm already running down the street, hoping to meet my suspect on the other side.

10

Shield

Phlegm builds at the top of my throat, making it hard to breathe. Everything around me is in a blur of motion, my feet sprinting down the narrow streets of Zorgossie. My mind wanders, going through the familiar motions.

She runs from my reaching hand, letting out a burst of frantic laughter each time I near. We both laugh and smile as we jump over the couch, rush through the living room, and dart through our tiny kitchen. I grab her in a tight embrace as she finally starts tiring.

"Tag, you're it!" I say through raspy breaths. Raena joins in and starts to tickle her. Zinny lets out a new wave of laughter.

Through her continual giggling, she says, "Daddy, I am supposed to catch you now!"

A smirk spreads across my face. "Oh yeah, right!" I bolt off the ground and hurry through our compact apartment. She giggles as Raena lets her free to chase after me.

Coleson's voice breaks the moment, snapping me back to reality. "I got his location! He's heading north through Zorgossie right now! Looks like he's heading back toward the city."

As if I'm jumping over my couch back at home, I vault over rolling street carts and teetering transport droids to keep my momentum going.

"Take the next left, then the first right! He's not far!" Coleson shouts.

My heart is pounding as I follow his directions. The case is about to end. My skin crawls with how close the bonus is. My hand inches closer. Debts need to be paid.

"You should be able to see him now, just twenty feet ahead!"

My gaze lifts to scan further ahead for any sign of Mirk. The end of Zorgossie is quickly approaching. Just ahead, ethereal neon light emanates from the tall skyline of Nox City, gripped by a cloud of haze.

My eyes harden, seeing someone sprinting ahead with a logo I recognize on the back of their jacket.

"Mirk! Stop now!" I shout.

Now, just outside the border of Zorgossie, Mirk stops and turns his head, staring back, purple eyes glaring. Slowly, he turns with one outstretched hand, facing me. A recent memory sparks from when I was skimming through Mirk's spec sheet.

Modifications. Mirk had something installed, and I'm sure one dealt with his hands.

A knot forms in my stomach. I skid to a halt and take cover behind an abandoned white cart that looks like it was to be used for selling vat-grown hot dogs.

Through the noise of Zorgossie behind me, I hear Mirk speak up in a loud and angered voice. "You just don't get it, do you? Are you so stupid, you don't see that I didn't do anything?"

Unsure of what Mirk is planning, I yell to the curious onlookers, "Everybody back up and get inside!"

"Harkones, I read over his spec sheet. I would watch whatever he's doing with his hands," Coleson says.

Peering over the cart, Mirk is still outstretching one pointed hand, which looks to be covered in chrome. It's just like that brute of a guy a few minutes ago. Hopefully, Mirk will go down the same way, with agonizing pain.

Speaking as loud as I can, I yell in Mirk's direction. "Mirk, there is no need to plead your case. You can tell it to the judge after we get you back to the station. How does that sound?" My unholstered hand cannon rests in my palm. I bounce on the balls of my feet, squinting over the cart.

"I ain't telling nobody shit!" Mirk shouts. "I was just doing my job, and you know... You are really starting to piss me off now." He takes a deep breath and squares his shoulders. "I think it's time to end this."

I couldn't agree more.

Mirk closes one eye and looks down his arm as if looking through the scope of a long-barreled rifle. I stare in confusion as his arm whips back, something launching with tremendous speed. Lights gleam off the metallic object zooming in my direction.

"Oh, fuck!" I shout while ducking under the cart once again. His metal hand smashes into the side of the cart. The impact pushes me and the cart's metal frame a couple of feet back. Sliding back into position, I hear a metallic tearing sound, ending in a quick pop as the cart jolts. Firmly grasping my Z4, I peer over the cart again in shock. His hand zips back toward his arm, reconnecting into his empty socket with a loud click. A deviant smile forms on Mirk's face.

Well... shit. He's got some sort of death boomerang hand.

Knowing that at least one of his hands is able to launch from him like a bullet, a plan begins to form. Taking a deep breath, I wipe the collecting sweat off my forehead as I ready myself, hopeful that I'm not making a critical mistake.

Thumbing the dial of my Z4 to the SHLD setting, I vault over the cart in a mad dash toward Mirk.

He tilts his head and lets out a cackle. "Wow, you really are a dumb plebo pig, aren't you?" He raises both hands in my direction, his purple eyes narrowing. His body jerks back in a sudden motion from the recoil, two hands launching like a rocket out from his arms, ripping through the air.

Two gleaming hands streak through the space between us, intended to tear me to shreds. At that exact moment, a small boy in a tattered smock stumbles between us. An older woman with oily, dark blue hair rushes out and grabs the boy by his shoulders. She looks up, and an expression of horror flashes across her face. The woman stands frozen in place, hands trembling.

It feels like a drum is beating against my chest. I halt close to the woman and boy, pointing my Z4 toward the ground. My finger pulls the trigger back, and a bolt launches out of the barrel. The bolt smacks the ground and instantly reconfigures to a black triangular device, making a rapid clicking noise. A rush of transparent blue energy domes around the device, creating a protective layer over the three of us. My breath catches in my throat. Mirk's hands smack against the shield, bouncing off and flying in different directions.

The modifier's eyes widen in surprise as he starts frantically moving his stub arms in the air, trying to call his hands back. Knowing that the shield dome only blocks high-speed projectiles, I pass right through it and run. I reach one arm down for a small disc attached to my belt.

"Oh fuck!" Mirk spits out, eyes still wide. One of his stub arms moves toward his waist as he tries to knock something off. A second later, a dark green ball falls from his side and rolls on the ground toward me.

What the hell is that thing?

Less than ten feet from me, I raise my hand cannon toward Mirk, flicking the dial to the PUSH setting. In my other hand, I tightly grip the EWEB disk. The ball bolts upward before I pull the trigger and hovers in the air.

My gaze darts from the hovering ball back toward Mirk. I blink and shake my head in confusion. Eight Mirks suddenly speed in various directions around me. My eyes bounce from each Mirk, trying to decipher what just happened. A tickle in my brain forms, recognizing something inconsistent amongst the Mirks spreading out.

Raising my Z4 toward the Mirk who's missing two hands. I pull the trigger back and a blast of air charges out of the barrel. The wave of concentrated air passes through clone copies of Mirk that remain unaffected until one topples over to the ground, the real Mirk. I step closer to the original, not paying any attention to the projection copies, and fling the EWEB disk.

Halfway before making impact, the silver disk unravels to an eight-foot web with electricity pulsing through the latticework of threads. It spreads out, ready to embrace anything in its path. Mirk, scrambling to get to his feet, falls to the ground as the EWEB wraps his limbs. Landing with a thud, his two flying hands career back toward him, slapping against both sides of his fallen body. He lets out a cry of pain from each impact of his hands. His body starts writhing from the electricity coursing through him. The clone copies of Mirk flicker out as the hovering ball falls to the ground, projections ceasing to be.

I hear the pop of my energy shield wink out behind me. The woman, finding her breath, lets out a terrified scream. Now able to move, she flounders and throws the boy over her shoulder, quickly hobbling down an alley. I stare down at Mirk and take a deep breath, relaxing my shoulders.

My god... finally. This took more effort than needed, but I finally caught the bastard.

"So you can do something by yourself?" Coleson's voice blares into my skull, our call still connected. "Scratch that." He scoffs. "I was the one who led you right to him."

I sigh and roll my neck. "Yeah... I don't know what to say besides thanks, and I owe you. There is no denying that, especially after today." I look toward my display. Coleson's lips are pursed while he nods.

"I'm glad we can both agree on that," Coleson says.

"Damn, what a day," I say and sigh. "I'll load him in the cruiser and head back to the station."

"Alright. Don't forget, though, you owe some grub!" Coleson's appearance flickers out as the call ends.

Tapping around my holo grid, I issue a command to my cruiser to head near my current location. Something still lingers in the back of my mind. I caught Mirk, but for some reason, this whole thing does not feel like it's over. Why did Pandemon come after me? What is Oblivion? How is Mirk connected to all of it, if at all? It doesn't make any sense, but I will find out.

Adrenaline dissipates as fatigue takes over my body. I'm more than ready to push these questions to tomorrow. I grimace and stare at Mirk, who still has murder in his twitching eyes.

Preparing to haul Mirk back to the station, fading questions bounce in my brain. He spits curses under his breath, squirming, bound within the web. After Mirk is questioned, I might still make it back before Zinny's bedtime. Will be great if I can get a confession out of him tonight. At that point, the case is closed. But something tells me he's not going to talk willingly.

11

Interrogate

I blink from a fist pounding against a metal table. The sound continues to reverberate in my head as if somebody struck a tuning fork next to my skull.

"You are going to tell us what happened to Benji Davis," Senior Detective Harvey Desson commands in a low voice, his fist still planted on the single metal table in the interrogation room. Devoid of any decorations or wall hangings, the eighty-square-foot room is brightly lit by LED light tubes recessed in the ceiling. The only furniture in the room is the metal table that separates Desson and Mirk, and two white plastic chairs that look very uncomfortable. I lean on the wall near the exit door, staring at Mirk, who is licking his lips while his furious eyes dart back and forth from Desson to me.

I feel lucky that Desson offered to help question Mirk. From what I've heard, he's one of the best interrogators on the force. It struck me as odd at first, since I know the old bastard doesn't *offer* help that often. From what I understand, he is usually a loner and likes to work solo, but I guess something about this case interests him.

Glancing down to my wrist, I check the time. I look back toward Desson and nod. I'll take any help I can get, even if it's from a supposedly short-tempered man who's wholly focused on physical fitness. He's been on the force for almost as long as I've been alive.

Desson stares at Mirk, his hard brown eyes unblinking, as if they were in some epic showdown. Desson's weathered and expressionless face doesn't falter. It's as if he's trying to make Mirk uneasy with only his no-nonsense demeanor. Mirk fidgets in his chair, his eyes twitching. I raise one eyebrow and purse my lips. The old detective might be on to something here or it could be that he is intimidating to look at. I trace a jagged scar running down Desson's forehead and cheek. Muscles strain the white fabric of his T-shirt around his bulging biceps and broad shoulders. His reputation for being some sort of health nut looks to be true.

I pray the old man has another trick up his sleeve, though, because, at the moment, it seems like Mirk's vocabulary is stuck with a select few words available to him, mainly including *"I didn't do shit."*

While restrained, Mirk stares up at Desson in quiet fury, his head shaking like a bobblehead figure. I expel a heavy breath and focus my gaze on the suspect. He is a thin man with a wild tangle of thin green hair falling over a receding hairline. Sweat shines off his forehead, and his cheeks are sunken. Overall, Mirk looks small without the oversized coat he was wearing earlier. My hand balls into a fist. This little scumbag caused me so many headaches. The room is silent for what feels like hours.

Three short and succinct beeps pierce the silence from somewhere within the room. Desson reaches for his holo grid and taps a button on the display. His hand moves toward his pocket and pulls out something grey and rectangular. He snaps it open with a click. Tilting it slightly, a mix of different-colored pills tumble onto his open palm. Bringing his hand to his mouth, he swallows the handful in one smooth motion, gulping them down.

Damn, that was a lot of pills. Why does he need all that? It looked like one of the pills was Senervamene, but I can't be too sure. I give the detective a curious glance. It doesn't look like he has any modifications. At least from what I can see.

Desson moves back off the table and raises his hands in a stance of surrender. His tone shifts from direct and threatening to something that sounds more like a late-night radio DJ. The detective sits in the chair across from Mirk and puts his hands on the table, his fingers interlaced.

"Listen, I just want to get to the bottom of this," Desson says in a low, calm voice. "You are saying that you had no part in this. If that is true, help us both out by shedding light on the situation." Desson pauses, the room going silent as he slowly scratches at his salt-and-pepper beard, which leads up to a sharp buzz cut. "It seems you are dead set that we are not here to help."

"You got that fucking right," Mirk spits out, ending with an annoyed laugh. "You're just trying to pin this on somebody who didn't do anything. I don't know how many times I have to say this." Mirk pauses and jerks his eyes toward me. "I didn't do shit!" Mirk roars, fire burning behind his purple-glowing eyes.

"Is that like your catchphrase or something?" I ask, shrugging.

"What? Are you mocking me after what you are putting me through?"

Desson moves one outstretched palm toward me. "It's alright. Let's just hear him out." Turning his head back toward Mirk,

Desson continues talking slowly and calmly. "Listen, there is no greater power than the power of choice, and you hav—"

Mirk snorts, interrupting Desson mid-sentence. "You are so full of shit." Mirk adjusts his tone to sound like Desson, spitting his words back at him. "No greater power than the power of choice... You sound like a lunatic!"

"You have the power here. You have the choice to chat with us and clear your name. How does that sound?"

It's silent again while Mirk stares between us. I can see him thinking, gears turning in his head on how he should respond.

Mirk takes a deep breath and exhales. "Whatever," he says with a reluctant sigh. "I'll walk you through what I know."

A subtle, warm grin forms across Desson's face. "Great. Let's start at the beginning, but before we do that, can I get you any water or coffee?"

Mirk stares at the stump at the end of each of his arms and looks back at us with angered eyes. "And how do you expect me to drink it?"

"We'll give you a straw," Desson answers.

After a brief pause, Mirk mumbles a response. "I'm fine. Let's just get it over with."

Leaning back in the chair as far as he can, Desson crosses his arms and places one hand on his chin. "So, you work at RootX, right? At the Sentari Street location? South side of the city?"

"Mm-hmm." Mirk nods.

"And you're a modifier? What does that mean?"

"You goddamn know what it means. Don't play me like I'm dumb."

I hold my tongue and roll my eyes. Has Mirk always had such a punchable face?

"I just want to hear it from you," Desson says. "What do you do as a modifier?"

Mirk licks his lips and sighs, his shoulders slumping. "I install modifications for paying clients. Iris illumination, holo grid implantation, you know, legal stuff. Nothing unregistered."

My brows rise at the mention of the words *legal* and *unregistered*. His boomerang hands are both not *legal* and not *registered*.

"Sounds like tricky work to me," Desson continues. "Having to understand both the human anatomy and the technical details of the modies right? You go to school or go through any training for this?"

"Yes. I went to technical training at RootX. Everybody goes through training to become a contractor."

"Contractor?"

"What about it?"

"So you, as a contract modifier, how does RootX play into this?"

"Can't you guys just look this up on the web? This is all standard shit. You are just wasting my time."

Desson pauses while nodding. "We'll come back to that. Let's get to when you first met Benji. Can you describe when and where you met him?"

Mirk licks his lips and lets out a growling sigh. "Yes, fine. Yeah, that Benji kid came into the shop maybe two or three days ago asking about modies he was looking to get. I gave him a quote, and he accepted it. That's it. Nothing else."

A flat line forms across my mouth. I close my eyes and swallow my building annoyance. He damn well knows there is more to this. Why the hell would he have run from me in the first place if there wasn't? My eyes narrow at Mirk. Could he be involved with Pandemon somehow, or linked to Oblivion? Benji Davis's face flashes across my mind. At the very least, we have a kid stuck in a catatonic state one day after visiting this slimy creature.

"What happened next?" Desson asks.

"Exactly what you would expect. He came back the next day to get the modies installed."

Still leaning back in his chair, Desson scratches his beard. "What did you install?"

Mirk shakes his head. "I mean nothing out of the ordinary, just typical standard shit, really. He wanted some illumination added to his eyes, facial projector units, and uh, a nasal sensory enhancer..." Mirk chuckles while shaking his head. "The kid said he wanted to be able to smell better. Who in their right mind wants to smell more of this putrid city?"

Desson nods and bites on this upper lip in thought. "So... that's it. Anything else you do for him?"

"Like I told you, nothing unusual," Mirk spits out, glaring in my direction. "All of it was sourced from legit suppliers, like I already said earlier."

I shake my head and roll my eyes. *Like he said earlier.* Does he mean when he was sprinting away from me? Or when he shot his damn hands at me?

Desson continues, "You know why you're here, right?"

"Honestly, not really, since I did nothing wrong. It's you guys who messed up but you know, can't expect much out of you pigs. Especially you plebo pigs."

Plebo... burnout...

Clenching my jaw, my right eye starts to twitch. Vanya flashes across my mind. I'm so sick of hearing that fucking derogatory name being thrown at me. I look down toward my holo grid device strapped around my wrist. Mirk is right, though. *Vanya too.*

I speak up while narrowing my eyes. "You realize talking like that is not going to help your situation, right?"

Mirk's face tenses. "Like I give a fuck!" he yells. "It's going to be you who apologizes to me when you see I didn't do anything."

I take a deep breath through my nose and open my mouth to respond, but a loud, metallic smack breaks my chain of thought. Mirk flinches back deeper into his chair.

Desson's hand rests on the table and he uses it as leverage to stand up. His penetrating eyes stare down at Mirk. An agitated and threatening tone replaces Desson's friendly and calm demeanor.

"Then you also know that Benji Davis is GONE! Right? He was found one day after your *ordinary* installation service in a pool of his own spit." Desson leans closer to Mirk. "He might not be dead, but he might as well be. No brain activity, just an empty meat sack, lungs only pulling in air because of a machine hook up."

A holo display materializes above the middle of the table. Pictures of Benji start to cycle through, starting with a photo showing him on the floor, his face in a glistening pool of saliva, dead eyes staring blankly ahead. The display transitions to the next image of a close-up of Benji's face. Like a punctured rotten tomato, his face is red and bruised, his mouth agape, and drool runs down his chin.

Mirk makes a snarled expression, staring at the revolving window of pictures. "That ain't because of me! He walked out of my shop, transaction complete. Modies installed to the correct specification." He shrugs, lifting his stump arms above his shoulders in a position of indifference. "Wasn't me that caused that."

Desson crosses his arms. "Let's walk through those modies you installed again." After a pause, he continues. "You also realize that we have the video recording of you installing the equipment, right?"

Mirk snorts. "Wouldn't surprise me if you do," he mutters. "Every RootX installation is recorded, no matter the person performing the service."

"Every installation is recorded?" Desson mirrors.

Mirk narrows his eyes. "Yes, that's what I just said."

The room is silent again. Desson sits while chewing on his lip. Staring at the two, I understand what Desson is trying to do. Silence is sometimes the best tool to get people talking. A few moments of absent voice can serve as a catalyst for many to fill the void.

"Every installation is recorded." Mirk's eyebrows rise while talking, as if he were speaking to children. "Supposedly, it's for the protection of the business and the protection of the modifier."

Opening one palm, Desson gestures in the direction of Mirk's stumps. "So you're telling me there is a recording out there for your hands?"

"Well, like I said, every service should be recorded," he says with a grin.

"Alright, fine." Desson moves his hands and taps around his holo grid. A moment later, the display changes from pictures of

Benji to a video clip, ready to play. "Since we have the recording of you installing the modies into Benji, why don't we walk through it together."

Two sharp knocks sound at the door before it swings open. Officer Palmer peers through the doorway with one hand still grasping the door handle.

"Harkones, the lieutenant wants to see you."

A flash of confusion courses through me. Amix wants to see me? Why? It could be about my run-in with Pandemon. Other than that, I have no idea.

Through a grimace, I respond, "I'll be right there." I look back toward Desson.

"You mind handling this for a bit? I'm going to see what the lieutenant needs."

Our eyes meet, and he gives a sharp nod. "Mm-hmm, no problem. We're going to spend a little time here talking about this installation."

"Thanks. I'll be back soon." I step through the doorway and shut the door behind me. With a deep breath, I make my way toward the lieutenant's office.

12

Assignment

Ambient light glares at the corner of my vision. Fifty-two stories high, I'm on the third-to-highest level of the building, which is occupied mostly by NCPD leadership. An all-too-familiar hum sounds in the distance belonging to the air filtration units, pushing clean air throughout the floor. Walking down the hallway, I glance out the window and see NCPD cruisers zipping from the station in different directions. My gaze shifts toward the ground. A throng of people bustle through the city. From this height, it looks like bugs skittering around in a sea of neon decay.

Is this how the people of Veridian see us? As insects they can stomp on? My eyes flick up toward a glistening tower connected to the web of bridges and walkways that make up the city. It's pointless to stare, but how can I not when towers loom above? Why do I keep finding myself glancing up? I'm not sure what I expect to change. Maybe that their wealth will come streaming down someday. If I had all that money, would I be any different? I don't know, but I would like to think so.

Shaking the thought from my head, I continue walking down the brightly lit hallway. Glancing at my wrist, I check the time and nod. I can still keep my promise. A couple of hours max, though. I don't want to disappoint Zinny again. My chest tightens at the thought of seeing the corners of her mouth turning downward, her shoulders slumped, and her watery eyes. Her disappointment shatters me. I can't keep doing that to her.

Hopefully, Desson is working his magic on Mirk. The faster the bastard talks, the sooner I can close this case out.

"What did I tell you about your posture?"

By reflex, I straighten my back and lift my gaze. Walking in my direction, Lyra Nekova moves with fluid grace. A close-fitting dark jacket with an almost armor-like quality wraps around her lean frame. Each shoulder is adorned with glowing yellow letters spelling out *NCPD*.

"Nekova. How's the Strike Force going for you?" I ask, studying the two hyper coils holstered to her hips. It's been a while since I last saw her, ever since she moved to a new division— one of the most dangerous ones, too. A whole squad, all skilled and focused on neutralizing level nine and ten threats that require immediate attention.

The corners of her lips curl up into a smirk. "As you would expect." She pauses and furrows her brow. Her black hair sweeps across half her forehead and rests behind one ear. "How's the family doing? Zinny is what? Four years old now?"

"Five," I say.

"Has it been that long?" she asks, her eyebrows raised. "It seems like just yesterday you were talking about having her."

"I know. I don't believe it myself."

She shakes her head and nods. "What do you say to a spar here pretty soon?" She gestures to my belt.

I glance at my weapon and suck in air through my teeth. "So you can kick my ass again?"

She snorts. "No. I want to see if my training has stuck with you or not. You might need a refresher."

I offer a smile, remembering the bruises and sharp pains from countless sparring sessions with her. "I'm getting by just fine, thanks."

"So you're saying you don't need practice?"

I chuckle. "No, I'm fine."

She looks at me and smiles.

In a flash, an activated hyper coil is slicing down toward my face. My breath catches as I gape at the oncoming tendrils of electricity. I spin on my heels and lunge out of the way of the attack. Pulse pounding, I back away and stare at Nekova.

"What the fuck was that for?" I hiss.

She purses her lips and nods. "Seems like some of the training stuck after all," she says, gesturing at my hands.

I look down and notice my hyper coil is firmly in my grip, thumb planted on the activator.

She sighs and holsters the weapon back to her hip. "But... you need to work on your breathing."

"Oh, come on. Was this necessary?"

"We don't want all that training to go to waste, do we?"

I scoff and shake my head. "You're unbelievable. It's no wonder you're in the Strike Force."

"I can't say it's not exciting, but I miss training the newbies." She steps closer and rests a hand on my shoulder. "I need to meet with someone, but it was nice seeing you."

"You too. Keep safe."

She nods, retreats her hand, and moves past me. She pauses and looks over her shoulder. "Remember, control your breathing and maintain posture for the love of god."

"Mm-hmm, will do." I nod.

Taking a couple of steadying breaths, I continue down the hallway. Nekova is a beast with the hyper coil. It's like they were made for her. I'm not sure I'll ever reach that level of mastery with the weapon. I shake my head and purse my lips, thinking of her using two at the same time. Whoever she is after should be afraid, and I have no doubt they are when they see the two coils twisting in the air.

I approach a wide, transparent glass door with the words "Lieutenant Lacet Amix" embossed to the right of it. I hesitate before knocking.

From my few encounters with the new lieutenant, I don't know what to make of her. New to the role, I can only assume she wants to make a name for herself and her superiors here at the station.

A hollow knock sounds on the door as I tap one knuckle against the glass. I stand silent, waiting for a response.

An instant later, a strong feminine voice sounds, "Come in."

I push the door open a few feet and enter the office. "Lieutenant, you needed to see me?" She looks out the window to the sprawling city beyond. Her hands are held behind her back.

"Yes, please close the door behind you and take a seat." Amix unclasps her hands and turns in my direction, bright blue eyes piercing. She might be short, standing slightly more than a foot lower than me, but a commanding and formidable aura exudes from her. Her brown hair is tied back in a tight bun, and not a single hair is out of place. She takes pride in her appearance because her blue NCPD uniform is immaculate, crisp, and perfectly tailored to her lean body. I bite the inside of my cheek, looking down at my clothes that need a wash at the maximum setting. Maybe even twice, to somewhat remove the smell of musk.

Anticipation trickles into my fingers, unsure where this conversation is heading. Closing the door, the glass flickers to opaque. I move to sit in one of the two chairs in the room in front of her desk. She places one of her hands on the top of her rolling chair, a thin smile forming across her angular face.

"Harkones, I heard you had a little trouble earlier today with Pandemon, correct?" Her eyes narrow, her head lowering in my direction.

Pandemon, ah, yes, so this is what it's about. I relax.

"A little trouble might be understating it, but yes, I ran into a couple of thugs from the gang. I should say they ran into *me* while I was hunting down a suspect."

Amix's mouth twists into a frown. Her eyes continue to stare into me. "Pandemon..." she pauses, taking a small breath while nodding. "Always poking around where they shouldn't. Did you find anything as to why they tracked you down?"

An image of the scorpion flashes across my mind, making me shudder. I let go of a held breath and shake my head. "Mm-hmm, they were convinced I was searching for something..."

I hesitate, rubbing at one temple. Should I be telling Amix about this? I might be stirring up a bigger mess with Pandemon. Sabine made it clear they did not want anyone from the NCPD tracking Oblivion. To hell with that. I'm not going to give them what they want.

"Something called Oblivion," I finally say, my shoulders relaxing as if a weight fell off of them.

Amix purses her lips in consideration. "Oblivion? Hmm, that doesn't sound familiar to me. What else have you found about it?"

I suck in air through my teeth. "Nothing. It's still a mystery, but it must be important to them. They went through a lot of effort to *speak* with me. A clean-up crew should be surveying the scene now."

"Good. Please keep me up to date on what you find. Especially anything that deals with Pandemon." Amix swivels her chair and moves to sit.

Sabine's malicious laugh echoes in my brain. My heart rate quickens, remembering her threats against my family. I run one hand through my hair while the other tightly grips the armrest of my chair.

"Ma'am, they also talked about visiting my family at home." I purse my lips. Amix's eyes focus on me.

After a pause, she folds her hands and places them on the table between us, her eyes hardening. "Understood. As you already know, we take any threat to an officer seriously, including their families. Do you have any reason to suspect they will continue seeking you out?"

I frown, shaking my head. "I... I'm not sure. It's possible, especially when they realize two of their thugs were taken out. Other than that, I really don't know. They were adamant that I don't speak about Oblivion." I anxiously laugh. "I don't even know what it is!"

"I'll send a request to the surveillance team to spin up a couple of drones for you, eyes in the sky. One is to monitor your home, and the other is to be your shadow for a few weeks. Until things settle down."

My brows rise in surprise, not expecting that response. It seems like she cares, which is something new to me. People showing empathy in the NCPD are few and far between. A memory of my last lieutenant forms in my head, him barking out orders and not giving a flying fuck about his people. It felt like we were just warm numbers thrown at open cases. Hopefully, there isn't a catch to all this generosity, but this is something I can get used to.

"That would be... great," I say.

"Good, let's hope they aren't necessary."

Something nudges in the back of my mind while thinking about a drone tailing me. Oh yeah, Coleson. I run my tongue along my teeth, thinking I almost forgot to tell the lieutenant... again.

"One more thing. I would probably be dead in the ground right now if it weren't for Agent Coleson." I sigh. "He's helped me out on more than a few occasions."

"Noted," Amix says.

I blink and try to hold down a laugh from bubbling out. After all this heated talk today with Coleson, I finally let the leadership team know, and I got a single-word response. Maybe Amix isn't what I think she is. Either way, I won't be lying to Coleson when I tell him I gave him props.

After a pause, she continues. "Now, for what I called you in for."

I lick my lips, a pang of worry forming in my mind. What else could there be?

"I understand that your current assignment deals with a case of brain trauma. The Benji Davis case, right?"

Where is she going with this?

I nod. "Yes, exactly. Detective Desson is helping me and questioning the primary suspect now, a modifier from RootX."

Amix's brows furrow. "You're thinking the brain trauma is most likely due to defective or counterfeit modifications. Do I have that right?"

"Mm-hmm, that's right. That, along with him running the moment he saw my badge. I think this is our guy. Desson is working on getting a confession right now."

"Good. Good work, Harkones." Her thin eyebrows rise and lower again. "I want you to look into something else for me that might or might not be related."

"Oh really? What makes you think that?"

"An influx of new cases have come in dealing with people experiencing episodes of brain trauma, similar to the case you are working on now. It's not so much that it's outwardly apparent just yet, but something else might be going on here."

My initial shocked reaction quickly shifts to concern. More brain damage cases? I wonder if modifications are the culprit or maybe even another modifier like Mirk. If that's the case, we might have something else that's more widespread than I thought.

"How many cases are we talking here?" I ask.

"Like I said, only a handful. Only five so far, but they all came in over the past two weeks."

I rest one hand under my chin and nod. Only five cases out of the hundreds that are called in every week. This could be a coincidence. "What are you thinking I should check out first?"

"We have an active crime scene with officers on site that I want you to scan through. This could be a coincidence and nothing unusual, but it's always better to be proactive on these hunches."

"You said it's an *active* crime scene?

"Exactly. We got a call from a father saying that his son is not breathing and that he hit his head on something. Deputies arrived on the scene less than an hour ago and found a young male sprawled on the ground in a pool of blood."

I place one hand on my chin, considering. "Are we sure this is a case of brain trauma? Or that it isn't a case of suicide?"

"It could be precisely that. The father also informed us about a new modi installed just a day ago in the victim."

My ears perk up at the mention of modies. "Oh really? What kind of modi and was it installed at a RootX location?

"I'm not sure, but the deputies on scene should be able to help with those questions. They set up view casters throughout the home, ready for you to tap in."

Pushing off the armrests of the chair, I move to stand. "I'll head down and see what I can find. Anything else you need from me?"

Amix pushes off her desk, rolling her chair back, giving her room to stand up. "No, that will be it. Treat this as a level two case for now. I'll have Palmer send over the details." After a pause, she continues, "Also, please let me know if you learn anything more about this Oblivion business."

"Will do. Thanks again, Lieutenant."

She nods and turns toward her large holo display above her desk, flickering with a constant flow of new notifications.

Grabbing the handle of the office door, the glass reverts into a state of transparency. When the door closes behind me, I place one hand on my forehead and let out a long sigh. A sinking sensation forms in my stomach as my promise to Zinny keeps inching further from my reach. At least this should be an easy assignment that leads toward more credits.

13

Elexor

Darkness descends as I lower an Infinity rig over my face, blocking any light from seeping in. With my eyes open, I am enveloped in a black void until something tiny pops to life. Like a glittering jewel, the logo for Infinity shimmers and quickly enlarges. A swooping icon that looks like a sideways number eight with one loop larger than the other. The logo charges toward my face, a rainbow of colors swirling. When just inches away, the logo suddenly bursts and color washes over me. As if a breeze is carrying away smoke, the colors dissipate, leaving me staring into the virtual world of Infinity. Stretching what seems hundreds of miles out, I gaze upon rolling fields of grass to the left. Turning my head right, I peer across an endless ocean of choppy waves with a stereotypical tropical island in the background. I flick my eyes up at the crystal-clear blue sky and make out the blackness of space filled with hundreds of planets and stars.

A chime sounds through the headset's speakers with a text menu materializing in front of me. Above the menu, "Welcome to Infinity" text is superimposed and looks like it is breathing.

Why does this Infinity startup process always have to be so fucking dramatic? Just let me put the headset on and piss off so I can do what I need to do. I mean, it's probably a setting I could disable, but I don't want to waste any more time than I need to here fiddling around with settings.

Using controls gripped in both of my hands, I navigate the menu and select a button named "NCPD Login." Ocular sensors inside the headset scan my eyes, confirming my identity and allowing me access to the NCPD network. *"Welcome, Detective Sol Harkones"* text appears in my view before snapping the background to a large, enclosed space without any decoration. Deep blue walls are on my sides. The wall to my left displays current news feeds discussing recent and upcoming events happening within the city. To my right, NCPD announcements and department statistics scroll horizontally across the wall. Directly in front of me is a barren mahogany desk with one display window hovering above it. Beyond the desk, the wall ahead is black with large yellow letters spelling out NCPD.

Infinity is a place of limitless opportunity, and I'm in an office. Granted, it's a big, exaggerated office, but still... depressing.

I navigate the menu until I land on a screen that displays the NCPD Caster Network. Glancing up at the top of the menu, I notice a notification for an unread message. Clicking the icon brings up the message in a new display window to the right of the home menu. Details about the case fill my view. I scan the message from Palmer, looking for the case number, address, and other relevant details. My brows arch while reading the building's address and the name of the tower: Elexor.

Of course, it has to be Elexor. I run my tongue over my teeth and sigh. What a hell of a day. Strolling through filth one moment and the next, I will be visiting the center of Veridian. I don't want to deal with these rich bastards staring with their noses turned up in the air as if they are trying to avoid smelling me. Well, thank god for them, they won't have to deal with that today. I sniff and get whiffs of an earthy odor mixed with the smell of dried sweat.

Tightly pressing my lips together, I continue to read over the case details. It looks like I'll be visiting the Rhyner family on floor 152. Reading over the victim's age, I blow out a puff of air. Tito Rhyner, son of Damian and Lucinda Rhyner, was only twenty-three years old. This kid has a squeaky-clean record with no criminal history. This might indicate he was a good kid, or money had a helping hand in keeping his record spotless.

Can this Tito Rhyner case be related to Benji Davis and Mirk? With it involving brain trauma and a recent modi installation, yeah, it's possible, but I am not convinced. The people of Veridian, especially this Rhyner family, can afford the best modi installations. I don't see why any of them would make a trek down to the surface to visit a RootX location when they have premier services at their disposal.

Either way, looks like he was set to graduate from Titus Institute of Engineering, one of the most prestigious universities in Nox City. My eyes perk up at the mention of Titus Institute. I know the annual cost to attend this school is exorbitant and out of reach for millions here in the city. I've looked at their website, I don't know, a countless number of times now. Titus is my dream school for Zinny to attend after she's done with Eligere. I suck in air through my teeth, knowing I am already in debt to her school.

With the family living in the Elexor tower, it makes sense that they can afford the enrollment and tuition costs, but what do they actually do? Where does their money come from?

Back in the station, one of my legs starts to go numb. I shift in my cushy faux-leather seat in the Infinity transport room. While my right leg slaps the ground, trying to regain normal sensation, I picture what I must look like to those who can see me back in the real world. A disheveled man, a large black headset covering half his face, tightly holding on to hand controls like a kid gripping lollipops and kicking like a jack rabbit.

I pull up a new window that materializes above the center of my virtual desk, pushing my other screens to the side. Clicking on the background search program, I run a query for Damian Rhyner. A second later, a list of Damian Rhyners who live within Nox City materializes. I scan the list, focusing on the address portion of the results. I come to a halt on the third entry. There he is, Mr. Rhyner, who resides in the Elexor Tower.

Damian Rhyner
    Age: 56
    Height: 5ft 10in
    Weight: 184lbs
    Occupation: Chief of Product at Sicarius Pharmaceuticals
    Time in Occupation: 8 years
    Recorded Implants: 1
    Criminal Record: Misdemeanors: 0, Felonies: 0

"Sicarius Pharmaceuticals... that makes sense," I mutter. I think back to the countless advertisements shoved in my face for Sicarius products and grimace. Almost everywhere I look when traveling through the city, Sicarius is pushing their shit, trying to pull credits out from my account. No, thank you. I don't need your pills.

Frowning, I envision the piles of credits the company takes in every single day. Millions of people lining up, getting a script for their bullshit Senervamene just so their modies continue working in their bodies, the pill acting as some sort of immunosuppressant. My eyes flick back to Damian's record. With him being on the executive board, I am sure he is handsomely rewarded.

In the Caster Network menu, I find my case in the list of active crime scenes. Selecting the case number, a new menu pops up with a list of feeds to tap into. I select the top option, labeled "Caster 1", and click a second button, named "Transport."

A whoosh emits from the headset's speakers with my view shifting like I'm being pulled through a wormhole in space. A few seconds later, a million pixels come together, and I'm greeted by opulence. From where I materialize, I stare up a small set of marble stairs that lead to two massive, intricately decorated copper doors that are opened inwards to the residence. From what I can see, everything looks spotless and untainted from the grime coating the city below. Through the arched doors, an incandescent orange glow illuminates a round room where large pillars of white stone stretch from floor to ceiling.

Peering inside the entrance to the home, my brows rise and my jaw hangs open. It's as if I'm a spectator at a pit fight waiting for gladiators to charge out from rooms deeper within.

A fleeting sense of vertigo escapes me as I turn my head and notice that I am extremely high up. Standing on the home's balcony, my eyes widen and stare out toward the neon mosaic of the city below. Glancing upward, clouds swirl and look only an arm's length away. Quick bursts of light dance within the clouds. A crack of thunder booms only a few seconds later, making me wince even though my ass is inside, sitting in an oversized chair back at the station. It looks like it will rain soon, but what's new?

I take a moment to reorient myself, knowing I'm not actually on this balcony. As much as it pains me, I can see how so many people would believe that Infinity is real. I shake my head. It's not real, though. I only think this because I see the natural world through Infinity, not stuck inside it in some bullshit virtual world. There is a difference.

Using my hand controls, I take a few steps toward the balcony ledge and peer down. I let out a whistle that emits out of the view caster's speakers, lost in the wind that whips the tower. It's hard to make out anything on the ground through the layers of pollution looming over the city. Like a rotting sandwich speckled with mold, this city is squished between layers of neon, ads, and, of course, the ever-present haze of Nox City.

My gaze trails from left to right, staring at neighboring sky-scrapers connected to the lower floors of Elexor. Extensive, immaculate walkways connect the towers, creating a labyrinth in the sky. I can make out sections of floors that are dedicated to serving the people in the clouds, the Veridians. Comfort and privilege to all those who can afford it, while bottom dwellers like me are stuck in the cesspit of Nox City, trying to claw our way out.

My chest feels tight. I close my eyes and take a deep breath. I snap my eyes open and blow out a puff of air. No, I don't live in Veridian, but at least I don't have the family living in the gutter or in the Swamplands. It could be worse. I just need to focus on now. One thing at a time.

To the side of me, red and blue lights strobe from thin slits that wrap around a couple of NCPD police cruisers. The cruisers are sitting next to what must be the homeowners' vehicles on the side of the floor, on the parking pad built into the tower. Lifting my head, I scoff. Each floor of this building has a private parking area.

Lightning flashes above, shining off the homeowners' pristine vehicles. The Veritas GXT and Celestia Model Z alone are signs of affluence, but the parking pad is just another *"Fuck you, I have money"* display of substantial wealth.

Sighing, my gaze pulls back to the center of the balcony, where I notice a half-foot-tall gray cylindrical device planted on the ground. Tripod legs hold it upright while a transparent black dome sits on top, emitting a soft whirring noise. Using my hand controls, I raise my palms and stare through my avatar's translucent, grainy blue hue. Peering ahead, I nod while seeing another view caster planted on the ground about four feet away.

A deputy walks onto the balcony through the massive doors, with blue energy rippling behind him. An energy curtain? Really? I shake my head in disgust as the cost alone to power it is astronomical. All to simply keep the filtered air within the home.

I can tell it's Deputy Gerson walking down from his wobbling steps and the shaven sides of his scalp. Below a plop of slicked-back hair, sweat glistens on his forehead and trails down his face. Continuing in my direction, his bulbous nose is in clear view behind the transparent layer of his mask.

Oh god, not this guy again. Sure, I like to close cases quickly, but I at least attempt to ensure I am doing my due diligence. This guy is a paper pusher who puts no effort into his work. Everything is surface-level, never digging deeper. The only reason I can think of why this guy is still employed is that he closes many cases—even if he is booking the wrong people—innocent people.

Gerson opens his mouth with a yellow display of teeth. "Detective Harkones," he says in a high, whiny voice. "I was told you would be paying us a visit, though I'm not sure why."

My brows furrow. "What makes you say that?" I say flatly, my voice sounding through the caster speakers.

Gerson shrugs with a smug face. "The way I see it, nothing here to... I don't know, inspect? The case is closed. Just an accident. So you'll just be wasting your time."

Shoving my annoyance down, I say, "The lieutenant wanted me to check out the scene, so that's what I'm going to do."

"I mean, it makes no difference to me. It's your time that you're wasting. I already scanned through everything. No evidence of foul play. So whatever you're about to do, I'd hurry it up. The father wants us out pronto."

"The father?" I ask. "What do you mean? I thought the family were the ones who called us?"

"He keeps going on about how we're intruding and that they need to be left to grieve."

"Hmm, I'll keep that in mind. So you didn't find anything suspicious?"

"That's what I said. If it looks like a drunken accident, and it smells like a drunken accident, chances are, it's a drunken accident. A stupid one at that." He chuckles.

The corners of my mouth twist into a scowl. "Don't you think we should wait for the medical examiner, toxicology, or the results from the autopsy? You know, before making any judgments? Could be something here we're not seeing just yet."

Gerson curls his lips and shakes his head in defiance. "Nah, no medical examiner is coming. Sometimes, what it seems to be is exactly what it is. Alcohol doesn't care who you are, poor, rich, it doesn't matter. Still fucks you up even when you live up here in the clouds. A bedside table of all things! Can you believe that? The boys back at the station will die of laughter after hearing about this."

A joyless smile pulls at my lips. "Thanks for the info. Can you do me a favor and just keep anyone from entering until I'm done?"

With a dismissive display of hands, he shrugs. "Yeah, yeah. Hurry up, though."

"Right," I say.

I thumb the dial on my controller and move toward the huge copper doors.

So Damian Rhyner doesn't want us to intrude? Well, it's too bad that it's my job to intrude. Does he have something to hide, or is he a parent in actual grief?

Gerson's cackle fades behind me. I roll my eyes, approaching the entryway.

14

Residence

I expect to feel a slight tingling sensation, like walking into spiderwebs while moving through the energy curtain. Instead, I feel nothing—only the stale air of the Infinity transport room clinging to my body. Shifting my stiff legs around, the chair squeaks like a rodent trying to break free of a trap.

A sliver of relief forms in my mind, thinking I can finally give my aching body a break from all the running I did earlier today. A lingering throb in my chest reminds me... I was fucking stabbed and paralyzed by a droid scorpion a couple of hours ago. I do not want to go through that again. It was close, way too close for comfort.

Raena will not be happy with the new bruises blooming like rose buds across my body. I keep telling her that I'm going to be more careful, but they keep welting up regardless of how careful I am. Unfortunately, it appears that it's just a part of the job. At least it's not from training sessions with Nekova anymore.

I pull in a deep breath and let it out slowly.

It could be worse.

Back at the entrance of Rhyner's residence, I study the impressive interior. White marble floors interlaced with swirling gold run throughout the entrance into the hallways and rooms beyond my sight. The entryway pillars are made of the same material, each stretching to meet the high ceiling above. In the middle of the ceiling, oscillating rings of orange light hover and act like a living, breathing chandelier, throwing warm light around the room. Mesmerized by the display, I pull my eyes back to eye level. Large paintings are hung on the wall between each pillar, depicting what looks to be chaos. Each painting is encased in glistening, ornate black and gold frames.

My eyes narrow while examining one painting that seems like a frantic mess of colors. Lines and swirls intersect with no apparent meaning, as though a mix of colors were thrown haphazardly at the canvas.

A bark of laughter escapes my lips. This is art?

As I'm about to dismiss it, I flinch back. A screaming feminine face suddenly snaps into focus in the mix of colors. Now, in clear view, the face looks to be in a tremendous amount of pain.

I don't know how I missed it in the first place. Why the hell would somebody want this in their house? I bet this bullshit sells more than what I pay for my tiny apartment for an entire year. A sigh escapes my lips, thinking it's probably even more. Do I want to know how much it really is? Probably not. It would only make me more upset.

Angered whispers break my focus as they bounce off the stone walls in what I think is the next room over. Looking down the hallway, view casters are planted at intervals of every three to four feet. At least Gerson did something right, if he had even set these up.

I move my thumbs to walk my avatar toward the source of the hushed commotion. It feels strange not to hear my footsteps, as if I were gliding like a phantom across the home.

Thin strips of orange light, the same color as the chandelier in the entrance, streak through the hallway walls. I round a sharp corner that opens up to a spacious room that stretches in a curved arc around what seems to be half of the floor in this tower. Large floor-to-ceiling windows glimmer, allowing a striking view down toward the city. The room is massive. Maybe six or seven copies of my apartment can fit into it with room to spare. I shake my head and scoff. I can only imagine the people living in this tower must feel like gods staring at the city below.

Blue reflections ripple off a few windows that I trace back toward the center of the room. Hologram birds flap and swirl through the air. They shimmer and dance around a tree that stretches toward the ceiling. My jaw hangs open as I stare at the majestic trunk, rising to a full canopy of leaves. It looks like the heavens are shining down, creating an ethereal glow, but staring at the light source, it's just recessed LEDs from the ceiling shining on the canopy.

My eyes glaze over, taking in the sight. This is something I will never see on the ground of Nox City's concrete jungle. A memory surfaces of clicking through holo books of pictures of lush landscapes of green. Forests, fields of grass, gardens of flowers, enormous trees, and so much more. I was just a kid back then, clicking through the book, staring at the pages, wholly transfixed. How life is now is how I've always known it. A polluted shithole nowhere near resembling what I saw in that book. A bitter annoyance creeps down my spine, knowing that only the people living in Veridian get to walk through gardens of greenery and have shit like this in their homes.

Sighing, I focus. The blue hologram birds continue swirling around the tree. Below the canopy, a short white couch stretches around in a U shape that can easily seat twenty people, with a stone table in the middle.

Angered whispers sound again. I turn and see what appears to be two people in the living space. Still walking, I thumb my control to zoom my vision toward the whispers. I have to admit, there are some benefits to using this view caster.

My vision focuses on a man who I can only assume is Damian Rhyner, hovering over a sobbing woman in an elegant white dress, her face buried in her hands while sitting on the couch. The woman sniffles and stares at the man dressed in formal business attire. A suit, tie, polished black shoes, and a sharp haircut to pull it all together. Exactly what I would expect some corporate bigwig to wear.

One of his hands is tightly gripped around one of the woman's pale arms. He leans toward her ear, his mouth moving. The woman trembles and nods at whatever Damian is saying. As she glances toward his eyes, tears roll down her blushed cheeks, scarlet red hair framing her face. A gleaming gold necklace traces around her neck, leading toward a pendant blocked off from my view as it rests right below the deep V-cut of her dress. Her chest shudders as it rapidly rises and falls.

"You need to listen—" Damian says in a low and gravelly voice before noticing my silent approach, my footsteps not making a sound.

The man's gaze snaps in my direction. Anger flares in his dark brown eyes. He releases the woman's arm, leaving red marks behind. Damian stands to his full height, his chin raised and eyes narrowing on me.

Glancing to the couple's right, I nod, seeing another view caster planted on the ground. I make a mental note to check the recording later. I zoom out and clear my throat. "Damian Rhyner? I'm Detective Sol Harkones, and I wan—"

"I thought I was clear when I told the other officers that we are to be left alone," Damian interjects with a cool tone of authority. Half his face is shadowed by slow-blinking blue and pink lights outside the windows. One of his hands gestures toward a view caster a couple of feet from where he stands. "Remove all your equipment and get out. Is that understood?"

My brows furrow, confused as to why he is so persistent that we leave and not check for anything that could be suspicious. If I were in his shoes, I would demand to know exactly what happened, or it would haunt my remaining days.

"Mr. Rhyner, I will only take a few minutes, and then I'll be on my way."

The woman's golden eyes flash toward me. She licks her lips and rubs tears off her perfect, symmetrical features that only huge stacks of money can buy. Thin gold lines trace around her angular face and eyes, shimmering from light beyond the room. "Thank... Thank you, Detective," she says in a weak, shaky voice.

She continues while sniffling, "As my husband said, we need time alone before... they take him away." She bursts into tears, her slender body trembling more than before.

It almost seems forced, but it's her child. I can only imagine the void I would be trapped in if something were to happen to Zinny.

One of Damian's eyes starts twitching. He moves a hand to one of the woman's shoulders. "Lucinda, it will be alright," he mutters. Slowly, his penetrating eyes move in my direction. An uneasy silence hangs in the air, the only sounds coming from the woman's sobs and the low hum of nearby view casters.

"Understand this, Detective, my son doesn't need any more prying people." He pauses. "Searching through his life, his things, his being. You pulling for new non-existent threads will only hurt us further. Leave us with what remaining time we have with him."

I take a deep breath through my nose. I didn't want to escalate this, but I will survey the scene regardless of anything that these two say.

"Mr. and Mrs. Rhyner, I'm only asking out of courtesy. I will check out the scene, but I'll try to make it brief."

Even if he were to try and stop me, which I highly doubt, his hands will pass through me, breaking the illusion that I am there. The only way for him to stop me would be to destroy the view casters, which would only come back to bite him, putting him in deeper shit with the NCPD.

I shrug and offer a pained smile. "Listen, I know this situation is hard, but I'm on your side."

A few moments pass before he breaks the silence while moving his hands behind his back. "This is unnecessary. Officers have already questioned us and declared it an accident, but go ahead.

Waste more of our time." He waves one hand toward the hallway that leads beyond this great room. "Your superiors will be hearing of this. Acting against our wishes," he snaps before returning to Mrs. Rhyner.

"Mr. and Mrs. Rhyner," I say while nodding and thumbing my controller in the direction he indicated.

Why are they so resistant? It's as if he is trying to hide something and keep me from looking. Hopefully, I'll learn more from the other officer on the scene. It will be interesting to see what they pulled out of the couple during their interview and if they asked any questions. I am not optimistic, knowing that Gerson was here.

15

Investigate

My avatar casts a blue hue in the immaculate hallway. I follow the path toward the end of the floor, leading to a massive window overlooking the flashing cityscape sprawled beneath. On the left, an officer emerges from an open doorway, a view caster in one of his hands. When he looks up, he jerks in surprise and fumbles with the device, almost dropping it.

"Detec—Detective Harkones? I thought Gerson told you that we're wrapping things up here?" He tilts his head while looking back and forth from the view caster back to me.

I run my eyes over the officer, drawing a blank on who this is. He is tall, has a bushy mustache, glowing green eyes, and looks in good shape. Possibly, he's a newbie who just joined the force. Obviously, he knew I was coming, so that is something, at least. My gaze moves to his name tag stuck to the left side of his chest, spelling out *A. Wright.*

"You can go ahead and set that caster back up," I say. "We are not done here yet."

"Oh, yeah. Okay, but why?" He tilts his head and squints his eyes like a toddler trying to understand. "Gerson said there is nothing left to do but wait for the coroner to take the body."

I suck air through my teeth and nod. "That might be true, but the lieutenant wanted me to check the scene. Have an extra pair of eyes to see if I can spot anything unusual."

"Umm, alright," he says, shrugging. He lifts the caster and nods toward the room. "Give me a minute, and I'll have this thing set back up." He turns on his heels and steps back through the doorway, looking back toward me. "Just watch your step in here. It's a pretty grody scene."

"No feet... remember?" I say while turning my avatar's translucent palms up.

Wright scans me with a confused expression. "Right, right, yes!"

Fortunately, another caster is outside the room's entrance, allowing just enough range for me to follow to the doorway.

Looking past Officer Wright, I peer inside the room. It's large with movie and band posters slapped against the walls. Clothes are strewn everywhere, with a big pile in one corner. The bed is a mess with drool-stained pillows. A desk in the left corner is filled with junk, almost spilling out of each drawer. Beer and soda cans are scattered throughout the room. More large windows offer views into the city.

The room looks like a typical space you would expect to find with most young adults. One wall is emblazoned with a giant hologram poster that loops through Droid Battle Arena clips showcasing DBA 46: Argof vs. Kain. I nod while remembering watching this fight with Ranea. The poster flashes to various highlights of the explosive spectacle.

The only glaring thing in this room that stands different from most is a pool of blood in the middle that trails to the corpse of this room's inhabitant, Tito Rhyner. I stare down at the lifeless husk with his arms and legs sprawled out. His head is lying in a crimson puddle that sharply contrasts with the white stone floor.

A surge of ice courses through me, seeing the body. My mouth twists into a frown. All these years on the force, I still feel a sense of unease seeing the dead. It just doesn't feel right. A young person who was once full of life turned into an empty shell. I stare down at the body and wrinkle my nose. If I were actually here, there would be no doubt that the smell of copper would fill this room. Instead, I only smell someone who badly needs a shower and a fresh set of clothes.

"Heard you interviewed Mr. and Mrs. Rhyner. Is that correct?"

"That's right," Wright says, stepping over a trail of blood. He leans down and twists the bottom of the caster until the tripod legs stick out. A click sounds as he flips a switch on the side of the unit. Leaning down, he plants the caster on the ground in the middle of the room. The device emits a soft whirring noise, and small green lights illuminate the sides.

"Did you learn anything from the parents?" I ask.

"Not really." He shrugs and stands, then waves one palm toward the body on the ground. "Just that Tito here got back from a party, drunk beyond belief. He and his father argued. The kid stormed off into his room and slammed the door. Next thing, the father finds Tito on the ground, not moving or breathing, and blood all around."

Waiting for Wright to continue, I raise my brows and shrug with my hands raised. "Anything else?"

"Well, umm, when we got here, we saw the gash in his forehead with the glass shard sticking out. The bedside table looks like it was made of glass before it shattered. So, that's it." He moves his hands and points toward the pile of glass fragments beside the bed. "The kid must have accidentally fallen over and landed on the bedside table, shattering it." He sucks air in through his teeth and gestures toward Tito. "Which is what caused that to happen."

With the caster back online, I thumb my controller and move inside the room. I scan the space, searching. I'm unsure what I am looking for, but just trying to spot anything out of place. Now, a couple of feet away from Tito's body, I move into a squatting position and examine the gash that looks as if someone took a glass ax to his head.

"Did you ask anything about this party he came from? Are we sure he came home drunk?"

Tito's mouth is parted, and his eyes are rolled back, revealing his whites. Beads of blood still trickle down the glass shard like a leaky faucet.

"No," he says. "After looking at the body, Gerson said there was no refuting this kid simply fell and smacked his head. End of story."

"But why?" I spit out with annoyance. "Why would a kid suddenly fall? Being drunk isn't a catch-all answer for this."

"I'm sor... I'm sorry, Detective," he says. "Gerson is leading this case, and I'm following. You know, doing the grunt work."

I take a deep breath and try to calm myself. "Did you two ask anything about a recent modi installation?"

His eyes widen as a look of worry passes his face. "Uh, no," he stammers. "Should we have?"

"Didn't the father call in and offer that information to us? Might be important to know what he had installed, don't you think?"

"Again, I'm sorry, but I don't know anything more than what I just told you. If you want, I can ask Gerson to come back. Or you can call him?"

"Hmm," I grunt while rolling my tongue over the top of my teeth. I move back into a standing position, still looking down at the corpse. "Can you give me the room for a few minutes?"

"Yeah, sure, sure thing." He walks toward the hallway.

"Make sure to report everything," I say. "That also includes your notes interviewing the family."

"Yes, sir!" He exclaims before stepping beyond my sight, outside the room.

An uneasy feeling fills my stomach. Why is it that no one cares to find out what happened here? There could be more to this than simply falling over and smacking his head. The father wants me out. Gerson wants me out. Deep inside, I know I want out, too. To get back home and keep my promise, but a kid is dead, and no one seems to care to see why.

In the Infinity transport room, I roll my neck, hoping to get some relief. Wearing this headset for long periods is not the most comfortable. I stretch my toes in my shoes, which are finally somewhat dry now.

I'm still pissed that I wasted all those creds on these shoes. I am already dreading thinking about calling customer support to return them. I can hear it now, the waiting tone from the call:

"Customer satisfaction is our top priority." I scoff and shake my head. "Sure it is..."

I look from the gash in Tito's head back to the shattered bedside table. Large glass panels are mixed with glittering shards. My brows furrow, thinking that it takes a good amount of force to crack open someone's skull like this. A few cans, a narrow light tube, and a picture frame are settled over the mess. Nothing too unusual there. He must have just fallen in the worst possible position. A few inches to the left or right, and things could have ended differently for this kid.

Benji Davis surfaces to the front of my mind. This is another case where the victim suddenly fell over without an explanation. Walking around one minute and the next, he's crumpled on the ground in a catatonic state. Med teams got him to a trauma center just in time to hook up an oxygen supply to pump air into his lungs. Now, that machine is the only thing keeping his body alive. A husk without a soul.

Tito and Benji. Is it possible these cases are somehow linked? Both victims suddenly fell over and both had recent modi installations. Mirk's glowing purple eyes abruptly burst to life in my head.

"Mirk," I mutter under my breath. Benji Davis, brain-dead only one day after having some modies installed. Tito also had something implanted, but I don't have any details on what it was. Scanning Tito's body, I don't see any visible trace of implants.

Can this be traced back to Mirk? Back to RootX? I need to learn more about these cases, including who is installing the mods and what is being installed. Is this just a coincidence?

"Fuck..." I mutter through gritted teeth.

There is still so much we don't know, but yeah sure, let's go ahead and close the case and wipe our hands clean. Maybe I should accept it for what it is. Possibly, Gerson is right. Rule it as an accident and move on.

I pace around the room, ending back at Tito. Crouching, I narrow my eyes and stare at the blood dripping out of the hole in his forehead. My gaze hardens, noticing something out of place. I lean closer to Tito's unmoving face. Blood not emerging from the newly opened wound. Three tiny spots of crimson form in the shape of a triangle on his left temple.

Swallowing a lump in my throat, my heart rate quickens.

Blinding light makes me squint while I pull up the Infinity headset strapped to my face. Blinking, it takes a few moments for my eyes to adjust to the bright LED tubes recessed in the ceiling. With the back of my hand, I wipe the sweat from my forehead and rub it on my already filthy pants.

My hand moves toward my pocket, pulling out the white triangular device I pocketed from my encounter with Pandemon. Licking my lips in anticipation, I twist the device, revealing what I think is the backside. My heart surges. Three silver dots on each corner about an inch apart.

What the hell is this thing?

Holding the object higher, I spin it around while trying to make sense of it. I pull the device closer to my face and examine the ring on the front. My thumb glides around the ring, which feels like plastic and is smooth to the touch. Slowly, I inch my thumb to the middle of the ring. A flicker of hesitation courses through my mind. This can't be a *button*, can it? A button for what?

I shrug my shoulders, pushing the uncertainty away.

My thumb applies pressure. The circle inside the ring lowers, making a single click sound. A shiver runs down my spine. My brows rise in worried anticipation. What did I just activate? I hold the device, expecting something, anything, to happen.

Nothing happens.

I wrinkle my forehead, staring blankly at the device. My thumb clicks inside the ring three more times. Again, nothing happens. I turn the device over and focus on the three silver dots. Clicking the button one more time, I see movement. Almost imperceptible. The three silver dots rise a fraction of a millimeter whenever I press down on the button.

This piece of plastic came out of that Pandemon van. They must be involved with this thing. Is this... Oblivion? That was the whole reason they came after me.

Is this device, this tiny piece of plastic, it?

Unsure, I shake my head and stare at the object. If only the thugs had given me more detail on what exactly Oblivion is before things escalated. Maybe the clean-up crew picked up some evidence that will point me in the right direction. Slowly, I set it on the metal table to the side of my chair. Hoping to relieve some tension, I roll my neck and arch my back, which creates satisfying pops in my spine.

This could all be a coincidence. There are three pinpricks on Tito's left temple and three pinprick-sized dots on the device. Have I been holding onto a missing puzzle piece this entire time? My stomach churns at the thought of it.

I suck in a deep breath and let out a steady flow of air, readying myself.

Pulling down my headset, the familiar hum of this floor's air filtration unit fades as darkness descends again.

16

Evidence

With the headset snug over my face, the welcome chime of Infinity chirps in my ears. Once again, I'm in the man-made world. I am relieved I don't have to suffer through the melodramatic Infinity start-up sequence. My vision snaps open in the Rhyner residence in the same position as when I pulled my headset up, as if I had never left.

Sources of light surround me from every angle. Orange illumination strips run along the room's walls, emitting a candle-like glow. Clips from the DBA poster continue to bounce hues of color while the glow of the city beyond the windows remains omnipresent.

Like a pumping heart, the room pulses with life while the pooling blood and the pale corpse in the middle of the floor speak the opposite.

Sighing, I focus on Tito's unmoving head resting on the stone floor. My gaze moves to the three crimson spots of dried blood on his temple. About one inch apart, it looks like it would match the device I pocketed from the Pandemon van.

I thumb my controller to move into a crouched position and scan through the room again, looking up and down, my narrowed eyes searching for anything. My brows lower while my mouth morphs into a grim, straight line.

The view caster menu on my display superimposes in my field of vision, hovering in the room. I toggle through the menu until I land on the camera filter settings. Flipping the infrared filter on, my world is coated in a wash of purple and yellow.

Anything giving off a high amount of heat shines bright yellow like a screaming torch in the dark of night. Scanning the room, small and large bursts of yellow surround me, coming from several electronics throughout the room. The cold surface of the walls and floor bleed purple with no traces of heat. What would be a bright, burning yellow, Tito's body is a dim, dirty orange color similar to coals from a dying fire.

Rising into a standing position again, I slowly pace around the room. I study every visible inch, trying to find anything out of place. Cold stone walls, cold stone floor, and a body becoming more frigid by the minute. I stare back down at Tito's lifeless face and let out a long sigh.

"How did you end up like this?" I mutter as I crouch and grimace, staring into his blank eyes. My gaze moves back to the three red dots perched on his temple.

"Did you really just fall over? Is this all an accident?"

A glint of red catches my eye amidst an ocean of purple from under his bed. Turning off the IR filter, my vision flickers back to the normal visible spectrum. Adjusting my controls, I zoom my vision to locate what could be giving off a tiny ember of heat.

Under Tito's large, unmade bed, my eyes sift past clothes, boxes, a couple of cans, and some other junk. I continue scanning left to right, searching until something makes me do a double-take. My eyes widen. Something white and triangular is poking out in a bundled mess of dirty clothes. I can't be too sure it's what I think it is. It could be nothing.

Something is definitely down there, though. Even zoomed to the max setting, it's hard to tell what it is. View casters have their benefits, but they also have limits. Moving physical objects is one of them.

The plastic controls of the Infinity rig creak as my clammy hands tighten around each grip. Moving with precision, I bring up the menu that superimposes in my vision and call Officer Wright. A few seconds later, his appearance forms in a window in my field of view.

"Detective," he says in a surprised voice. "What ca—"

"I need you in the kid's room. Now!" I interrupt.

"Uhh, okay, alri... alright," he stammers. "You find something?"

"Possibly. I'm not sure."

"I'll be right there."

Gerson starts cursing in the background. "What the hell does he want now? Vexing bastard is just wasting time. The coroner team is here—"

Gerson's rambling ceases as the call flickers out.

Waiting for Officer Wright, I pace around the room, deep in thought. If it is Oblivion, how did it get here? Who or what was this kid's source? Why do the Rhyners want me to leave? What the hell does that button do? I keep thinking back to where this all started.

"Benji Davis," I mutter, the name hanging in my mind. I have his file, meaning I have pictures of his face. Amix said there were a few cases similar to this. It would be interesting to see if the people involved in these other cases have similar markings on their temples too.

Anticipation fills me, making my skin crawl. I clamp my teeth and breathe in through my nose. The transport chair squeaks as I shift, trying to get comfortable.

My hands move like lightning, pulling up menus and diving down lower into case files, folders, and details. Finally, I navigate to the Benji Davis case file. A flicker of hesitation passes through me before clicking on the folder that contains pictures.

I select the first thumbnail at the top of the list. A picture materializes in a virtual window in my vision that looks eerily similar to the Tito Rhyner scene. The most glaring difference is that the Davis kid is in a puddle of his saliva instead of a pool of blood. Clicking through the photos, I stop on an image of a close-up of his bruised face.

I suck in air through my teeth and let out a silent praise to the gods for high-quality photos. I magnify. My eyes widen in recognition. Almost unnoticeable without zooming in on Benji Davis's left temple, three pin-prick-sized indentions rest like three lit beacons waiting for somebody to take notice.

"There it is," I whisper to myself. The same three dots are placed in the same position.

Closing the window, I let out a long breath and sink back into the transport chair, my head slowly shaking. This is growing larger than just Benji Davis. If what I see here matches the other cases, something new and dangerous is spreading in the city. I need to find out what this device is, see if the other instances have similar marks on the persons in question, and find out how far this stretches. Is Mirk innocent after all?

Questions...

Questions that are keeping this case from being closed and preventing me from heading home. In frustration, I drop my right-hand control into my lap and ball my fist. Tears start to well in my eyes. A crushing weight feels like it was just laid on my chest.

I made a promise to my little girl, and I can't keep it. She looks up to me, and I continue failing both her and Raena. I want to be home for them. I want to take care of them, but this job keeps wrapping threads around my ankles, slowly slithering up, and keeping me put and away. This job pays the bills. It pays for us to live, but it's not enough.

Someone clears their throat from the direction of the hallway. My focus shifts.

"Detective Harkones?" Officer Wright says in a worried voice. "I would be, uhh, very quick about what you're going to do here. Both Gerson and the family seem"—he smacks his lips—"upset."

I take a deep lungful of air and let out one steady breath, trying to focus on what's in front of me.

"We'll be quick. I think I might have found something under the bed. Can you check for me?"

Confusion still lingers on his face, but his shoulders drop. "Sure. What do you see?"

"On the far left, something tiny and white is sticking out in that pile of clothes."

He reaches into his back pocket and pulls out a black latex glove. He carefully steps over Tito's body and moves into a crouched position. I hear the smack of the glove as he puts it over his hand.

"Right over here?"

"Yep, that's it. Just a little left, behind that wadded-up blue shirt."

"I think I got it." He moves into a standing position and turns back toward my avatar. An expression of concern forms across his face. Looking toward his hands, his head tilts. "This tiny piece of plastic? What is it?"

My heart jumps and blood rushes into my ears. I move closer and stare at the object resting in his palm. It's a gleaming, triangular white object that looks identical to the device I had stowed in my pocket. It looks the same, but something is different. A soft red glow emits from a portion of the internal ring. In the center, where the button sits, the number eight is displayed in a dim gray font.

"Bring it closer," I yell louder than I mean to.

If this thing was stuck to Tito's head, how did it get under his bed? Maybe it's possible that it just popped off when his head hit the table.

"What is this piece of junk? Why is it counting down?"

My breath catches. "What do you mean it's counting down?"

"Just a second ago, it said nine! Right here," he says in an anxious and worried voice while his other hand points toward the center of the device.

Panic prickles my skin. I have no idea what this thing is and why it's counting down. The one I had in my pocket didn't do anything like this.

"What... am I holding on to, Harkones?" he stammers. Beads of sweat glisten on his forehead. "Is this a bomb?" He starts taking quick breaths through his nose.

"Hey! Calm down, Wright," I say while holding my hands up. "We don't know what it is yet."

The number in the center of the device descends from eight to seven. His eyes widen further, and his hands start shaking.

This device is acting as if it's a countdown timer. A countdown to what, though? Do we need to call in the bomb squad? Should we evacuate the floor? The building? For this tiny object?

"Just set it on the bed and check for anything else under there. More of these devices, anything that can help point us to figuring out what the hell this thing is."

"Okay, okay," he stutters. Wright carefully moves his palm toward the bed and puts the object down. He licks his lips and shakes his head. "I don't like this, Harkones... I don't like this at all."

"You don't have to like it. Just check under the bed." I thumb my controller to slowly pace to the side of the bed, hoping to get a better vantage point.

"Yes, yes, got it." He lowers to all fours. His hand stretches back, pushing the piles of junk and clothes around. He inches his head further under the bed when a loud chime suddenly blares. Wright jolts and smacks his head against the metal frame with a loud clunk.

"Ow!" He yelps as his hand moves to comfort the back of his skull. He moves his head from under the bed and stares at his wrist. "It's Gerson... uhh, should I answer? Should I tell him what's going on?"

"Yes, just not right now. Keep looking! We don't have that much more time."

I stare at the device on the bed with narrowed eyes. It descends once again from six to five. I suck in air through my teeth, thinking of all the possibilities.

"You find anything yet?" I spit out.

Wright is frantically moving junk around the bed. "No! There is too much crap down here. Wait, this could be something. It's a box!" He slides back out from under the bed, holding a white plastic box about a foot tall and a foot wide. The box is unadorned: no text, no barcode, and no logos. Wright stands back up and stares from the box in his hands to the device counting down on the bed.

The object displays the number four in the same gray font. The red glow looks to be getting smaller, as if the countdown and ring are in sync.

"Hurry! Open it up!" I snap while my heart hammers against my chest.

Wright stares at me with horror-struck eyes. "I... I gotta get out of here." He moves to place the box on the bed.

"No!" I roar. "Just open it up and then evac this floor, the Rhyner family!"

"Okay... fuck!" he spits out.

Holding the box in one hand, he uses his other to grab the top flap. I move my avatar closer to peer in. Wright pulls the top of the box upward, revealing the contents. We both stare, dumbstruck. Worry courses through my veins. My hands grip my controls even harder.

There are more white triangular devices—at least twenty—all packaged in tiny square boxes with transparent plastic displaying the device sitting on molded plastic that perfectly fits the object. In the center of the devices, the letters "OV" are displayed in a static gray font.

"Oh, hell! It's more of them!" Wright shrieks.

We both glance at the device on the bed, now slowly blinking the number three.

"Get out of here," I command. "Get the family out!"

Wright doesn't hesitate and lightly places the box on top of the bed to the right of the counting-down device. He sprints toward the door and hesitates, swiveling his head toward me.

"What about you?" Wright pleads.

"I'm not here, remember?" I point toward the view caster in the middle of the room.

"Right, right. Okay." His footsteps echo in the hallway as he sprints out of the room, toward Mr. and Mrs. Rhyner.

I take a deep breath and stare down at the device and the box filled with more of these devices. These things are being produced and packaged by someone. There must be an operation behind this. How large, though? What the hell do they do? Well, it looks like I'm about to find out in one minute.

The device on the bed is now blinking faster than before, with the number one flashing. The red glow of the ring is a fraction of the entire circle, as if it was draining with power.

The tiny screen flickers to 30 and quickly changes to 29... 28... 27...

This is it. These must be the final seconds before it counts down to zero. My heart continues pounding even though I am not running; I'm not even physically in this room. I take a deep breath, trying to calm myself, but it doesn't seem to be working.

5... 4... 3...

My face tenses as I stare at the device through squinted eyes.

2...

My hands grip my controls even harder, making the plastic creak.

1...

17

Connections

Snap!

A sharp pain erupts in my right hand. "Fuck!" I scream, expecting a thunderclap detonation to sound out. Peeling open my eyes, I thought my avatar would be consumed in a blazing inferno, but... it's not.

Nothing happened.

All is silent besides the soft droning of the view casters and my heart thumping against my chest. I lean closer to the device. The numbers are gone, the ring inert and devoid of any glow. It now looks the same as the device sitting next to me at the station. What the hell was all that for?

I release a held breath and pull in more deep gulps of oxygen. Pulling up my headset, I blink and stare down at my throbbing hand. The analog stick on the plastic controller snapped off and is now digging into my palm. I stare at a red indention in my hand thinking that if I gripped any harder, the analog stick would have pierced my skin.

Of course the NCPD has cheap-ass controllers.

I drop my head back into the cushy foam of the chair. I am tired. The corners of my lips form a frown while I slowly shake my head. A joyless chuckle escapes my lips, thinking of the insanity of what just happened.

At least it's not a bomb. What it's counting down toward, I still don't know.

Pulling down the headset, I navigate the menus with my working controller and call Officer Wright. A couple of seconds later, he appears in a window in my vision within the headset.

"What... what happened?" Wright stammers. "Did that thing blow up?" He looks to be out of breath and is gasping. Gerson must be near him as I hear his voice as clear as Wright's.

"The fuck is this all about? Making us run around like rats. You're just wasting more time and making us look like fools, Harkones!" Wright's face winces with each word Gerson spits out. "All for what? For nothing! The Rhyner's are even more pissed off now! Threatening legal action!"

I sigh and roll my eyes. Ignoring Gerson's words, I respond to Wright. "Nothing happened. It just counted down to zero, then zilch. It's sitting on the bed exactly where you left it." I shake my head and chew my lip. "We need a team here to pick up these devices as evidence. We still don't know what they are or if they are dangerous."

"We are not doing shit!" Gerson spits out. "This case is closed. Harkones, I recommend you back off. You've given enough *help* already."

A fiery rage starts boiling within me. I am tired and want to go home, but I have to close the Benji Davis case. To do that, I need to figure out what the hell these devices are and see if they are connected. Gerson is not getting in my way.

I clear my throat. "Gerson, I'm not asking. I'm stating what will happen and what you nee—"

Gerson starts cackling. "Detective, you have no grounds to give me orders. I'm the lead on this case. What I say goes."

"Fine. Be the person who sweeps something potentially dangerous under the rug."

"I'll do exactly that. I'm glad we're on the same page. Wright, terminate that fucking call."

Wright mouths the words "*I'm sorry*" before the call flickers out, leaving me alone in the bedroom, my only companion being the corpse of Tito Rhyner.

"Bastard," I spit out.

Gerson is being ridiculous. Someone from the NCPD will have to return to this room and collect all the equipment throughout the house. These view casters are not cheap. He's being difficult because... I don't know. Maybe he's just a piece of shit and a difficult guy in general. At least, that is the way it seems from what I know about him. Either way, I will have to record his outburst in my report and let Amix know. Will he be slapped with any repercussions? I shake my head, thinking probably not.

I glance at the device on the bed before shifting my gaze to the box full of questions. I take a deep breath, drop the controls in my lap, and reach to pull the headset off. I blink, trying to readjust to the bright lights in the transport room. I run both my hands over my face into my hair, applying soft pressure to my skull, trying to massage away all my anxiety, my anger, and all my disquiet feelings. It doesn't work.

Groaning, I reach one hand to the end of the chair and pull myself up onto my feet. I slowly move my stiff legs to get the blood flowing again. My hand moves to grab the device I pocketed from the van. Holding it up, I stare at it with furrowed brows.

"What are you?" I ask.

The tiny cryptic device does not answer.

I could be like Gerson and not care, but I know that would leave me feeling worse than I feel now. If it were my child who randomly died for an unknown reason, I would drag this godless city deeper into the depths of hell to find out why.

Heat trickles up my face and into my ears. I take a deep breath, knowing I am on edge. Grinding my teeth, I pocket the device again. An overwhelming need to find out more washes over me. Zinny's smile suddenly flashes across my mind, easing my tension. With deep breaths, the blood rushing in my ears starts to calm.

After this case, I think it may be time to take some personal time. It might hurt the bank a little bit, but I need it. I need to spend time with Raena and Zinny without worrying about catching the latest scumbag in the back of my mind. The bonus from closing Mirk's case should help me get caught back up. I mean, I'll still be in debt to Zinny's school, but I should be fine. I sigh and lick my lips, remembering I need to zero my balance with QuikCred, too.

"Shit," I mutter. Scratch that idea about personal time.

I roll my shoulders and stretch my neck. One thing at a time. First, I should see if there are any connections with these other cases Amix mentioned. If these victims or these other people also have marks on their temples, something dangerous and large might be spreading its webs across the city. I hesitate and purse my lips.

A tiny thought sparks in my mind. This could just be the beginning of something massive. Something that leads to an equally massive payday. I drum my fingers on the side of my temples, thinking. This could be my break, a way to get ahead if everything pans out. Resolve ignites and blasts through my body.

I need this.

Pulling up my holo grid, I glance at the time: 10:00 p.m. It's past dinnertime now, and Zinny's bedtime was thirty minutes ago. My stomach plummets. I shake my head, knowing I broke another promise. I feel that I am slowly chipping away at her trust, and eventually, it will shatter into a million pieces. Every case, every night that pulls me away, I take a pickaxe and hammer it down on our wall of trust. Tomorrow, I will try to make it up to her. Tell her that I am sorry. Eventually, I know just saying sorry will not cut it.

The only thing I can do is focus.

I navigate the menus until I land on Officer Palmer. Clicking his name, I select the message button. Typing away at the virtual keyboard, I ask for the case file numbers for the other cases that Amix mentioned.

Waiting for a response, I start pacing along the hallway. I suck air through my gritted teeth, knowing I still have no idea what they are. I need somebody with extensive street knowledge or someone who is aware of new things hitting the streets. Someone who can enlighten me on what these cryptic devices are. Based on how they were packaged, it looks like they were ready to sell or distribute.

We have teams at the NCPD that specialize in gathering the latest intel from the mass of human activity online and in the physical world. Petabytes of data are stored within a farm of NCPD servers that are collecting an endless amount of surveillance. Given how new this is, it may be a good idea to check with someone from this team about these devices.

My mouth morphs into a flat line. Actually, I don't know when was the last time that the People Analytics team has helped with anything. With all this data and these machine learning models, we are playing catch-up. We are still responding to events rather than being proactive. Sure, they can tell me things after something big has happened, but I need to know now—not weeks from now. This is something new. I doubt they will be able to help me.

I scratch at the stubble on my chin. One thing that confuses me is how the hell Tito ended up with a box of these devices. Is he involved in the production process?

Still pacing, I move toward the end of the hallway. Voices ring out from officers and other staff going about their daily business. Within an arm's length of a window, I grimace, staring toward the ground. I lightly lean my forehead on the window and unfocus my eyes. The motion of humanity blurs into a blob of shifting colors. My stomach makes a bubbling, growling noise. I realize I'm starving.

"Jesus," I mutter. I haven't eaten since this morning when I left for work. I shake my head, knowing I should have gotten something other than coffee at that hole in the wall earlier. What was that place called again? Grubbies, I think.

A chime sounds on my holo grid, indicating I have a message. My eyes narrow, staring down at the hovering screen.

Rapid footsteps sound behind me. In the window's reflection, I make out a dark figure quickly approaching. My stomach drops, and my heart freezes. The figure's featureless mask stretching from chin to forehead is a dead giveaway.

A Torqueman.

I thought I had more time. Why is this guy here, and how did he get into the station? Turning on my heels, I hold my hands up to the loan collector. Any attempt to fight off this guy would be a mistake. Retaliation would only deepen my debt.

Before I can utter a word, the Torqueman shoves me against the window with my right cheek squished against the glass. An instant later, something cold and metallic clasps around my neck.

Instinctively, I gulp for air and reach my hands to my neck. I'm forced to my knees, still grasping at the cool metal. My heart rate climbs with each passing second.

"Sol Harkones," a robotic voice says. "This serves as your first reminder of your outstanding balance with QuikCred Loans."

Through squinted eyes, I stare at the broad-shouldered Torqueman. A dark, oversized jacket sweeps at his ankles, with the collar turned up. Unseen eyes look down at me behind the faceless inky-black mask.

Reminder... What kind of fucking reminder is this? What happened to just sending a message?

"You will comply with the repayment agreement or additional consequences will occur." The debt collector raises one hand and taps at something on his wrist. An instant later, two clicks ring out from the collar clasped around my throat. Something metallic grips my wrists and pulls my arms to my chest. My pinned arms fold over each other as if I were wearing a straitjacket.

"State that you acknowledge."

"Acknowledged," I rasp.

My arms suddenly go slack and drop to my sides. The collar pops off with a click and falls to the floor. The Torqueman grabs the collar and turns toward the hallway. Just as quickly as he came, the debt collector was gone.

"Fuck me and fuck today," I whisper through ragged breaths.

Rubbing at my neck, I try to steady my breathing. I knew that Torquemen were used to collect debts, but I never thought they would be sent out to serve *reminders*. A lump forms in my throat. I need to read over that contract again and see how long I have. What would be even better is if I could pay it off completely.

I climb to my feet and sigh. My heart is still beating like a drum. For what feels like an eternity, my mind is scrambled. It's hard to fixate on a single thought. Worry prickles my skin about what will happen next if I don't pay up. I don't have time to worry, though. What I need is credits.

Now, what the hell was I doing? Right, I was looking into the other cases Amix mentioned. I suck in one more breath before bringing my holo grid back up. I glance over my shoulder and back down the hallway, not seeing any trace of the Torqueman.

Focusing my sight, I read Palmer's message, which includes the additional case numbers. At the bottom of the message, he also mentioned that a surveillance drone is now in position at my apartment complex.

I grimace, thinking about an unmanned drone hovering around my home. I could send a message to Raena letting her know that we have a hunk of metal with firing capabilities scanning our building. Or maybe not. Doing that will probably just scare her and put her into a panic. I'll tell her when I get home, whenever that is.

Now that I have these case numbers, I need to dive into these files, pull up the photos, and see if these other victims have similar marks on their temples. I move my hand to position my holo grid to start searching, but something is tugging at the back of my mind.

"I didn't do shit—" The words ring like a hammer striking a bell in my mind.

A frown forms, thinking of Mirk, the grimy little bastard. If I find evidence or traces of these marks on these other victims, Mirk might be telling the truth. If that is the case, why did he run the instant he saw my badge? It still doesn't make any sense.

I look at the window and sigh at an oil mark where my face was pushed against the glass. Using the back of my jacket sleeve, I try to wipe it away, but the oil mark only smudges further.

"Damnit," I mutter. If only I had a window cleaner gun implant that could pop out of my arm, I could wipe this away. It would be a stupid implant to have, but I'm sure something out on the market does exactly that.

I shake my head and chuckle, thinking of how useless some implants are.

My eyes dart to my arm. Implants... Benji Davis was found in a catatonic state only one day after having some new modies installed. Tito Rhyner had something installed as well, just a day ago even though I am not sure what exactly the modies were.

Modi shops, brain-dead victims, and these mysterious devices. I sigh. How do these all connect?

Mirk is a modifier at one of the largest modi shop chains in the city. He must know something. Maybe it's the reason why he ran. Either he knows precisely why these people are dropping like flies, or he knows what these mystery devices are. Hell, he might have info on both.

I spin on my heels and walk the hallway back to the elevators. I wonder if Desson got any useful info from him. Possibly a full confession into what happened to Benji. Now, that would be interesting.

A dull ache still throbs at my chest where the scorpion speared me. I wince, running my hand over the bandage the med team slapped on when I got back to the station. Raena is going to be unhappy with me when she sees all the scrapes and scratches I got. I'd better leave out the scorpion part when she sees this bandage.

Should I look into finding another job? My mouth forms into a grim line. Is there any other job out there that pays these lump sum bonuses? I doubt it, but... I haven't looked, so I am not sure.

Walking toward the elevators, I bring up my holo grid and navigate through the menus until I see a familiar face: Tommy Coleson. I take a deep breath and tap on the call button.

"Booyah!" Coleson's voice booms out from the speaker; his appearance materializes above my wrist. "Found it!" He starts laughing while pumping one fist in the air. "Harkones? What the hell now?"

"What did you find?" I ask, with one brow raised.

"I found some breadcrumbs for this other case I'm working. Found proof of some bigwig who's been evading taxes."

I purse my lips and nod. "Is now a bad time?"

"You can't seriously be asking for *more help*? Also, where's my pizza?"

"You got me, and I'll get your food sometime this week, okay?" Coleson chuckles. "You're just adding to your tab."

"I told Amix about your help, by the way, so she is fully aware now," I say, not offering anything else about her response. There is no need to let him know that it seemed like she couldn't care less, at least for the moment.

"Finally! Was that so hard?" he says while shaking his head.

I chew on my lip and nod before continuing. "I need your technical wizardry again."

"Of course you do, and everyone else, apparently. Why should I keep helping you?"

"Hey man, I'm getting you a pie, remember?" I say.

Coleson scoffs. "You think one pizza will cover everything I've already done for you?"

"Maybe not one, but... how about two or three?"

He smacks his lips and sighs. "Okay, okay, fine. What is it now?"

I reach the elevators and click on the up arrow beside the doors. A moment later, the elevator doors slide open, revealing a couple of blue-uniform officers in conversation. They both turn to look at me and nod in unison. I nod back, step inside, and click the button for floor sixty-five.

The elevator doors close, and the floor shudders before it moves upward.

"I'm going to send you four case numbers, and I want you to check if they have any images attached."

"Okay... and?" Coleson asks.

"This might lead to nothing, but I want you to check each victim's face. See if you can spot three indentions in their temple area."

"Uhh, okay... That's strange. What is this about?"

My mouth forms into a frown. "It's just a hunch for now. One more thing, too, if you don't mind."

"My god, Harkones, just keep adding to your Coleson debt, why don't you?"

I close my eyes and push out a breath of air. *Debt...* He has no idea.

"I know, but this should be the last thing."

"Alright, just spit it out."

"Can you cross-check if these victims also have recent modi installations?"

He shrugs. "Uh, yeah, sure, I can do that. Give me a couple of minutes and I'll get back to you."

The call flickers out before I can say another word. I let out a sigh of frustration. He's too damn quick. I wasn't able to tell him to scan the photos for any sign of the triangular devices. I haven't even given him the case file numbers yet.

Shaking my head, I copy the case numbers from Palmer's message, paste them into a text box, and click send.

My fingers move to my temples. I lower my hands as I stare ahead at the stainless-steel wall of the elevator door. Through the soft whirring of the elevators, the two officers talk about an upcoming Droid Battle Arena match between two names I recognize. My eyes start twitching, thinking back to the Rhyner crime scene. The kid would have been excited, too, if he were still here.

A rumble of anger forms in the back of my mind. My hand moves and rests on the handle of my hyper coil. Something is going on, and I am going to find out what. All I have to do is pry it out of Mirk. He must know something.

My payday rests on it.

18

Answers

My eyes rise as the elevator comes to a stop. A chime indicates we have arrived. An instant later, the doors slide open. By habit, my eyes dart to the elevator's top, ensuring I am on the right level. Floor sixty-five flashes on the display.

I step into the hallway and hear the officers' conversation fade behind me. The doors close, and the elevator continues its ascent.

Staring blankly ahead, I let my feet guide me toward my destination. Mirk is blocking my path toward answers, and I think it's time to pull them out, even if he's unwilling.

As I walk the halls, the noise of ringing, typing, conversations, and news broadcasts fills my ears. I stop in front of a black metal door with the words "Interview Room 28" emblazoned above the frame. Taking a deep breath and exhaling, I steel myself. I knock twice before opening the door.

The first thing I see is the deep purple glow of Mirk's eyes darting in my direction, a feral scowl forming on his face. My gaze shifts to Desson sitting in a relaxed posture in the chair across from Mirk. He turns his head in my direction.

"Desson, mind if we talk?"

His brows rise. "Alright, sure thing." He places his hands on his legs and grunts, moving to stand.

"Hey! You said I was going to get out of here. Where are you going?" Mirk spits out, teeth bared.

Desson turns back toward Mirk. "Just give us a moment, okay? Then we can talk about what happens next for you."

Mirk's eyes flare in anger, but he keeps silent.

I step back from the doorway and Desson steps into the hallway. The door clicks shut behind him.

"How's our law-abiding citizen doing so far? You learn anything?" I ask.

"He's upset about a jacket you supposedly ruined."

I roll my eyes and snort. "It was a piece of wire. I'm sure he can easily replace it. But really, anything useful?"

"He keeps rambling about how we got the wrong guy and that he didn't do anything. I also learned that he is aware of other people suddenly dropping to the floor, and it's not because of him."

"He's aware... of others becoming incapacitated? Brain dead like Benji?" A lifeless body flashes across my mind. "Like Tito," I mutter.

"That's what he's saying. It could be that he's trying to place the blame somewhere else or point us in the wrong direction. We reviewed the recording of him installing the modies into Benji. He went through each step and gave details on everything he was doing."

"Really? He was that forthcoming? I was not expecting that at all."

"Me either, and I didn't notice anything unusual in the clips. So unless these recordings were altered, he could be telling the truth and completed the installations to spec. We need to check the modies and see where they came from. Grab the model number, the manufacturer, and see if they came from the supplier defective. Line it up against what Mirk is telling us."

I nod and grimace. "Agreed. I'm interested in these other people dropping dead that he's aware of."

Desson nods in the direction of the door. "Want to join?"

"After you."

Desson moves his hand to the door handle and looks back in my direction. "Everything go okay with the lieutenant?"

"Yeah," I say, looking toward the ground and sighing. "Just more questions, but I might have a new lead on Benji that could paint Mirk here in an innocent light. Doesn't change the fact that he ran and attacked me, though."

Desson snorts and raises his brows. "Oh, really? You'll have to let me know about what you found." He opens the door and positions his palm, indicating that I should step through.

I nod, enter the room, and stand against the wall. Mirk doesn't take his eyes off me and follows my every movement.

Desson steps inside and lets the door close behind him. He grabs the empty plastic chair, spins it, and sits. He rests his chin over his arms, which are crossed over the back of the chair, and pushes air out of his nose.

"Okay, let's continue where we left off," he mutters in a low, soothing voice. "Does that sound alright?"

Mirk's lips press together into a thin line. Signs of annoyance creep across his face. "I thought we were going to talk about me getting out of here? I shouldn't even be in here in the first place!"

"We'll talk about that when we're ready," Desson says. "We just have a few more questions."

Mirk folds his arms together and leans back further into his chair. "Yeah, whatever." He mumbles something under his breath, but I can't make it out.

"You were saying something about people randomly falling over? Similar to what happened to your customer, Benji Davis, right?"

Mirk takes a deep breath before responding. "Yep, and it has nothing to do with me."

"Can you give more detail on how or where you saw this take place?"

"I was at a party after work one day and I—"

"When was this party?" I interrupt.

Mirk's eyes dart toward me and narrow. "Just last week. On Tuesday, if you have to know."

"And where was this party?" Desson asks.

"It was at a club called Giest on the east side. Pretty chill place. I was there with some buddies from work, and a few randos joined in." Mirk pauses as both his eyebrows rise. "Should I continue, or will you two keep interrupting me?"

"No, go on," Desson says.

"Everything was ginchy. They seemed like normal guys. I guess they were friends with one of my buddies so I didn't question them joining in. We were drinking, getting a nice buzz then one of the new guys announced he had to go piss. He gets up and waddles over to the head. Next thing I know, I see him stumbling back toward our table, and then splat." He thumps his two stump hands together, which would probably make a slapping sound if his hands were still attached.

"Splat?" Desson questions.

"Yeah, splat. He falls onto the ground. Limbs sprawled everywhere like he got shot or something."

"Was he still breathing?" I ask.

"He was, but it was more like gasping. Like he was outside without a mask." Mirk stares at Desson with wide eyes. "That's all I saw. People were all freaking out trying to pick him up, but he was dead weight."

"You said he was stumbling back to your table, right? Before he collapsed?" Desson asks.

"That's what I said."

"Did you happen to see his face? His expressions? Did he look scared, happy, or what?"

"Uhh, hmm," Mirk says while resting his chin on one of his stump hands. "Now that you mention it, he looked pretty happy. Like he was super high or something. That's all I know."

"What was his name?" Desson asks.

"It was something like Reexe, uhh, I'm blanking on the last name." Mirk shrugs.

Something pings in the back of my mind. This name seems familiar.

"So you said he looked happy? Like he took drugs?" I ask.

Mirk's eyes narrow in my direction. "Mm-hmm."

"So, what happened after?" Desson asks while his fingers interlace, one of his thumbs tapping against his hand.

"What do you mean what happened after? What happened to the guy? Reexe?"

"Yes, what happened to this Reexe guy?"

"A trauma team was called, I guess." Mirk says. "I don't know by who. My buddy was on his knees trying to wake him up, but..." He rolls his shoulders and lifts his stump arms in a dismissive gesture.

A chime sounds on my holo grid. My eyes glance down and see that it's a message from Coleson. I tap the message and expand the details. My eyes widen seeing that he already checked each case and reported back. Damn, this guy always impresses me with how fast he can gather intel.

"What?" Mirk spits out. "Am I bothering you, Detective? So much that you can't even listen to me?"

I roll my eyes, look toward Mirk, and shift my gaze to Desson. "I'm going to step out for a second." Moving toward the exit, I grab the door handle, and look back toward the table.

"Sounds good," Desson responds, still staring at Mirk with a frown.

Stepping out of the room, I let the door click shut behind me. I run my hands through my hair and rub the back of my head. Slowly, I start reading the message while holding my breath.

CASE 1038405-33
  Victim Name: Josiah Walker
  Incident Date: 2038-02-17
  Photo Temple Markings: Yes
  Recent Modi Installation in Past Six Months: No

My eyes halt, reading over Coleson's notes. "Photo temple markings..." Another victim with a triangular mark on their forehead. A shiver of worry runs down my spine, thinking of the implications. I lick my lips as my mouth suddenly feels very dry. With the back of my hand, I rub the sweat forming on my forehead and wipe it on my jeans.

One thing that looks different here, though, is that this Josiah did not have any recent modi implants installed. At least no recorded implants.

I take a deep breath and continue reading.

CASE 1038432-29
Victim Name: Mandi Walton
Incident Date: 2038-02-15
Photo Temple Markings: Yes
Recent Modi Installation in Past Six Months: Yes

A knot forms in my throat. I lower my hands and stare at the ceiling. Another case with markings. So far, all these cases including Benji have these pinprick markings on their temples. I lean against the wall and scratch my chin. This cannot be a coincidence. These are connections. Connected by threads of something dangerous, something new. Something that is making these people suddenly topple over. All connected by what must be the device I found in the Pandemon van.

What am I dealing with here? I close my eyes and let out long steady breaths. After a few seconds, I open my eyes and bring up my wrist. Reading the victim's name, my breath gets caught in my throat. I blink, not believing it.

"Reexe Fuello," I hiss. "Mirk, you sack of shit." He is more involved in this than he is letting on. What did I expect though?

Everyone in this city seems to want to fuck each other over. Mirk is no exception.

I pull out the cryptic triangular device from my pocket and raise it in the air. Twisting it around, I narrow my twitching eyes.

"If you won't tell me what you are, let's see what our buddy Mirk has to say." The device does not respond.

Pocketing it, I move back toward the interview room. To the side of the door, I navigate a display mounted on the wall. Tapping through menus and controls for the interview room, my fingers stop on the camera options, wanting to disengage the camera from recording. My fingers come to an abrupt halt. I tilt my head in confusion while reading the screen, "INTERVIEW ROOM 28 CAMERA - NOT RECORDING". The camera in the room is already set to not record? I'm confident it was operational when we first brought Mirk in. Is it a glitch, or did someone else purposely deactivate the camera?

I shove the thought from my head and brace myself, pushing the door open. Stepping inside, I glare at Mirk and walk toward him. I lean my hands on the table and press my lips into a tight line. A grin creeps across his face.

"What the fuck is wrong with you?" Mirk says while laughing, spittle flying from his mouth.

Mirk's head jerks back as one of my fists collides with the side of his jaw with a loud smack. He falls back and lands sprawled on the ground while his chair topples over. Desson jerks to a standing position. I hold a hand out toward him. "Mirk knows more than what he is telling us."

Mirk stares up at me, astonished. He closes his mouth and winces. Moving his jaw, he spits out a blob of blood and stares at it as if he were looking at some alien creature.

My hand throbs. I clench my fist and hold it for a moment, feeling the tension build and slowly stretch out my fingers. Taking a deep breath, I move toward Mirk and pick up the chair. My face leans toward Mirk and stops only inches away.

"Get off the floor," I say through gritted teeth.

Before I can react, Mirk quickly gurgles and spits out a glob of red-tinged spit that grazes my cheek. My right eye starts to twitch again. A grin returns to the little bastard's face. I slam a fist into his gut, making him grunt in pain. Moving behind Mirk, I position my arms under his shoulders and heave, pulling him up off the ground. I shove him back into the chair.

Desson stares at me, confused. I walk to the other side of the table. I reach into my pocket, fish out the device, and toss it onto the table. It clinks as it bounces on the metal surface before landing with the button side up, devoid of any numbers or glow.

For a moment, the room hangs in silence.

"What is this?" I spit out while pointing toward the device. Desson glances at it and back up at me. Mirk's eyes widen. He knows exactly what the hell this thing is.

"I shouldn't tell you anything after what you just did. Fucking corrupt cops. Can't trust 'em, and that will always be true."

Hearing the word *corrupt*, a dull pain aches in my chest. I am not corrupt. I just want answers, and I want to go home.

"You know what this is, don't you?" I ask.

Mirk moves his head to the side and spits out another glob of blood that lands on the ground. His eyes move back in our direction. Desson still looks confused, with a sliver of amusement etched across his features. The old detective sits back down in his chair and crosses his arms.

"I told you I didn't do shit, and you didn't listen," Mirk says in a low voice. He moves one stump arm and tries to push away the hair that had fallen into his eyes. With no success, he jerks his head and puffs out a quick breath, causing more hair to spill into his face. He lets out a growl.

Tension presses down on the room like a stack of weights.

Mirk smacks his lips. "Fine..." He pauses. "That's an Oblivion chip."

19

Zilch

Oblivion. I freeze, my lungs keeping any air from escaping. As if somebody were firing bullets into my brain, the events from today flash in my mind. Benji Davis, Mirk, Pandemon, the device, the Rhyner family, the similar cases, and now Oblivion.

"Oblivion?" I finally spit out. Lifting my gaze from the inert device on the table, I stare directly into Mirk's glowing purple eyes. "Tell me everything you know."

Mirk's mouth twists into a grin. A low bubbling laugh spills out of his mouth, trailing into his words. "I'll tell you, sure. But you're going to have to give me assurances since you know my hands are clean." He shrugs and waves his stump arms in the air. "Clean of anything dealing with Benji Davis besides a completed transaction. So... I'll tell you what it is, and you let me go. We got a fucking deal or what?"

Beads of sweat form on my forehead while I hold Mirk's gaze. We still do not know with any certainty that Mirk isn't the reason Benji is hooked up to a ventilator. Tests still need to be given on the modies that were installed and if Mirk knew they were defective or counterfeit. There is no way we can let him go just yet, but he doesn't have to know that.

"Understood," I say, with a stern look.

Mirk shakes his head and leans back into his chair, exhaling a long breath.

"Harkones, a moment outside, please?" Desson asks, with one brow raised.

I nod and stand with a grunt. My hand still throbs from punching Mirk square in the jaw. I repeat opening and closing it into a balled fist. Was it worth it? I run my tongue along my teeth while nodding.

Desson steps out of the room. I follow behind into the hallway. He turns his head and levels his eyes in my direction. "What the hell was that? What are you doing in there? If word gets out that you assaulted a suspect in our custody..." He pauses and shakes his head. "It's not a good look, Harkones."

I lick my lips, knowing that it might appear that I've snapped. Today feels like it's never going to end. New things keep rising to the surface. So maybe I did snap but it's getting us closer to the truth. Does it matter what I do if the result is knowing the answer? Closing out this case with certainty? I need to find out what these devices are and see how far it spreads. Credits are at the end of this tunnel. We just need to find all the pieces of the puzzle.

"Desson, that device, that thing I threw on the table, is what I was talking about earlier. It could potentially prove Mirk is innocent." I sigh, my shoulders slump, and fatigue creeps up my spine. "It could prove that Benji Davis did not suddenly go catatonic because of Mirk but instead, that thing he is calling Oblivion." I point one index finger toward the door. "That device could be the reason for several other victims with similar afflictions, and I... We need to find out what it is."

"You're saying that piece of plastic is causing people to fall over dead?" Desson asks.

"I don't know, but it's possible." Tito Rhyner's gashed face flashes across my eyes. "I found a similar device at a crime scene the lieutenant had me check out. The victim dropped dead, just like Benji. Agent Coleson checked out a few more cases that could also be linked to this thing."

Desson scratches at his beard. "Hmm. It would have been nice knowing that before we went back into the room."

"I know," I say. "I'm sorry. I should have told you sooner."

"If what you are saying is true, we should know what we're dealing with, but you need to cool it. We're getting answers. Just be patient."

I nod. "I'm sorry. I didn't mean to react like that. It's been a long day."

Desson rests a heavy palm on my shoulder and lets out a sigh. "It seems like we're having more days like that. But keep your head up. I know you do good work."

Blinking, I stare back at the old detective. I lose my cool, beat a suspect, and get complimented? I chuckle to myself, not sure what to say. Only one word comes to mind.

"Thanks," I say in a grim tone. After a brief pause, I continue. "Desson. I appreciate your help on this."

"Hey, I'm not doing this for free, so no need to thank me," he says, with a gentle smile. "How else do you think I afford this physique?"

"I was wondering about that," I say. I'm still wondering, but that's a question for later. "Let's get back in there and see what that device is capable of. Maybe Mirk has info on who is creating it, whatever it is."

"Agreed," Desson says, pulling his hand away and moving back toward the door. The door clicks open, revealing Mirk. A flicker of rage courses through me. Why does this guy anger me so much? I take a deep breath, step into the room, and lean back on the wall, trying to temper myself.

Desson sits down and leans back in his usual calm manner. "So this is what's going to happen. You are going to tell us what this thing is." He opens a palm and gestures toward the table. "And your information might just help you out in your current situation. Either way, you attacked an officer. You know that, right?"

Mirk's grin goes flat. One of his eyes starts twitching. "I attacked? Me?" He scoffs. "I was the one who was just attacked!"

Desson leans closer to Mirk and lowers his brow with a serious expression. He nods toward Mirk's arms. "Are you saying you did not fire at Detective Harkones earlier today?"

"I think it's... a bit obvious." He nods at his stump hands and waves them in the air.

"There we go. See, I knew we could agree on something. So, if you help us, we'll help you, okay?"

"Holy hell, fine, I'll tell you what it is, okay? I'm just fucking tired of sitting in this chair. Fucking ass is going numb." He points one stub at the white triangle on the table. "Like I said, that is an Oblivion chip."

I feel the hairs on the back of my neck stand up. Oblivion, finally, I will find out what the hell this thing is. Maybe I'll get an answer as to why Pandemon attacked me earlier and the reason they wanted me to stop searching for it

"An Oblivion chip?" Desson asks while rubbing one thumb against his interwoven hands.

"Yeah, these chips are the latest drug hitting the streets. Super fresh. Just started getting into people's hands. Like, in the past couple of weeks, from what I know."

"You said it's a drug?" I ask, trying to make sense of it.

"Uh-huh, a banger one too. Really good shit that hits like nothing I've ever tried before."

Staring at the device, I question how this tiny thing can possibly be a drug. I now have at least four cases that can potentially be tied to it. Four people, one a cold corpse. The others are now empty sacks of warm meat, including where this all started: Benji Davis.

A shiver of worry creeps down my spine, thinking of Bronk's gleaming hammer from earlier today. It's as if my skull took a blow from his hammer, leaving my brain scrambled and confused. Pandemon... they must have a stake in all this. The Ogre's bloody and headless body flashes across my mind. I shake my head, trying to focus on what's in front of me.

I walk toward the table, pick up the *chip* between my thumb and index finger, and hold it out in front of Mirk's face. "How is this a drug?"

"How is it a drug?" Mirk frowns and shrugs before continuing. "I can't tell you how it works, because I don't know. I would tell you to try it out for yourself, but you got a dud right there. All used up. Won't do shit."

"Let's back up for a second," Desson says while raising his hands. "Drugs, as far as I know, are inhaled, swallowed, or injected." He points one index finger toward the chip held in my grip. "How does this chip act as a drug?"

I study Mirk's face for any sign of deceit. He could be lying straight through his perfect, artificially white teeth, and we're just soaking it up. But it makes sense. Another drug hitting the streets. Another way to escape from the reality of Nox City. Another drug killing its users.

"That's how it's different from any other drug out there. You slap it to the side of your forehead, click the button, and whoosh." Mirk raises one stump in a swaying motion. "Pure bliss, euphoria, a clean high. Feels like you're floating in an ocean of, hmm, I don't know... you just feel like you're flying."

Click the button... So that's what that button is for. To start or activate the chip somehow. It doesn't explain the countdown though.

"What about the countdown timer?" I ask.

Mirk's eyebrows rise. His purple eyes stare back at me in surprise. "Oh, so you already have experience with Oblivion, do you, Detective? Why are you wasting my time if you know what it is?"

I tightly shut my eyes, trying to contain my building annoyance. "Let's just say, I saw one of these chips count down with no other details about what it's counting down toward."

Mirk shakes his head and chuckles. "Not only are you a plebo pig, but you're also an ignorant one too, aren't ya?"

I slam my fist on the table which makes a low hollow ring echo in the room. "Stop playing games! Just tell me what the countdown means."

"Is it not clear? It's just counting down to when the drug stops hitting your system. That's it. Damn, you're so fucking clueless."

A bubbling laugh spills out of my mouth. Wright and I freaking out and scrambling around in the Rhyner bedroom because the chip was counting down to completion. The chip isn't a bomb counting down to detonation. It's counting down to when the person comes back to reality. All this still needs to be confirmed, but it sounds plausible.

Desson clears his throat while leaning forward and points at the chip in my hand. "You mentioned that this particular chip is a dud?"

"Yeah, these chips are one-time-use devices. One click, one high." He shrugs and raises his arms in a stance of indifference. "Actually, it's not always one click because you have options here."

"Options?" Desson asks.

Mirk smacks his lips and sighs. "Yep, that's right. You click the device once for sixty seconds, twice for six minutes, and three clicks will get you sixty minutes. That countdown you saw is just the chip coming to an end."

"Three options? Why at those exact intervals?" Desson asks.

Mirk scoffs. "I don't know, man. I didn't fucking make it. That's just what it is."

"How do you know this is a dud?" I ask while extending my hand in his direction with the chip resting in my palm.

"The screen is blank. If it weren't all used up, you would see OV on the display in the middle."

An image of the box of devices in Tito's room surfaces in my mind. This kid had at least twenty of these devices packaged nicely and ready to use because they all had OV visible on the front. How the hell did he manage to horde a box of twenty of these *fresh* drugs? Maybe he was a seller? A seller for who, though?

Pandemon? I picture Tito's face in the pool of blood and the three pin pricks on his temple. A seller or a user, this kid had access to these chips somehow. Now, he's most likely dead because of it.

"You sure do know a lot about these chips," I say while twisting my hand around with the device pinched between my fingers. "How do you know so much when these are fresh on the market as you say?"

"I wasn't born yesterday. I have to know what's hitting the streets. Need to see how it can potentially interact with modies, if at all." He squints in my direction. "I don't want to cause unnecessary harm to my paying clients."

My eyes roll back. Really? Don't want to cause harm to his clients? It doesn't seem like he gives a shit about his clients.

"So what happens after you use this chip? Any side effects?" Desson asks while scratching at his beard.

"Zilch, nothing, that's it. When that countdown hits zero, your trip is done. That's what's so great about this drug. Pleasure with no risk."

No risk, my ass. I can think of four or five people who would disagree with that. How the hell does he know so much about this drug? He sounds like a goddamn spokesperson for it, as if I were listening to an advertisement.

"No risks?" I ask, tilting my head.

Mirk sighs and smacks his lips. "Nothing. I think whoever created this thing is a genius. True engineering masterwork at its finest. We now have a way to escape without any consequences."

Bullshit. We still don't know who is creating this drug, how it works, and what the ramifications are of using it. Mirk continually saying there are no side effects doesn't mean shit unless proven otherwise. I ain't buying it for one second.

"Reexe Fuello," I whisper at first, letting the name hang in the air. "Reexe Fuello!" I say again.

Mirk's laughing stops. His eyes lower in my direction.

"I think your buddy would disagree with you."

"What the hell are you talking about?"

"That's your buddy, right? From a few nights ago? The one who suddenly toppled over?"

"Yeah, that's him. How do you know his last name?"

"I wasn't born yesterday," I say while bringing up my wrist. The hologram display flickers to life. My other hand navigates through layers of menus and screens until I end up on CASE 1076032-18.

"What the hell is this guy doing?" Mirk asks while shifting his gaze toward Desson and lifting one stump arm in my direction.

Desson must know where I am going with this as he speaks to Mirk. "You said Reexe suddenly collapsed, right? Coming back out of the restroom?"

"He must have been drunk or high. I don't know, man. I barely even knew the grody fucker."

Clicking through the case file, I pull up a list of thumbnails taken at the trauma center Reexe was transported to. Scrolling through them, I find one with a close-up of his face.

"How do you explain this?" I swipe up on my display, which streams the photo to the center of the room. A photo of a scruffy, narrow-faced man with wild brown hair materializes in the center of the table. The man's head is tilted to one side, his eyes open, and he stares blankly ahead.

Mirk stares at the photo in confusion. "Oh, for fuck's sake, it's just a photo of him at the trauma center. I told you the trauma team was called, didn't I?"

I pinch the photo on my holo grid with my thumb and index finger, zooming in to Reexe's temple. The image in the middle of the table mirrors my motions and zooms in. Three pinpricks can easily be identified.

"Listen, I don't know what the hell you guys are going on about."

I smack one hand on the table with a loud cling, causing Mirk to wince. "You know what these indentations mean, don't you?"

Mirk stares with defiance, silent.

"Don't you?" I yell.

Mirk takes a deep breath and exhales through his nose. "Those are after marks of using Oblivion. That's it. They go away with time."

My heart starts thumping and blood rushes in my ears. I need to relax a little bit and cool it down. Breathe in and out, just like how Nekova taught me. Damn, today is just never going to end.

I need to focus on the positive. Mirk is in our custody, and he isn't going anywhere. He has the answers. We just need to keep asking the right questions. I lean back against the room's wall and nod in Desson's direction.

Desson nods back, an unspoken understanding between us.

"You can agree that Reexe used Oblivion? Most likely on the night he fell over?" Desson asks while crossing his arms.

"I have no clue. Like I said, I didn't even know the guy. He was just there that night."

Once again, the room is silent except for the tapping of Desson's hand against his other arm.

Desson leans in before speaking. "I need to remind you that you are here as a suspect in the death of Benji Davis. I also want to remind you that you have the power here. You have the power to clear your name. So I think it would be best for you to cooperate with us."

"You with that shit again? I have the power? Yeah, okay." He shakes his head. "Your buddy over there made that clear when he sucker punched me that I have the power." Mirk scoffs. "What the hell do you think I have been doing these past few hours? Sitting in this hard-ass chair. I have been answering all your questions all goddamn day."

I'm about to lose it again. My hands push off the wall. I move to stand at the corner of the table. Desson's chair scrapes the floor as he stands up, holding one arm out and blocking my path. I give Desson a questioning glance while he moves directly in front of Mirk. His eyes bore into the modifier, his gaze unwavering.

"I have one more question for you," Desson rumbles.

Something flickers in the back of Mirk's eyes. He licks his lips and stares up at Desson. "Alright."

"Where do you buy it?"

Mirk's lips part as if he's about to answer, but he pauses and lowers his gaze toward the floor, then back to the hovering picture of Reexe's face. His eyes swivel back toward Desson, then shift toward me.

"Dorsett and Sumerian, you'll find what you're looking for."

20

Plans

"Do you think we're walking into a trap?" Desson asks while picking at tight clamps around his arms and chest. A thin, dark metal skeleton is strapped to Desson's body, which gleams from the passing light outside the cruiser as we streak through the sky toward the street corner Mirk gave us.

I stare at the cruiser's floor and trace my vision up my legs, which are also tightly clamped by a lightweight NCPD exoskeleton suit. A pang of worry runs through my mind, thinking of this hunk of metal strapped to my body. I shake my head, knowing it's only temporary—only for a few hours, as these things have a limited charge anyway.

"A trap?" I ask while furrowing my brow. "No, I don't think Mirk is the planning type."

"True, but that doesn't mean he couldn't have given someone the heads up before you caught him."

"Based on his reaction when he saw me, I doubt it, but there's only one way to find out. Plus, if there is a trap, I think we should be able to handle it." I raise my hand up and slowly twist it around, staring at the metal secure around my palm and knuckles that trails up my outer arm toward my shoulder.

I reach into my jacket pocket, pull out a NitroMAX bar I grabbed from the station, and unwrap the thin plastic. The wrapping makes crunching sounds as I peel the plastic down and bring the protein bar to my mouth, biting off a chunk. The dry bar is supposed to taste like chocolate cinnamon swirl, but a better description would be a sticky pile of cardboard. I grimace, staring at the remainder of the bar. Hopefully, this settles my stomach somewhat.

"I gotta say, I enjoy suiting up in these things," Desson says. "Gives an old man like me a way to even out the playing field. Especially when these punks are chromed to the neck with illegal modies."

I sigh. "They can help. If they don't glitch out, that is." I raise my arm over my head in a dramatic arc, activating the back control unit underneath my jacket, which emits a soft whirring noise. "And they're not exactly the quietest things in the world." My jaws continue biting down on the rubbery, dry bar, which makes me thirsty.

Desson chuckles. "You might be right on that, but still, I'll take any chance I can get to strap into one," he says, admiring his partially encased hand.

"Hopefully, we don't need to use them. Just thought it would be better safe than sorry." I suck in air through my teeth and sigh. "Now that I'm pretty certain that Pandemon is involved in this."

Desson stares at me with lowered brows. "Pandemon," he says while shaking his head. "Not the best bunch of people there. Always getting into trouble with their droid animals, causing even more trouble."

"Yeah..."

It's all I can manage to say. The screeching metal scorpion echoes in my brain. Desson purses his lips and stares toward the ground. Silence fills the cabin with the only sound coming from the low hum of the propulsion units pushing us forward and my throat trying to swallow the remaining clumps of cardboard protein.

A familiar chime of three quick beeps sounds. Desson reaches into his pocket and plucks out the grey-silver pill container. Just as before, he gulps down a handful of pills and wipes at his mouth with the back of his hand.

"What is all that for?" I ask, with one palm pointed toward the container.

Desson glances at the pill case. "Just a bunch of supplements. Have to make sure the body has what it needs."

I raise one brow. "Seems like a lot."

"Well, when you get old like me, it's the only way to keep up." He snorts. "Supplements, diet, exercise, and having the drive to push yourself is all you need. If people did just two of these things, they would live happier lives. Longer, too."

I nod and leave the subject alone.

My gaze shifts up through the transparent dome of the cruiser toward the hazy night sky. An ethereal glow radiates within the smog, making the city look like it's burning with flames of purple, green, blue, orange, and whatever other color is twirling from the city below. It would be a beautiful sight, a cityscape enveloped in a cloud of colors as if an artist hand-painted the scene on a canvas.

My lungs say otherwise, knowing the colorful haze is a continual reminder of the filth and history gripping our city.

I can't even remember a time when the sky wasn't tainted. Polluted air and advertisements. Either way, corruption always lingers above. It seems we are in a never-ending decline as things continue to get worse and worse. Crime, food, trash, air, and for fuck's sake, the coffee too. Everything is getting worse day by day.

Maybe spending time in Infinity isn't so bad after all, even if it's not real.

I shake my head, refocusing my sight and my brain to now. Turning my head, I look behind us. Lights, buildings, and air traffic blur together until a glint of something shiny catches my eye. A flash of disquiet courses through me until I realize what it is. An NCPD drone moves at the same speed as our cruiser and follows our every direction. Amix did say there would be a drone tailing me for a while until things settle down.

I am relieved that Amix kept to her word. Even though I don't have a reason to doubt her. The drone following us reminds me of the other drone that should be circling my apartment building, looking for any sign of a disturbance. My apartment building... my home... my bed... my shower... my family. I gaze toward the clock on the front display of the cruiser and grimace, seeing that it's 11:23 p.m. I roll my eyes and shake my head. My god, it's almost the next day already.

Should I have just gone home after Mirk told us about Oblivion? He gave us a lead, and it's a path that could end with a big payday. It's already past Zinny's bedtime. I might as well stay out a little later, anyway. That book of hers will be waiting, and hopefully for not too much longer.

"What do you make out of this whole Oblivion situation?" Desson asks.

Zinny's smiling face suddenly cracks into a thousand pieces in my mind. The pieces collect and morph into the triangular white device, Oblivion. My mind flashes to Benji's drooling face, flashes again to Tito, and flashes once more to the list of other potential cases. I take a deep breath and exhale quickly before responding.

"I don't know what to make of it yet, but from everything I've seen today, it can explain a lot. There's so much we don't know, though. We don't even know if we can trust what Mirk was telling us. This could be an elaborate ploy to buy him more time." I pause, pursing my lips while staring blankly ahead. "But... Mirk really *could* be innocent in all this. That doesn't excuse the fact that he ran from me. Or shot at me."

"It's the first I've heard of this apparent drug, so I'm right there with you. A lot to figure out still about all this." Desson rubs at his temple and slightly shakes his head. "I'm still trying to wrap my brain around how it works."

The cabin glows with a dull blue that slowly gets brighter before it eventually dims again. A modulated voice speaks through the cruiser's internal speakers, letting us know we're about to land.

"Just another question waiting to be answered. Desson..." I sigh, dropping my shoulders. "I also wanted to thank you for joining me this late in the day. You didn't have to stay with me this long." I offer a solemn smile in his direction.

"I'm happy to be here." Desson's gaze settles on me. "It was fun seeing the guy squirm. I'm interested in seeing how this all turns out with the new drug hitting the streets."

"Plus, I'm sure there will be a good payday for the officers who bring in more than just speculation about this new drug. It was great to see your work in action. Word around the station is that you're our best interrogator."

Desson slowly nods. "I do enjoy the questioning process. You can learn a lot by asking questions or being silent. Throwing surprises in there, too, can help kick a person's mind into high gear, spilling out even more information."

A jolt passes through the cruiser as it lands with a clunk. A hissing sound comes from the vehicle with the propulsion units winding down. I stare out the window and see we are on an above-ground parking pad filled with several other vehicles. My brows rise, looking at some of the battered and beaten, rusted-up scraps of metal that form into the shape of a car sitting on top of four rubber wheels. These cars have seen better days. I would be surprised if they can even move or start-up.

I look around the cruiser and nod. I guess flying around in this NCPD vehicle is a luxury. I don't even have to steer the thing. I just say an address and a proximity to the location, and it just zooms off. It even parks for me.

My hands reach for my mask attached to my belt and move to pull it up. The activators on the back unit of my exoskeleton quietly wine and whir from the motion of my arms. I'm about to strap my mask over my face when I notice that Desson isn't doing the same. I let my arms fall to my sides, holding the unit.

"Where's your filtration mask? You looking to breathe in some of this fresh air?" I ask, pointing to my mask with a questioning look.

"Oh, I haven't told you yet?"

"Haven't told me what?"

"I got a pair of iron lungs a couple of weeks ago. I mean, they are not actually iron, but that's what people are calling them."

"Oh wow... you got a modi installed?" I ask, with raised brows. I guess one of those pills was Senervamene after all. "Out of all the potential modies you could get, I can see the reason behind that one."

"Yep, it wasn't cheap either, but I don't have to worry about fiddling with masks anymore. Those bulky things are such a pain."

"What about your eyes? Doesn't the raw air mess them up at all?" My gaze shifts to my mask, and I look over the transparent dome that covers my mouth, nose, and eyes.

"Nope, I got that covered."

I lean toward Desson and squint, scanning his features. "Are you sure? You got eye implants but didn't opt in for any glow?"

"I find glowing eyes a bit tacky if you ask me. I got the latest version of the OptiSync ProMax." The corners of his lips curl up before he scoffs. "The ad said *see like never before,* and they weren't lying."

His eyes at least look better than the tubes attached to the Pandemon woman from earlier. They don't even look like implants and could pass as completely organic.

"I guess I can understand that. Man, you must have spent a lot of creds to get those."

Desson shrugs. "Yeah, well, I know a guy," he says with a grin.

"More power to you then," I say while shrugging.

I grunt out of habit while moving to stand, which feels effortless as the activators in the exoskeleton amplify my movements. I scratch at the straps clinging tight against my chest, the suit holding me in a fierce embrace. The fragile flesh of man, bound within a skeleton of metal, and becoming something more than human. It's not natural, and I don't like it at all, but I'll do what is necessary.

I reach down and make sure my hand cannon and hyper coil are attached to my belt. I nod, feeling the familiar grips at my sides. I bring the mask over my face and strap it in place. As the filtration units kick in, green lights on the sides flick on.

Moving to the front of the cruiser, I click a couple of buttons and activate a map of Nox City which flickers to life. It hovers in the center of the cabin. Using my hands to control the pitch and yaw of the map, I pinch my index and thumb together and expand my hand out, zooming to our current location.

A flashing red dot pings on the street corner of Dorsett and Sumerian. Desson moves a little closer to the map, walking into the hologram projection, and squints.

"So, we're right here," I say while pointing my hands at our current location marked by a flashing yellow triangle. "Should just be a two-minute walk to the intersection Mirk gave us. Then we'll know whether he was full of shit or not."

"Do you have a plan in mind?" Desson asks.

I nod while staring at the map. "We're about ten stories up right now and I'm pretty sure that we can have a vantage point from the end of this parking pad with direct vision to the corner. So, I say one of us gets to a position from this height, surveys the scene, and checks if anything looks suspicious.

"What about the other person? What are you thinking?"

"Street level. Don't draw attention, and scope the area out on foot. You might best fit up top with these new bionic eyes."

Desson nods. "If you say so. Mirk said we can buy Oblivion here. I wonder what that looks like. I doubt there will be a guy below with a big red arrow pointing to his face with the words, *Oblivion Sold Here* flashing in big bold letters."

"It's too bad we couldn't get more out of him after he told us about this intersection," I say, shaking my head.

"Oh, I'm sure he'll be talking soon. If he's innocent, he won't shut up about it."

I rub my chin, hopeful that this plan will work and that we find something. Anything more about this drug. Something that I can at least report back to Amix with. I don't want all the shit I've been through today to go to waste. I need the bonus and I need it soon.

My hand moves to press the door button, but I hesitate. I turn back and stare at Desson, who looks completely ordinary with no modifications at all. *Plebo* by all accounts.

"You sure you can breathe fine in this air? No mask?" I ask, with raised brows.

Desson chuckles. "Yeah, I'll be fine. Let's go."

"Okay then..." I say. The button clicks when I press it down. An instant later, a whoosh sounds as the door opens vertically, allowing us to step out. I place one foot on the concrete and duck my head under the doorway, moving to exit the cruiser.

In the middle of stretching my shoulders back, a bone-shattering boom erupts in the distance. I jolt, panic rushing through me. Again, another monstrous boom sounds, echoing from what could be the direction of our target area. Again and again, large booms sound like gunfire from a high-caliber weapon. Next, I hear tires screeching, ending in a loud crash.

Desson and I stare at each other in shock.

"What the hell was that?" I mutter.

21

Dealer

We dash forward, each step creating a metallic clank as we near the edge of the garage level. Surging in motion, the wind whips at my hair while my suit emits mechanical whirrs and hydraulic hisses. Moving faster than I ever humanly could, a slight grin spreads across my face. Maybe this suit isn't so bad after all. I can get used to the enhanced mobility and strength.

The sound of distant screams becomes louder. Whatever made that noise, it can't be good. Did it really come from the street corner we were about to scope out?

We approach the parking pad's edge and peer toward the ground, scanning for motion or anything that could indicate what caused the large booms of noise. A mass of people are shouting and running in every direction.

"Do you see anything?" I ask, my eyes searching the scene.

Before Desson can answer, I notice a car smashed into the corner of a building, the front crumpled. Something crimson glistens in the light. I realize it must be blood as I make out bodies near the smashed car. Limbs and unmoving bodies are sprawled out everywhere, making it hard to tell how many victims there are. I squint harder, trying to get more details, but it's still blurry from this distance.

"What the hell just happened?" Desson asks while surveying the scene. "Looks like a guy is pinned between that car and the building. He's still alive!"

I lean further down, but it doesn't help my vision. "How can you make that all out? I can barely see shit."

"OptiSync ProMax!" he yells while turning on his heels. "Let's get down there!" He starts sprinting away from the edge.

Oh, right. I forgot about his modified eyes. Damn, the old man's vision is probably ten times better than the mine now. I bet he was able to zoom in and see everything crystal clear, as if he was down there in the commotion. Enhanced eyes. I can see their benefit, but still, I wouldn't trust it. My mind still wonders how Desson can afford it all. Does it even matter, though?

My organic eyes scan the scene one last time before running to follow Desson.

"Over here!" Desson yells, not looking back.

My heart rate spikes as I make my way to a door that I assume leads to a staircase for access to all the levels of this garage. I pass through the doorway, still following Desson's direction, and head down. Graffiti and trash litter the walls and floor. The narrow stairway reverberates from our quickly descending feet. Beads of sweat start forming on my forehead and roll down my cheek.

Descending stairs once again. It seems like I just did this only a couple of hours ago. Why can't places just have normal functioning elevators? Is that too hard to ask for?

With about five levels to go, Desson jumps over the railing and falls toward the ground. I freeze and my eyes widen in shock. I lean over the railing and stare at the falling mass of flesh and metal. A second later, he lands with a loud crack. He swivels his head and stares up at me.

"Come on!" Desson yells.

Right, the suit! The crazy old bastard wasn't lying about loving to strap into a suit. It's like he's a different person now.

I suck in air through my teeth and ball my fists. "Fuck me!" I scream while grabbing the railing and throwing my body down the stairwell. The different levels blur. Wind rushes past my face. The floor is getting closer. I clench my teeth and brace for the impact. My feet slam against the ground with a hard smack that should have splintered my bones into a hundred pieces. The hydraulic system in my legs' exo suit pushes out a loud hissing whoosh.

A grunt of pain escapes my lips. It is still jarring to fall five floors, but it's manageable. I lift my gaze and see Desson sprinting toward a door with an inert EXIT sign above it. I push out a puff of air and dash forward.

Just ahead, I hear Desson yelling at his raised hand. "We need units on the corner of Dorsett and Sumerian! Threat in progress! Medical assistance needed!"

The exit door flies open as Desson careens through it. Following behind, I exit the narrow confines of the garage hallway into an open street of chaos. The air is hot and humid. People are still running and yelling in random directions. Looking through the mass of people, I focus on a hanging street sign with the word "Dorsett" brightly displayed. Glancing at the adjacent street sign, I laugh.

Sumerian. What are the odds? Mirk just tells us about this street corner, and on the same night, mayhem lets loose? Maybe we are walking into a trap. From the look of things, it has already been sprung.

Staring straight ahead through a clearing in the disarray of people, an orange rust bucket of a car is smashed into the side of a building. Smoke billows up from under the crumpled hood. My eyes narrow, taking in the sight. In front of the mangled hood, a person is groaning and moving. His head is lowered, making it difficult to make out his face.

I start scanning the scene, trying to make sense of what just happened. The concrete is blood-streaked from what looks like three people. Unmoving bodies. Flesh torn and shredded as if they went through a meat grinder. Is this the aftermath of those booms from a few minutes ago? I would have thought to see bullet wounds or something other than this bloody mess.

My hand moves toward my hand cannon, ripping it from the holster. I hold it tight against my chest. Desson is first on the scene and moves toward the person trapped by the car. His backside blocks my view from seeing the person up close.

While taking deep breaths, my head swivels, looking for answers.

"Sir, are you alright? What happened?" Desson asks.

I hear the trapped man chuckle, leading to manic laughter.

"Sir, are you okay?" Desson asks.

"Oh... I will be," says a shrill and scratchy voice.

Something sparks in the back of my mind. That voice... it sounds familiar. I move to the side of Desson to get a better view of the pinned man. My heart drops as a pang of recognition courses through my veins. I know this guy. I saw him just earlier today. Black jacket, glowing white eyes, and a wicked smile spread across his face behind a filtration mask. Descent. This is the demented guy who was trying to give me something. Something new.

"My god..." I mutter.

I remember now that he was holding on to something white. I never saw what it was but it had to be Oblivion.

"Sir, what did you say?" Desson asks.

Slowly, I walk up to Desson and stare down while shaking my head.

The man licks his lips and arcs his head back, resting it against the wall with closed eyes. He releases a breath of air and violently coughs. Spit shoots out from his mouth, hitting the wall of his mask. It sounds like a struggle for him to pull in more air.

My gaze traces down his jacket and focuses on his trembling hands. I furrow my brow, noticing they are not trembling at all. Split open down the center, a circular blade slowly spins between each hand. The blades are gleaming discs of razor-sharp teeth, each smeared with ruby-red splatters.

I glance back at the ripped-open bodies and swallow. Shaking my head, I breathe in through my nose and return my gaze to the coughing man.

His eyes open and flick in my direction, meeting my stare. He chuckles while coughing at the same time.

"Oh, Officer, so you do want to try it out after all?"

Desson's head snaps in my direction. "What's this guy saying? You know him?"

"Oblivion?" I ask in a low, hushed voice.

His smile widens. "Yes, yes, so you already know. Soon, everyone will know. Everyone will experience. Oblivion is the future."

Sirens wail in the distance. Responders en route to the scene.

"I would offer you some, but it seems…" He looks to the left and right. "It seems I just have the one here." His split hand moves to his interior coat pocket while the blade retracts. He reaches in and pulls out a triangular white chip. Holding it between his index finger and thumb, he moves it closer to his temple.

"Wait!" I shout, with one hand outstretched. "What happened?"

The small chip is now resting on his temple, and his finger is holding the center button, which has not yet been depressed.

"Word is getting out. People want an escape and Oblivion is their answer. When they want something, someone is there to provide." The man speaks in a nonchalant tone as if half his body isn't smashed into a wall.

"You are saying people attacked you for… Oblivion?" I ask.

"It would seem so, Officer." He lets out more violent coughs and sucks in more air. "This group must have known I have it and that I'm selling it. Only, they didn't want to pay." He starts laughing again with a mix of wheezing while still holding his fingers over the device pressed against his skull. "They might have managed to get my stock but not without sacrifices." He looks at the bodies on the ground and shakes his head. "Now they are in an oblivion." He takes a deep breath through his nose and exhales. "Where I will be soon as well." He closes his eyes and clenches his jaw.

"Hold!" Desson shouts while moving closer to the pinned man. "Where is your source?"

The man's eyes slowly open and shift in Desson's direction, staring for what feels like an eternity. Desson mouths something that I can't make out. Finally, the dealer responds after a violent cough. "On the edge of the swamp. But it doesn't matter. You're too late. Word is out. There is nothing you can do." He closes his eyes. Splatters of blood are on his chin and against the inside of his mask.

Three rapid clicks sound out as the man presses down on the Oblivion chip. An instant later, his body jolts. He lets out a gasp of air while his head falls back, resting against the building. His glowing white eyes roll backward. A smile creeps onto his face. The chip displays 59 on the center button. "Finally," he says in an almost whisper. "Sweet oblivion."

His breathing becomes labored, a struggle to continue pulling in oxygen.

Screaming sirens are now behind me as deputies and trauma teams arrive on the scene. Blue and red lights flash in my peripheral vision. As I stare down at the dealer, I hear doors opening and closing behind me. Officers shout commands, and I hear spectators being instructed to stay back, along with the unsettling creak of something nearby. A shiver of worry runs down my spine.

Something creaking, something groaning, and something hissing. What the hell is making that sound? My eyes narrow, searching to pinpoint the noise.

"The swamp? You think he's talking about the swamplands?" Desson asks. "Also, you still haven't answered me. How do you know this guy?"

"Wait!" I shout, with one palm pushed out. "Do you hear that?"

It sounds like something is straining, like something is about to pop.

My exo suit whirs with each movement. I squat and scan for the source of the hissing. A soft whistle comes from under the car and is gradually getting louder.

"Mm-hmm, I hear something," Desson says while crouching down. "Is that coming from the car?" Desson leans his head forward and points to under the car with raised brows. He sucks air between his teeth. "You see that?" His eyes dart from under the car to me and back. He continues furiously pointing. "We need to move!" He quickly stands. "The battery is compromised! It's expanding!"

Hiss...

22

Motion

Straining my eyes, I look under the car again, searching for what Desson is pointing at. I wince from a loud pop. Something skitters onto the ground next to me. Something tiny and black.

Is that a screw?

My eyes dart back under the car and widen. I finally spot the source of the noise. The battery compartment under the car is rising like a balloon about to burst, and the casing holding the battery is straining from the pressure.

Hiss...

Oh hell... I flick my eyes to the dealer trapped between the car and the building. The man smacks his lips as his eyes continue rolling back and forth. The number 57 now displays on the chip. He starts laughing again.

"Everybody back!" Desson screams while swaying his arms forward. "It's going to blow!"

Adrenaline pumping in my veins, I heave myself up and turn to run from the car. I glance at the man's face before he's out of my line of sight. I could swear he was smiling and staring at me, his glowing white eyes shining bright.

Hiss...

Our feet smack the pavement as Desson and I sprint away, our suits pushing us forward. A thunderous boom erupts behind us, sending a shockwave of vibration through my bones. Flaming debris flies in all directions and plummets toward the ground.

I turn back and stare at the scene. The scorched orange car blazes in an inferno of fire with black smoke ballooning outwards. I don't see any trace of the man. It's as if he vanished, leaving behind nothing but unanswered questions and the crackling fire amongst the wreckage.

"Jesus..." I mutter.

The back of my hand wipes the sweat off my forehead. I shake my head, stare blankly ahead, and deeply breathe through my nose. A bubble of laughter rises from within me. I don't get paid enough for all this shit I have to deal with. Explosions, drugs, robot animals, gangs, and no elevators? Fuck this shitty day.

I clear my throat, which feels like sandpaper. I'm still parched and hungry. I need a drink. Actually, I need a lot more than a drink.

"So, are you going to tell me how you knew that guy?" Desson asks, orange light shining off his face from the rippling flames.

It still strikes me as odd seeing him with no mask on at all. How much did that all set him back? How can he afford it all when I am just barely scraping by? I know he's a senior detective, but his base salary shouldn't be that much higher than mine.

I draw in a deep breath and let out a long, steady sigh. "I'll tell you, though it's not much of a story." I grimace and scratch at my stubbly chin. "What do you say? We make one more stop before we call it a night and head home? Just a little recon."

"The Swamplands?"

"Yep, it's on the way to the station anyway."

"On the way to the station?" Desson asks.

"I know... it's not on the way. I wish it were, though."

Footsteps approach us from behind. "Detectives, what the hell happened?"

I turn and take in a short deputy with an arched nose. He scans the scene while his meaty palms turn upward. A second explosion from the car booms, jolting everyone in surprise.

Twisting back toward the car, I point at the columns of flames reaching into the sky. "That happened."

"I can see that. How about before?"

My gaze darts toward where the dealer once stood. The corners of my mouth form into a flat line. *"On the edge of the Swamp."* How can a drug like Oblivion come out of that wasteland? It doesn't make sense.

I turn back and stare at the deputy. "Find out what happened here. Let me know when you submit your report so I can read over it." I shrug and roll my neck. "We have somewhere we need to be."

The deputy stares back up at me with an annoyed expression written across his glistening, sweaty face. He purses his lips before responding. "Uhh, sure. Yes, sir."

"Harkones? Twice in one day?"

I turn to my right and narrow my eyes. "Nekova? What are you doing here?" She steps through the crowd of responders, her jacket glimmering with a metallic sheen. A low-profile mask contours around her face.

"I can ask you the same thing," she says, hand on hip, fingers close to one of her hyper coils.

Looking from Desson back to Nekova, I shrug and tilt my head. "We were the ones who called this in."

"No. No, it was already called in when you two reported it." She glances at Desson and nods. "Desson, nice to see you."

"Likewise," Desson says.

"We got a report about a questionable weapon being spotted in this area. Could be an illegal modi, too." She gestures to one of the bodies on the ground and smacks her lips. "Looks like the report was right."

The deputy clears his throat. "Umm, sir. Is there anything else you nee—"

A high-pitched whine sounds from down the street. I look past the deputy and spot a shirtless man hunched over a silver hoverbike hurtling in our direction, one hand in the air. It looks like he's holding something, but I can't be sure.

Desson squints and lets out a gasp. "Grenade! Take cover!"

A sick feeling intertwined with panic shoots down my back. What the hell is this bullshit? What does this guy think he's doing?

From behind us, I hear a concussive boom. I twist to the source of the new sound and feel the heat of something pass me. An instant later, a squelching pop rings in my ear. My eyes go wide as something wet splatters against the side of my face.

Where the deputy once stood, I stare at a cloud of crimson mist. What's left of him plops to the ground. I snap my eyes toward the origin of the blast and see another shirtless man with black pants slowly walking in our direction, clutching some kind of weapon with both hands. A panel of blue energy is directly in front of him.

We burst into motion.

Desson and I sprint toward the cluster of parked cruisers. Nekova dashes to the incoming hoverbike, hyper coils buzzing in each hand. I reach for my Z4 and hold it against my chest. My heart races with adrenaline coursing through me. Peering over the door of a cruiser, the shirtless man is still approaching our line of officers.

"They're pinning us in!" I cry out.

What kind of gun is that? Are these the same guys who fought with the dealer? Why didn't they get out of here?

Officers fire a volley of bullets toward the walking man with no success. Rounds of metal bounce off the layer of energy.

"He's got a mobile shield!" Desson shouts.

"I can see that!" I yell back. "How do we get to him?"

"We need to flank him!"

I clamp my jaw and stare at the walking man. He appears to be organic and ripples with muscles. He raises the blocky weapon again and aims in our direction. The blue energy shielding the man winks out.

"Incoming!" I shout.

Another boom rings out. The cruiser next to us explodes, sending a tremor through the earth.

"Jesus," I rasp.

Peering over the door again, the man's energy shield is reactivated. Bullets ricochet off the protective layer and spring away in different directions.

I swivel my head behind me and spot Nekova streaking toward the incoming hoverbike. Her movements are fluid and smooth as if she's dancing. The man on top of the bike moves his hand back and jerks it forward. The grenade sings through the air with a constant beeping.

My breath catches in my throat, staring at the oval-shaped metal overhead. I raise my Z4 and glance at the side display. I gulp and scrunch my face. Positioning my aim, I wait for the right moment. I need the angle to be perfect. I need luck on my side.

Not yet... and... NOW! I squeeze the trigger. A blast of air charges out of the barrel toward the falling grenade. The wave of air catches the grenade and flings it forward.

The man behind the layer of energy moves to fire another blast and hesitates. He looks up and tilts his head. The grenade falls to the ground behind him and skitters to a stop. He jerks to get out of the way.

Boom. The grenade goes off with a deafening roar. Blinding light sears my eyes before I close them. A sharp crack sounds out as panels of glass shatter from the nearby building.

I take a deep breath and look around. The thug is gone, replaced by a thick layer of dust and billowing smoke.

Darting my head back in the other direction, I tighten my jaw. It looks like an electric tornado is twisting in the air. Nekova is upside down and spinning, falling back to the ground. The hoverbike careens forward, passing underneath the vortex of electricity. The goon looks up with his mouth agape. Nekova's hyper coils take hold and grip the broad-shouldered man, constricting. He separates at two points, head and body falling to the pavement. Nekova gracefully lands on her feet and straightens her back. The hoverbike hums and slows to a stop.

"Goddamn good work, Harkones," Desson says while patting my shoulder.

I suck in a sharp breath of air. "What the hell was that all about?"

The clustered officers and responders around us ease their shoulders, taking panting breaths.

Desson shakes his head and purses his lips. "If I had to guess, it's probably something to do with Aspire. The gang is known to have bulky hotheads like that." He gestures toward the split corpse of the man at Nekova's feet. "Though, to come directly at us like that is unusual."

"Whatever it was, I guess we have an answer to what was making those booming sounds earlier."

Nekova approaches us, her mouth in a flat line. She shrugs and shakes her head. "Just another day on the job, right boys?"

I chuckle. "You could say that."

Glancing at the time on my holo grid, I growl and shake my head. It's getting late and we still have so many unanswered questions. This incident with potentially another gang is only adding more questions to the pile.

"Gotta be somewhere?" Nekova asks.

"We have a new lead I want to follow up on."

"Well, go on then. I'll handle it from here. We'll exchange notes later."

"Thanks, Nekova. We'll talk soon."

She offers a smile and turns toward the group of idle officers. "Move your asses! You know the drill!"

I turn toward Desson and clear my throat. "You ready to check out a swamp?"

"I'm here and alive, aren't I? Let's get it done."

23

Swamp

All around, the only thing I see is filth, rubble, and dilapidated structures in a body of stagnant septic water. The cruiser flies forward over mounds of trash that resemble bodies of land in a green-tinged ocean. Islands of filth connected by makeshift bridges and pathways lit by dim lights strung together. It's almost a mirror image of Veridian but far, far worse. I bet this place was once beautiful, a pristine lake, but now it's just a dumping ground for the waste of our society, relics of our past.

The Swamplands... the nickname suits the area. My face contorts, thinking of this place being home to an uncountable number of residents. I shake my head, envisioning what life must be like here. Toxic air above you and toxic water below you? Sounds like a worse hell than Nox City already is.

"How can the source of Oblivion come from this shithole?" I ask, not believing it to be possible.

A part of me feels grateful that my life decisions have not led me and my family to sink to a point as low as living here, in a shadow even darker than the bottom of the actual city. At least not yet.

"I'm not sure. There is a lot of scrap here to pick from," Desson offers, with his palms raised.

"Enough scrap for an entire production and distribution line? The dealer was making it seem that this new drug will be the future. I doubt the future of anything is coming out of this... this cesspit," I say, swaying my hand toward the ground.

"Maybe Oblivion isn't tied to this place at all. Maybe he was just pointing us in the wrong direction?" Desson says while shrugging.

I draw in a deep breath and exhale. "You might be right. We've been scanning this area for twenty minutes now?" Leaning against the side wall of the cruiser, my gaze drifts downward, searching the piles of discarded waste passing us by. "Even if it came out of here, I'm not sure we'll be able to find it tonight. It's like searching for a needle in a haystack."

This time, I don't have a map loaded on my wrist and pointing me where to go. We could be wasting time. I despise wasting time, but sometimes, you just have to see if anything comes out of it. It's a risk. What's the saying again? Not all efforts will bear fruit? Sometimes, though, risks will reap rewards.

Right now, I'm not seeing any fruit come my way. It's just another dead end. My stomach lets out a low, hungry rumble. No fruit or any food, for that matter. That protein bar from earlier didn't cut it. I smack my lips in distaste, thinking about how dry it was.

At this point, from the shit I went through today, I have stacks of reports and notes to scan through. A problem for tomorrow. My eyes shift to the clock, knowing I will not be happy regardless of the time. 12:03 a.m. I guess it's a problem for today, now.

Slumping back into my chair, I drop my head against the headrest, and close my eyes. A thick cloud of disappointment hangs over me. I press my fingers against my forehead, rubbing in a circular motion. The slight pressure helps, but my lingering headache refuses to go away.

I wanted to wrap this new case in a bow and hand it over to Amix. Maybe I still can tomorrow or the next day or whenever things line up and start making sense. A feeling of unease chews at my stomach. I have a debt to pay, a debt with a hard deadline. Not just one, either. I reach for my neck, remembering the chill of the Torqueman's collar. I still have over twenty-four hours for Zinny's school, so that's something at least.

"We may need to involve others in this as well. Get a squad of drones set up and scan the area. We could also bounce ideas off with different team leads." Desson nods while pursing his lips. "Don't forget we also have Mirk sitting in a cell. We can question him some more. Maybe he was holding something back."

I nod and stare blankly ahead, feeling today's fatigue take hold. My hand moves and rubs against the dull ache in my chest. Did I go through all that shit tonight for nothing? I let out a groveling sigh.

"I think it's time to call it a night," I say in a tired and defeated voice.

Desson reaches out and rests a hand on my right shoulder. "Hey, don't feel like you've lost. We'll rest our eyes for a few hours and get back at it." He offers a warm smile. "We learned a lot today and I think we're on to something big."

A breath escapes me. "You're right. Okay... let's head back."

I hold a button down on my armrest, activating the cruiser voice command. "Take us back to the station."

A modulated voice sounds through the cabin speakers, "Confirmed, rerouting." A second later, the cruiser's propulsion units veer us in a new direction, back toward the city.

"On the edge of the Swamp." What edge was the dealer talking about? Logically, I would think he meant the border of where The Swamplands starts. Or ends?

Blue, purple, and green lights wash over the approaching hazy city of metal, concrete, and glass. Home. Finally, I'll be able to lie in my bed. I sniff at the air, smelling the musky odor coming off my clothes.

A thought flashes into my mind that makes me snort and start laughing. I see it clearly in my mind. Creeping into bed and waiting for Raena to catch my rancid smell. Her cute face scrunching up, her eyes snapping open, her grabbing a pillow and smacking it against my head. "Sol, get in that shower right now before I smack you with something other than this pillow!" We both laugh as I step out from under the covers. "Alright, alright," I say, with my palms raised.

"What are you laughing at?" Desson asks.

"Ah, nothing. Just that I stink."

"I was going to say something," Desson says, with a grin.

I roll my eyes and shake my head. "It will be nice to get out of this skeleton, though. It's making me sweat even more than normal." Raising my hand, I stare at the dark, thin metal wrapped around my palm. Stretching my fingers out, I focus on a circle of silver wrapped around my ring finger. Traces of blue and black swirl in the manmade metal. One corner of my lips curls upward.

I picture Raena's smiling face on our wedding day. Her delicate hands hold the silver ring between two fingers as she places it around my ring finger. She stares up at me with sparkling green eyes.

The moment I met her, I knew she was something special. Something rare in this city. She left me breathless. A flicker of light that radiated warmth throughout my body. I never thought I would find someone so beautiful in this world, especially after my last *relationship*.

I grin, thinking back to the first time I held Zinny in my arms. Her tiny body squirmed in my careful grip. The warmth I felt for Reana only compounded and grew while staring at Zinny, her little hands clenched into shaking fists. My heart swelled. Tears formed at the corners of my eyes. A sense of worry crept over me and still does to this day. I will not let anything happen to her.

"Hey! You see that?" Desson says, pulling me out of my deep trance.

I shake my head and blink, trying to focus on the direction Desson is pointing. Something flying at an unusual speed, bobbing up and down in the air.

Is that my tailing drone? No, it's the wrong color, and it's too tiny. This thing looks like it is made of metal, chromed on the surface. I stand out of my chair and lean my head forward, trying to make sense of it.

"Is that thing flapping?" I ask. "Use those new eyes of yours and see what it is."

I don't remember the last time I saw an actual bird flying through the air, especially here in the city. It can't be real. It must be a recreation or a droid.

A *droid...* Pandemon. No, it can't be.

Desson rises out of his chair, steps toward the front of the cruiser, and squints. "Hmm, that is odd. It is a bird, but it doesn't look like any bird I've seen."

"It's metal, right?" I ask, with furrowed brows and clenched fists.

"Yeah, looks like it." Desson turns toward me and tilts his head. "Are you alright?"

I suck air through my teeth and grimace, focusing on the bird still flapping through the air. My gaze shifts to the ground. I spot a few buildings that appear to be warehouse-type structures, about nine or ten stories high. Squinting, I spot something glowing.

"What? What are you looking at, Harkones?" Desson asks while scanning the ground, trying to follow my line of sight.

On the rooftop, I make out the shape of a person with glowing orange eyes. The person appears to be standing still with their neck craned back, staring up toward the sky, where the metal bird is flying.

"Oh shit..." I mutter.

"Harkones, what are you seeing? The guy on the roof?" he asks, pointing toward the building.

"Pandemon, it must be. The edge of the city. The edge of the Swamp. I think this is it."

"This is it?" Desson asks. "You think Oblivion comes out of there?"

"I'm not sure... but I know Pandemon is involved somehow, and look at what we find out here. A metal flying droid and a Pandemon thug who is controlling it."

"I don't know if we can be too sure about that. It could be a nobody with modified eyes, just bird watching."

The cruiser is now inside Nox City air space and continues toward the station. I follow the flapping bird as it zig-zags through the air and plummets toward the ground. Defying gravity, the metallic creature shoots back up and lightly lands on one outstretched arm. The arm of the man on the rooftop.

"I don't think he's just bird-watching."

Desson purses his lips and nods. "Okay, you might be right. So, what's your call? Keep heading back to the station or...?" He stares at me, his eyes urging me to act.

I look toward the clock, now displaying 12:13 a.m., and sigh. It's not the latest I've been out, but it's still pretty damn late. My gaze shifts back to the rooftop. The man is walking toward a large box on the roof. His glowing orange eyes are shining bright like a beacon. A beacon guiding me toward answers. Toward credits. This could be my break. This could make all this shit I've been through today worth it.

"We're already here. Let's see if this building bears any fruit."

"Fruit? What the hell are you talking about fruit for?"

I let out a snort and shake my head. "You know what I mean." Stepping back toward my seat, I activate the cruiser's voice command. "Park us in the first available spot inside a quarter mile of this location."

"Confirmed. Proceeding to the next available parking within 0.25 miles of the current location." The cruiser starts veering left, our path taking us closer to the warehouse. I don't take my eyes off the man walking toward the large box. Now, closer, I can make out that his arm is covered in metal. Two claws wrap around it, trailing up to the entire body of the chrome-winged creature. I grimace, remembering the scorpion from earlier today, and rub at the fading ache in my chest.

"That bird looks smaller than I expected. The scorpion I ran into earlier was about double the size. This thing looks to be—"

"Wait, what?" Desson asks, brows arched. "Did you say a scorpion? When did this happen?"

"When I was tailing Mirk. I was tracking him to Descent, and surprise. I got a metal stinger shooting toward my face. Pandemon goons were trying to scare me off from pursuing Oblivion."

"That happened today?" Desson asks.

My mouth forms into a frown, thinking of the headless corpse of Bronk. I blow out a breath, knowing how close I came to death myself. I blink and refocus. The Pandemon thug is getting closer to the box.

"Maybe an hour or so before I brought Mirk into the station. The crazy thing was that I had no idea what they were even talking about. I was just trying to catch Mirk... Wait, are you seeing this?" I point toward the rooftop. "I think he is about to put that bird in the box or shed."

Desson looks back to the rooftop and narrows his eyes. "You're right. The little thing just hopped into that cubby. Maybe it's a charging dock of some sort? Hmm..."

"What is it?" I ask.

"Now that I'm looking at it, there are more cubbies in the box too."

"More metal birds, you think? What do you call that? A murder?" I ask while picturing a flock of these things ripping through the city.

"I guess you could call it that. No telling how many are in there."

"Jesus... This has to be Pandemon, then. What the hell would they be doing with an army of birds? Surveillance?"

"I wouldn't put it past them. Seems like something they would do."

"Well, shit... we're going to need to let the lieutenant know about these little chromed pheasants, regardless of what they are used for." My shoulders slump. "Another thing we have to be on the lookout for."

"I agree... if that's what these things are used for. They could be harmless. We still don't know if it's even Pandemon." Desson rakes his fingers through his hair and moves to sit back down in his chair.

I shudder at the thought of Pandemon having several of these creatures flying across the city, gathering whatever intel they can get their claws on. We may need to have a team send out some drones and shoot these birds out of the sky. Drones... don't I have an NCPD drone tailing me? Where is that thing? My head swivels as I search for the drone I saw earlier. I know they don't have an unlimited power supply, so it's possible that it was routed back to base to charge up, but I would think if Amix put a tail on me, there wouldn't be a gap in *when* the drone is tailing me. I chew on my lip, searching the smog-choked night sky.

My eyes spot the drone, maybe ten or fifteen feet above us. A wash of relief mixed with concern fills me. Hologram letters spelling out NCPD shine bright above the unit. I know I have limited control over what I can tell the drone to do from my holo grid, but... an extra pair of eyes getting us into this building might not be a bad idea.

We clunk onto the pavement on top of an above-ground parking pad. The cruiser whirs down. As I navigate my holo grid, I come to a familiar name. I think I'm on his good side now, so hopefully, he won't mind helping out. I grimace, staring at the time. It is late, though.

"What do you say I call for more backup?" I ask.

"More backup?" Desson says, with concern in his voice. "Who are you thinking?"

"I think Agent Coleson might be happy to pilot that drone for us." I nod toward the sky.

Desson licks his lips and shifts his gaze up. "That's fine with me. I won't complain about having an actual human watch our back. Even if it's through a drone."

I nod in agreement. Now, just got to see if he's up for it or if he's even awake. I tap on the call button and wait as a ringing chime sounds. A few seconds later, I raise my brows in shock because the call is answered. At first, I think my holo grid is glitching because no one is on my display. Coleson's face suddenly whips up into the frame. He looks bleary-eyed with hair sticking out on one side and a confused expression on his face.

"Huh? Harkones? Do you know what time it is? Wait, are you still out? Jesus, do you ever go home?"

"Yeah, yeah... I'll be heading home right after we check one more thing out tonight. Wanted to know if you would like to be our eyes in the sky? Scan a couple of networks, maybe?"

"Wow, Mr. Hotshot is asking for my help again. Isn't your debt to me already sky-high?" Coleson asks while trying to pat down his hair, with no success.

"I know, I know. Isn't this your job, though?" I smile. "You're also getting paid by the lovely taxpayers of Nox City."

"True, but... you are calling me after hours," he says while tapping one of his wrists.

"Hey, look on the bright side. This will be fun!"

Coleson sucks in air through his teeth. "I don't know... I mean it is pretty late, and you already owe me, so..." He shrugs and purses his lips.

"What do you owe him?" Desson interjects.

"Hey, who is that there with you? Is that Desson? What's up, man? What the heck are you doing here with the Scorpion King?"

Desson's brows narrow. "Scorpion King?" He chuckles. "Oh right, your run in with Pandemon."

"Are you able to help out?" I ask. "We have a drone already in position right above us."

Coleson rubs his hands together while biting his lip as if he were in deep consideration. After a pause, he lets out a snort. "Yes, of course. Just give me a few minutes to get me set up here. Also, send me the drone number."

I navigate around my holo grid, looking for my active connections. Locating the drone ID, I read it off to him.

"Ginchy, I'll let you know when I'm in." Coleson's face flickers out.

I nod while reaching down toward my belt and grab my mask. Pulling it up toward my face, I meet eyes with Desson and pause. "Iron lungs... I can see the benefits."

Desson twists his palms out and shrugs. "All the filtration I need. Automatic too. My body isn't getting any younger but... these implants sure do help."

I bet the bucket of pills he takes every day *help*, too.

"Ready to see what these bastards are up to?"

"As if my life depends on it," Desson says.

I strap my mask over my face, and a second later, the filtration unit kicks to life. One more thing before I go home. It's just going to be a little scouting trip, that's it.

24

Infiltrate

"You guys are fucked. Mega fucked," Coleson's voice blares in my earpiece. "This place has security out of the wazoo. It's like a full-on spaghetti diagram around the entire building. What kind of grody place do you guys have me looking at here?"

I stare up at the ten-story warehouse with a deep frown. The exterior of the building is plain gray concrete. Small rectangular windows are placed throughout the different levels. Scanning the top floor, large windows stretch around the perimeter of the building. This must be the "office" floor that overlooks the city.

"You look into those windows on the top floor?" I whisper while resting my hand on the grip of my Z4.

"Of course I did. Do you think I'm new to surveillance? The windows are reflective. I'm already concealing all NCPD markings on the drone." Coleson laughs. "Did I look into the windows? Really?"

A couple of streets over from the warehouse, I lean my other hand on an alley wall and search the building for signs of the security network Coleson is describing. I try to act as inconspicuous as I can, but it's hard to do with an exoskeleton strapped to my body.

Luckily, my jacket covers most of it, with just the ends of my hands and legs gleaming from the suit. I glance toward my right wrist and check the power level of the skeleton. Twenty-three percent. Already? It feels like we just put these things on. I haven't needed to use it yet besides jumping down that stairwell.

Hopefully, I should be good for at least half an hour before the power drains out on me. Power... Electricity... Heat... My eyes harden as I stare back up toward the top floor of the warehouse.

"Infrared," I spit out. "You try that yet?"

"Infrared?" Coleson says in a sharp voice. He smacks his lips. "Infrared, hmm. I have to come in from a different angle. Don't want to raise any suspicious eyes."

I crack a smile and shake my head. "Not new to this, huh?"

"Oh, piss off!" Coleson says.

"With so much security, there must be something important in there." Desson's voice sounds over our three-way communication channel. "I'm not seeing movement from my angle. All the exterior doors appear to be closed."

My gaze shifts down to ground level. I scan for any open access points in the warehouse. The exterior wall is lined with wide warehouse doors a few feet off the ground. I shudder at the thought of this building being a Pandemon logistics hub where they conduct who knows what inside. Something seems off, though. Pandemon has a reputation for being organized, but to this extent? This building looks to be a commercial center for an actual corporate entity.

"I'm not getting much on thermals," Coleson announces on the channel. "It's all muffled from the glass, but... it all looks clear from my angle. No moving heat signatures."

"We know at least one person is inside the building. How many cameras did you say you saw again?" I ask while tugging at my exo suit chest strap.

"Sensors are picking up a boatload on the ground level and more trailing up the building."

"Are you able to get into the network?" Desson asks. "See what the cameras are picking up?"

"It's possible, but it would take time. Plus, I usually only go down that route with an authorization letter tied to a specific case." Coleson sighs. "And it sounds like what we're doing is just working off a hunch, right?"

I grimace while staring at the building. Everything is pointing to this warehouse: the dealer's instructions, the goon on the roof, and the chrome bird in the air. Oblivion is in there. For my wallet's sake, it has to be.

I'm sure we can go through the proper chain of approvals to give Coleson the go-ahead to breach the network, but it could take a couple of days to get the thumbs up. If it comes to it, this might be a time to act and ask for forgiveness later.

"How much time are we talking?" I whisper.

"Could be an hour or maybe five, I don't know, without probing the network. Their security barriers could be made out of hay that I can simply blow over with a puff of air. Or... they could be fortified to the balls. Steel balls which would take a considerable amount of time to crack."

"We have to get inside," Desson says. "Coleson, go ahead and see if you can tap in. If anyone gives you shit about it, tell them they can speak with me."

"Okay, if you say so. Give me a sec, and I'll see what I can find."

I'm not going to complain about Desson using his superiority. If things go south, at least I have someone to back me up. Studying the building, my lips tighten. Security all around the perimeter. Our exoskeletons are losing power. It's not looking like we'll learn anything else tonight. Maybe coming back at this with a fresh pair of somewhat rested eyes will be good. I need to sleep anyway. I close my eyes, thinking of resting my head against the soft pillow on my bed, Raena sleeping beside me. I can almost fall asleep now just thinking about it.

"Hey!" Coleson yells. "One of those metal-looking birds just flew out that box thing on the roof. It zipped off somewhere westbound."

An idea sparks in my mind. My eyes snap open, and a smirk forms on my face. The birds. The door that leads into the building. Can it be that simple? Would whoever is in this building think to lock a door that's a hundred feet up in the air? How would we get up there without raising too much suspicion? The cruiser screams NCPD and is bulky. I purse my lips and shake my head.

"Coleson, what's the max payload on our drones?" I ask while staring toward the sky, my heart rate quickening.

"A few hundred pounds, why?" Coleson responds.

"Harkones, you can't be thinking—" Desson snorts. "Are you insane?"

"Oh, hell yeah!" Coleson says, laughing.

"Come on," I say. "It's basically the same as jumping down a stairwell."

Desson scoffs. "No, no, it's not."

"I guess you can stay on the ground and keep watch. It might be a good idea anyway, to monitor for movement on the street if we do get in."

"Oh no, I'll be joining. I need to see what is hiding behind these walls," Desson says.

"Coleson, did you see any cameras up on the roof?" I ask.

"I was able to pick up on one. Let me scan it again and see if I can tell which direction it's pointing."

My feet clack against the ground while moving away from the building. I purse my lips, thinking of the best way to get on the roof. Shooting straight up from the ground from where I am would be too close to the warehouse. I need to come in from a different angle and from a spot where security sensors won't pick me up.

"Desson, meet me two blocks east in a back alley off Huxelo Street. It should be far enough away from the warehouse and a good distance from any foot traffic. We don't need the boss hearing about this from a good Samaritan calling about a couple of lunatics flying through the air."

"Alright. Meet you in five."

"Good news!" Coleson exclaims. "Only one camera is on the roof."

"Okay... so does that mean you have bad news too?" I ask.

"I have more good news. It is a 360-degree camera, so it's pointed in all directions right above the doorway."

My brows furrow. "That sounds like bad news. Are you sure you're okay, Coleson? Are you still sleeping?"

Coleson snorts. "Yeah, I'm fine. The good news is that I can shoot off a targeted static blast from the drone. Should make the camera look like it's glitching out, but..." He takes in a sharp breath. "Whoever, if anyone is watching the camera feed might take notice of anything lasting more than a few seconds."

I nod while approaching a dimly lit alleyway. "So, you're saying we're only going to have a couple of seconds to land on the roof, sprint to the door, possibly deal with the birds, and hopefully just stroll inside?"

"Yep! Sounds about right," Coleson says.

"Jesus Harkones," Desson interjects. "I mean, I'm with you, but this is just getting crazier by the second."

I let out a sigh. "Welcome to my world."

Now, at a good distance from the warehouse, I'm in the middle of an alleyway between two buildings that are a little more than a hand stretch apart from each other. Water runoff from earlier today mixes with ripped-open bags of garbage that fester and give off rancid smells of decay. I take in my surroundings and hear skittering from rats, bugs, or both. Neon lights from the main street bounce and streak down the dark hall, giving some illumination. I glance toward the hazy, brightly lit sky. It looks as if I am trapped in some sort of dark well, staring up toward salvation. I smack my lips and let out a puff of air. There should be just enough room for the drone to fit in.

A chime rings out from my wrist. I bring the display and notice I have a new message. My brows furrow, reading a preview of the message's contents. *COMPLAINT FILED.* I shake my head, clicking into the message.

On behalf of Damian Rhyner, Deputy Enzo Gerson has filed a complaint against you, Detective Sol Harkones. Please be advised that this is your first warning. Further complaints will result in—

I stop reading and swipe the message away, letting out a low growl.

"Gerson," I spit out.

What bullshit is this? Did that Rhyner asshole really file a complaint against me? Or is it just Gerson being a prick and trying to get back at me? Why can't I catch a break today?

I take a moment and close my eyes. My chest rises and falls as I take controlled breaths through my nose, slowly releasing my tension.

"Listen, we're just going to get in and get out." I say, anger still trailing into my words. "That's all we're going to do. See if any indication of Pandemon or Oblivion is coming out of the warehouse, and then we'll be out. No mess and no noise. Just recon."

"Let's hope it's just that," Desson's voice sounds from behind me. I turn on my heels and nod. A deep pinkish light shines on half of his features, highlighting the deep scar running down his face. He appears to be calm and ready.

"Coleson, you can fire off another round of that static, right? When we're ready to make a quick exit?" I ask.

"That shouldn't be a problem. I'm here, by the way."

A heartbeat later, a quiet hum sounds above me. The drone descends into the alleyway, with the resonating hum getting louder. The propeller blades send a gust of wind toward the ground. I stare up at the machine while holding one hand in front of my face, unsuccessfully trying to block some of the wind. My jacket and hair whip from the torrent of air being thrown down. Cans, dust, and other debris stir from their eternal resting place.

"You couldn't have chosen a narrower alley, could you?" Coleson's voice sounds muffled by the air.

"Just playing it safe," I say while glancing at Desson.

"After you," Desson says, gesturing one palm toward the drone above us.

I reach toward one of its landing feet. I would be worried about holding on to the drone and letting go, but my exo hands can grip it with minimal effort. My hands wrap around one of the protruding feet at an awkward angle. Desson moves to do the same, bringing us almost face-to-face under the whirling blades.

"You realize you're working with genius here, right?" Coleson's voice is barely audible under the resonant thrum of the drone. "I have to account for the equilibrium of you heavy fuckers when flying this thing up."

"We're ready. Let's go!" I yell.

Without another word from Coleson, we lurch toward the sky. The buildings blur and then quickly disappear as we increase speed, shooting up like a rocket. The force of acceleration pushes down on our upward ascent, slightly straining my shoulders. Clenching my jaw, I stare at the shrinking city, hoping no one is looking up.

We jerk as the drone shifts in direction, making our bodies sway while we dangle in the open air. I spot the rooftop directly below us. The drone suddenly stops ascending further. For a split second, I'm weightless.

"Get ready!" Coleson shouts.

We start hurtling to the ground. A rush of adrenaline courses through me. A slight grin forms across my mouth. My stomach drops while the wind whips at me from all angles. The rooftop rushes up to meet us.

"Activating the static blast!" Coleson yells. "Drop in three... two... one!"

Panic shoots down my spine before letting go. I unclasp my hands. It feels like gravity is nonexistent until my feet slam into the rooftop. My instincts kick in, and I drop into a roll. I bounce back on my feet and stride toward the door. Desson is right next to me, only a second behind. I hold my breath, scanning for trouble, but everything looks clear. I can see the cage now in closer detail. Small red and green lights shine above each square hole. Not seeing any movement, my eyes flick toward the door. I spot the camera unit behind a dark, translucent dome.

A pang of worry flows through me, seeing the camera. I trust Coleson will come through.

The door is only a few strides away. I search for any means to open it. It looks like a typical lever handle. Our feet skitter to a stop before the door. Desson and I quickly glance at each other and nod before I reach my hand to the handle. I suck in a sharp breath of air before my hand takes hold. Pushing it down, my hand immediately comes to a stop. My eyes widen. Blood rushes into my ears. Come on, it can't be locked.

I spit out a curse, still holding onto the handle. Chewing on my lip, I move my hand up. The handle lifts without resistance and makes a clicking sound. The air-tight seal pops as the door opens an inch. I pull on the heavy metal door and stare down into darkness. Blinking, I make out small yellow LEDs lighting each step of a stairwell. I quickly scan for any signs of additional cameras, but it all looks clear.

Taking a step into the doorway, I look back toward Desson. "We're in."

25

Camera

The rooftop door closes with a hollow clunk, making the city's hum go silent. I wince at the sound, hopeful that our mad dash to the door and entering the building didn't trigger any alarms. My feet take hesitant steps down the stairwell, expecting a siren to sound at any moment. I grip my Z4 with one tight fist and hold it close against my chest.

"Coleson, you read? We're in and moving forward," I say in a whisper.

Our feet clank with each step on the concrete staircase. Glancing ahead, the stairs lead down to another door just a few steps further. It's quiet in the stairwell. My nerves are on edge, trying to hear any movement. I lick my lips and taste salt from the sweat above my lip. Our exo suits make soft whirring noises with every little movement.

"Ginchy, it worked!" Coleson's voice spits out, making me wince. I run my hands alongside the smooth stone walls of the stairwell, balancing myself. "Yeah, I read you loud and clear. Nothing to report outside either."

"What about street level?" Desson asks, following me.

How does he always look and sound so calm? We were just dropped onto a building by a drone and sprinted our asses off. It seems like he didn't even break a sweat. Maybe there is something to all those pills he's taking.

"Nope, looks the same as before. No movement. Hmm..." Coleson pauses.

I step onto the floor landing and peer around a corner that leads to more descending steps. Approaching the door, I reach out and feel the surface. It's smooth and cold to the touch. To the left of the door, a face plate reads "Floor 4." I lean one ear closer and squint my eyes, trying to focus.

"What is it, Coleson?" Desson asks.

"Oh, nothing. I thought I saw something new pickup on my network scanner, but it looks the same. I'll keep circling the building for now."

I close my eyes and place my ear on the door, trying to listen. The door feels like ice against the blood rushing in my ears. My eyes shut while I take a deep breath and exhale, calming myself. It's silent. I don't hear anything beyond the door. A mix of relief and concern flows through me. I know there is at least one person in this warehouse. If it's Pandemon, there must be more. There has to be if this is a supply hub.

"I don't hear anything," I whisper, looking back toward Desson.

He scratches at his beard and gives a slight nod.

"Coleson, I'm about to open the door and head in. Keep watch and let us know if anything changes."

"On it!"

Backing myself from the door, I stare at it and swallow. There better be answers here.

Sweat trickles down my back. A constant thump hammers against my chest from my pounding heart. I reach for the door handle that looks identical to the one outside. My fingers curl around the lever. Inching up my hand, I pull until a soft click sounds out. A second later, air hisses out. I grind my teeth at the sound and lightly push the door outwards. Holding one palm up in Desson's direction, I move my head to peer around the door.

Steeling myself, I expect someone to swing a hammer the moment I look inside. Breathing heavily, I peer into the room and shake my head in disbelief. It seems like an ordinary office. It's dark, the only illumination from the city beyond the windows. Inert lights run along the ceiling. Desks and chairs litter the floor as far as I can see. It looks organized, clean even. I don't see a living thing, and there is no movement. I push the door wide enough for my body to fit through and sidestep into the office. Not taking my eyes off the floor, I motion for Desson to follow.

Desson moves out from the stairwell into the room, the only sound coming from his suit and the hum of filtration units pushing air into the space. He gently pushes the door closed behind us. I unclasp my mask, attach it to my belt, and sniff at the air. It smells clean, with no traces of anything.

"No one is home. It's dead," I whisper.

"We know somebody is here. Where they are is the question," Desson says.

I scan the room again. The floor has giant windows that stretch around the entire level. One side overlooks the flashing city while the other offers views of the swamp. A row of large offices with glass separating the space runs alongside the wall facing the city. Glancing to the right, the gleaming doors of an elevator rest closed to the side of us.

This does not feel like Pandemon. This looks like an everyday corporate office tied to a warehouse. Did we just break into the wrong building? None of this explains the birds, though.

I turn back toward the office and shake my head. This doesn't make sense. If this was Pandemon, I should be seeing goons, drugs, illegal tech, or some sort of sign of gang activity, but I see none of that. What even is this warehouse? What are they holding up in this place, and where the hell did that one guy go? My gaze halts on the wall directly ahead of us. A beam of flickering light streams from a room with a slightly cracked open door.

I look back at Desson and nod my head in the direction of the door. He nods, understanding my intention. Check the room out and see if anything helps show what is going on in this warehouse—anything that gives me answers.

My feet start moving toward the door. I grip my Z4 even tighter. My eyes trace the room, scanning for any more signs of cameras. With Coleson spotting so many outside, I think they would have some interior cameras, too, but I don't see anything. I suddenly halt, hearing small traces of something... something laughing. One of my palms shoots up and points to where I think the source of the noise is: the room with the flickering light. Unease chews at my stomach. I begin walking again and swivel my eyes around the office, trying to make sense of what goes on here.

The desks are unadorned, with nothing sitting on top. There are no mementos of life outside these glass walls. I lean toward one of the desks, peer into a small black bin, and see scraps of trash.

It's filled with plastic wrappers and what looks to be a half-eaten sandwich.

Finally something points to people being on this floor. It must be recent, too, from what it looks like. There is not a speck of mold on the sandwich at all. My stomach grumbles. For a split second, I picture myself pulling the sandwich out and taking a bite. I shake the thought out of my head as the laughing continues, which now has a malicious tone. Tendrils of worry coil around my chest.

Now close enough to peer into the room, I glance back and see Desson scanning the office. Our eyes meet. He offers a small nod while clutching his hand cannon. I turn back and peer through the small gap. Flashes of light come off from what looks to be a holo display. I squint, straining to make out the scene with no success. Holding my breath, I approach the door and lean my ear in. Another cackle radiates from somewhere within the room. Slowly, I move one hand to the door and hesitate, hearing a chirping screech. My eyes widen, hearing another bellow of laughter. I place one palm on the smooth door, trying to minimize the sound of my exo suit. Cautiously pushing forward, the gap opens further, revealing the source of the sound.

In a black crescent-shaped chair, a man leans back with an Infinity rig strapped over half his face, wires trailing up toward the ceiling. His hands are wrapped around two control sticks. Another screech sounds out again. My eyes flick toward the holo display.

At first, I see the city from a high angle. The view suddenly plummets toward the swamp. It looks as if the display is zooming toward the mounds of trash, but it's not as smooth as a typical camera should be. As the view descends, white noise, like rushing wind, emits from a speaker somewhere in the room.

My eyes narrow. What am I looking at? It somewhat resembles footage from a drone, but it's too choppy, as if the drone had a damaged blade.

The ground rushes up. I start to make out the shape of people, a group of three in ragged clothes huddling together. A man with a long, wiry beard holds a hand up toward the source of this footage. A young girl is cowering behind the man while an older woman holds the girl close.

The man in the crescent chair displays a violent show of teeth before licking his lips. "Old grody fucker, get out of the way," he mutters. A piercing screech sounds, and the view darts toward the man's hand. I see what looks like a metal-pointed jaw snap toward the man and jerk back, pulling flesh from the man's hand. The view shifts so I can make out the shape of a wing. A chrome-plated wing.

I start to make connections. This guy is controlling one of the birds we saw earlier. This must be the man we saw on the roof. I glance at Desson, who is staring at the scene.

"Daddy, no!" the girl screams, echoing in the room.

My eyes flick back to the display, and I see the bird rush forward again, this time toward the man's face. Heat travels up my spine. This disgusting person is tormenting what looks to be a family—a family just trying to survive—a family like my own.

My fist clenches tighter around my Z4. I raise it, flicking the dial to the BLST setting. I grind my teeth while pointing the gun toward the man's head, ready to pull the trigger. A firm hand rests on my shoulder. I rip my eyes away and peer into Desson's gaze. He shakes his head while mouthing the words, "*Pandemon.*" His hand points to the chair. He shifts his finger and gestures to the right of the room to another holo display. Camera 53 shines in small red text on the top right of the screen.

It takes everything in me to swallow the anger bubbling in my throat. I lower my Z4, not taking my eyes off of the lowlife. Desson is right, though. If something were to happen to this fucker, the rest of Pandemon, wherever they are, will go on alert. This sadistic, smiling man proves that Pandemon is here. They are up to something in this building, and I will find out what.

The man laughs more as he flies the bird back and forth, toying with the father. Pleading screams sound through the room. I flick my eyes off the man and slowly inch toward the other display. Below the projection, an old-school keyboard rests on a white countertop. My gaze shifts from the arrow keys on the keyboard to the screen, which displays footage from the street outside the warehouse. Traffic looks light on this side of the city, with only a few cars passing by.

Desson steps beside me and tilts his head to the screen. He leans forward and clicks the right arrow key. The display flickers to *Camera 54,* showing the same street from before but from a different angle. Desson squints his eyes and clicks the keyboard again and again. The screen flashes to different angles and heights around the building.

Another scream echoes in the room. The thug lets out another cackle. I look back at the bird's view. The father is on his knees and covers one eye with a hand, blood trailing down his cheek.

A sick feeling ripples through me. Frustrated tears start to burn my eyes. My skin starts crawling more than before. Something starts lightly tapping on my arm. Turning back to Desson, I rub my eyes and wipe the moisture away. I look to where Desson is pointing. He managed to adjust the screen to display multiple cameras simultaneously. Ten live video feeds are displayed in a grid, showing cameras one through ten. The footage all looks to be from inside the warehouse. My eyes widen, focusing on camera four.

Desson selects camera four, which expands and takes up the entire display. One of the warehouse floors has rows of cargo containers double stacked on one side of the floor. A fleet of at least ten dark, gleaming vans sits to the right of the containers. The vans look similar to the Pandemon vehicle I was trapped in earlier today. Desson points to the right of the projection, where I see what looks to be a giant elevator shaft that is at least ten times wider than what you typically see in a building. I can only assume it's used to transport the cargo and other heavy items around the warehouse. Just to the right, on the adjacent wall, is another elevator of the standard size. It must be attached to the one we passed earlier.

Something orange, something bright, enters the view. My eyes dart to the moving illumination. Eyes belonging to an Ogre.

Oh god, not another one of these bastards.

Somehow, this abomination is even beefier than the Ogre I dealt with earlier. The brute clings to something that glitters and shines in a certain light. Not a hammer, but a large sword that looks as big as me. He is just walking up and down the rows of containers as if he were a security guard. The sword rests over his shoulder and brushes against the metal sides of the containers as he slowly walks along the row. He steps out of view behind another cargo container.

An Ogre stalking the floor of this warehouse is just another reason to confirm Pandemon operates out of here. If what the dealer said was true, Oblivion must be somewhere in this building.

With what I know now, it should be more than enough to report to Amix, but... I want more. I want to know with certainty this drug is coming from this warehouse. The more information I come up with, the larger the bonus will be... hopefully. Plus, I think Amix will be happy knowing we found a supply hub for the gang.

I rub a temple, thinking of Oblivion. With how clean and organized it looks here, it's possible that Oblivion is manufactured here, but I haven't seen anything to indicate that. How did they create something so intricate and powerful that it can be used as a stimulant? Something that works as a drug. A product that is becoming a thing to kill for.

No matter how, Pandemon is involved in all this, whether as the manufacturer, distributor, or both.

The man in the chair chuckles. The view shifts toward the sky. My stomach churns, making me feel as if I am going to be sick by not blowing this guy's brains out. I shake my head and glance toward Desson who is studying the screen. His eyes flick to me. I mouth the word "*Oblivion*" and point to the display. Desson nods and navigates back to the screen of camera views. He starts paging through screens, his eyes scanning left to right while I do the same. We pass more views of the different floors and various rooms filled with boxes, tech, and weapons. Now, this is what I was expecting to find.

We need to move and hurry up. There is no telling how long this goon will be in this chair. The second he lifts the rig off his head, he can cause us a world of trouble.

Desson continues paging through view after view. My breath catches, and I quickly stretch my fingers, indicating that Desson should stop. I point toward the block that indicates camera 34. The feed expands as Desson selects the screen.

My heart jumps to my throat, and my pulse starts racing. On top of the black plastic pallet are white boxes that look identical to the boxes in the van with the scorpion—the same box I found under Tito's Rhyner's bed. The pallet rests on the concrete floor in a dimly lit room and looks to be the only thing present.

This is it.

It has to be. I point to the screen, stare at Desson, and mouth, "*Where?*"

Desson navigates the display, searching for more information. He squints and looks left to right as a new screen appears. His eyes look back to me while holding three fingers up. He mouths, "*Floor three.*"

I nod and gesture back to the stairway we came through. I take a silent, deep breath of air and slowly head out the door. Glancing over my shoulder, Desson is quickly typing at the keyboard. He clicks one more button and nods, then moves to follow.

As we move to our last stop, the sound of anguished screams mixed with delight fades.

26

Elevator

Twelve percent. I double-check my wrist making sure my eyes aren't playing tricks on me. I only have twelve percent left in my exoskeleton's power supply. I hope it's enough. It has to be.

"We need to make this quick," I whisper, pointing toward the suit's power-level display. "Not too much juice left." Running into that Ogre would be bad news alone, but running into it with no power in our suits would be even worse.

Desson nods while pursing his lips, staring down at his power level. "I'm right there with you. Fourteen percent."

The narrow stairwell is more of the same, with concrete floors and walls. Our feet resonate and echo with a light clink from each step.

"What were you doing on the computer?" I ask, looking over my shoulder.

Desson licks his lips. "I set all the cameras to stop recording."

I stop and look back, confused. "How did you manage to do that? You actually disabled the security in here?"

I don't know where Desson picked up that skill or how he did it so fast. From what I know, security systems are not that intuitive. It looked like he knew exactly what he was doing and where to go.

"Just something I picked up over the years," Desson says.

"You did what?" Coleson's voice bellows in my ear. "How?"

"Come on, it wasn't like a light switch. I had to navigate the menus and enter a few commands, but we shouldn't worry about being seen in their recordings. The live feed, on the other hand, is still operational."

I nod. "Well, it's something at least."

It will be interesting to see how long it takes for whoever is running this hub to find out there is no playback. No footage to scan back through. No trace of our presence here at all, no echoes pointing back toward the NCPD. With all the info we're gathering, Amix should be happy. She may even be able to work with different teams, Strike, and whoever else to take down this hub before they even know their cameras were compromised. That should make a decent dent in Pandemon's operation.

The next floor's door is at the end of this flight of stairs. I take a deep breath while running my hands along the walls and clear my throat.

"Coleson, still no changes outside? We're in the clear?"

"Actually, a bunch of them are outside now dancing in a circle..."

"What?" I snap.

"No, of course not. I would have told you otherwise. Come on, Harkones, give me some credit."

"Alright. I was just checking." I place one hand on the door. "Desson, you know which direction to go when we step inside? We need to make this as fast as possible."

"Yep, that room with the pallet you saw is on the east wing, which shouldn't be too far.

"Alright, good. What about that Ogre? What floor was he on?"

"Floor two. Shouldn't be a problem."

"Okay…" I roll my shoulders and stretch my sore back. "In and out, then we head home."

Desson nods.

"I'll keep circling the building up here, all by my lonesome," Coleson says.

"We'll let you know when we're heading back to the roof, so be ready. It might get messy in here."

"I'll be ready."

I grab the handle and lift. The air-tight seal pops, and the door opens outwards. Clenching my jaw, I push. With just enough room for my head, I peer into the floor beyond. It's an open room with gray stone walls that run up at least thirty feet high. The ceiling has pipes and support beams that stretch across the level. Dimly lit LED lights dangle down. More rows of cargo containers, some double-stacked. Scanning the ground, I see what looks to be rails built into the floor between each row. I scan left to right, searching for any movement. Not seeing anything, I step inside.

Swiveling my gaze, I look to my immediate right, and see another set of rails that leads toward the giant elevator shaft. The platform must be on another floor below as a black gate is lowered, blocking anyone from accidentally falling down the pit. Looking left, three cargo movers are attached to the floor rails with two steel arms protruding outwards.

"Where to?" I say in a hushed whisper, looking back at Desson.

Desson points to the right wall and nods. "Should be in room 304."

My eyes dart in the direction he is pointing. More rails lead toward various rooms that run along the wall. Each room has wide doors that look like they slide open. These rooms must be used to store sensitive or important things compared to whatever else is stowed out here in the open on the ground floor of this warehouse. Would make sense not to stow a new drug out in the open. If it's so desirable and new, though, I think there would be more security guarding it.

I slowly start moving my legs, the activators in my suit whirring. I unholster my Z4 while nearing a row of cargo containers adjacent to the wall of storage rooms. I rest my back against the metal surface of a container and slowly peer around to see if I can spot room 304. I jerk my head back, seeing a bulky figure.

Desson looks at me, confused, lifting his palms in the air. He mouths the words, "*What?*"

"*Ogre,*" I mouth, over-emphasizing each syllable, making it as clear as possible.

Slowly, I glance toward the door and see the glint of something steel in its hands.

I growl and shake my head. Another one of these bastards, and it's not the same one we saw earlier. This one holds a giant ax with sharp blades on both sides topped with a spiked point. Death from three angles and not even including this brute's amplified strength. I frown, thinking of how I barely escaped the grips of the Ogre from earlier. I need to get in that room. I need to see if Oblivion is really in there. I need to play this smart and make sure I get out of here alive.

Ideas start bouncing in my brain on how to handle this metal thug. I wipe sweat off my brow and pinch the bridge of my nose. A firm hand rests on my shoulder. My eyes flick toward Desson, not comprehending his silent words. He mouths again, "*I'll handle it,*" while pulling his hand off and turning on his heels.

"Desson, wait," I whisper through clenched teeth. He rounds a corner, out of sight.

What the hell does he think he is doing? Splitting up is never a good idea, especially when dealing with one of these metal bastards. The two of us together should be able to handle him, but one one-on-one? I'm not a fan of those odds.

I glance back toward the Ogre. His unblinking eyes shine like a neon light in a dark alley.

A clanging sound like falling metal pots and pans resonates from somewhere distant within the floor. The Ogre instantly seizes his ax with both hands, gripping the shaft. He moves in the direction of the sound, leaving the door unattended.

"Desson... what the hell are you doing?" I whisper with furrowed brows.

"Go, get in there and find your answers," Desson whispers back through the comm channel.

I shake my head and move, not wasting another second. My heart starts thumping against my chest as I near room 304. A touchpad is anchored to the wall to the side of the closed doors. Standing directly in front of the room, the door does not automatically slide open. How am I supposed to get inside? Panic rushes through me. I need to act fast. The Ogre could come back at any moment. I wave my hand in front of the display and the screen comes to life, presenting a grid of numbers.

Fuck... a passcode. There are an infinite number of possibilities for what this code can be. There is no way I will be able to guess it, either. I am out of time. I don't want to cause any suspicion about us being here, but I don't have another choice.

I grip the center of the two doors, trying to wedge my fingers in as much as possible. I tense my face and heave, trying to pry the doors open with all my strength. The activator on my backside whirs as I fight the door's locking mechanism. I hear metal straining. The crack in the door jerks open, allowing my fingers to get a better grip. The veins on my arms and neck bulge. A sharp snap sounds out and the doors suddenly slide open, revealing the room beyond. Glancing at the power level of my suit, I let out a curse. Nine percent. This is going to be close.

Rapidly blinking, I let out a puff of air, feeling slightly dizzy. Panting, I step into the room and see the black pallet. It's the only thing in the room besides one light that hangs from the ceiling. My feet step closer to the white boxes stacked on the pallet. I reach for one of the boxes and grip it between my hands. My heart hammers, finally so close to ending this day. I lick my lips and grab the top of the plastic box, flinging it open.

I let out a sharp breath. More boxes. Small boxes containing white triangular chips, just like what I found in the Rhyner residence.

"Oblivion is here..." I whisper.

Something tugs at the back of my mind. Where does it come from? Who developed it? Who is manufacturing it? Who is providing it to Pandemon?

I scan the room, searching for answers with the little time I have left.

"You found it?" Coleson asks in an anxious tone. "Alright, get your ass outta there!"

My vision blurs. Neurons in my brain fire off, trying to make connections. The dealer's words echo in my mind: "Oblivion is the future." If this is just the beginning, there must be more. Someone is creating it, and I don't think the source is inside this building. I haven't seen anything that resembles a lab or manufacturing plant—just rows and rows of Pandemon supply. So, who is the supplier?

I shake my head, focusing on the box. I shut the lid and turn it around on each side, looking for anything that can help point to where this drug came from.

It's blank, just a plain white box. I quickly move and pull other boxes from the pallet, searching for anything that stands out.

If Pandemon didn't already know from the forced open door, they will certainly know now that someone was in this room. I push a stack of boxes that topple over. One box opens up, spilling Oblivion packages on the ground. I frantically search through them and find nothing.

Ringing footsteps quickly approach from outside the door. I pause, not moving, and strain to listen. It doesn't sound like the Ogre. I would hear heavy footsteps compared to the small clinking sound, but I can't be too sure. I hold my breath while unholstering my hand cannon and pointing it toward the door. An open hand pops into view, followed by a second.

"Harkones, it's me. It's Desson, don't shoot." His head pops into view as he walks into the room, staring down with wide eyes. "Come on! We need to leave!"

I shake my head in frustration, scanning the sides of more boxes. Who is the supplier? Why can't I find anything? There must be something here!

"Harkones, we have enough for a report. Come on, let's go."

"Hey, what's the holdup? You guys coming or what?" Coleson exclaims.

"Fuck..." I grunt through clenched teeth, while kicking down another stack of boxes. My eyes harden, staring at the contents.

"That's not Oblivion," I say in a low whisper.

"Let's go, Harkones, come on!" Desson says.

I bend down and grip a transparent plastic bottle in my hand. I hold it up and twist it around in the air. All my focus shifts toward reading the label wrapped around the bottle. Desson talks more, but I only hear muffled sounds.

"Senervamene," I whisper.

I read the label again and again. "This is... this is Sicarius's drug. Why is a box of Sicarius drugs in this pallet?"

My pulse quickens, and my eyes go wide. Connections form in my mind as if a veil has been lifted. Who else has the means to produce and manufacture a new wave of drugs? Sicarius Pharmaceuticals.

"Harkones!" Desson yells. "We have to go."

I take my eyes off the bottle and stare at Desson. "Sicarius... it's them." My eyes widen thinking back to earlier today. Damian

Rhyner, the chief of product for the company. Tito Rhyner, dead on the ground. A box of Oblivion under his bed. That's how he was able to secure a box of packaged chips. He must have got it from his father.

"My god," I mutter.

We have to get out of here. We have to let Amix know of everything we found. This goes beyond just street-level gangs and this is only the beginning. Produced and packaged by Sicarius while Pandemon funnels the shit into the streets.

Stepping toward the door, I raise my holo grid and snap a couple of pictures of the scattered boxes on the ground. A low rumbling noise sounds from outside the door. The floor vibrates. The hairs on the back of my neck stand up. That can't be the Ogre. It sounds like an elevator. A big one. Tendrils of dread unfurl in my stomach, making me feel like I'm about to be sick.

"Harkones! Desson!" Coleson shouts. His voice is choppy, as if there was static on the line cutting in and out. "I... out... calling... help... birds!"

A bleep tone sounds in my ear, signaling Coleson's connection dropped from the call.

Did he just say something about the birds? Did someone sound the alarms? I don't hear anything besides the deep rumbling sound. Whatever it is, we need to leave now.

Desson and I sprint out of the room toward the door leading to the stairwell. The deep whirring continues and clamors to a full stop. We round the corner with the doorway in sight. I turn my head left and stare at the elevator shaft. A buzzing chime sounds out, and a green light flashes to the right. The black gate rises. I can't make out anything, as if whatever is on the platform is shrouded behind a curtain of darkness. For a split second, I think I see the glint of something moving before I skid to a stop, almost running into Desson. His head is lowered, staring at the ground.

"Desson, come on! Open the door!" I yell while throwing my arms up. "What the hell are you doi—"

A low guttural roar erupts through the warehouse floor. Holding my breath, I slowly twist my head to where the noise emanates. Two small orange orbs spark to life on the elevator platform, illuminating an angular, feminine face. The figure steps forward onto the warehouse floor. Recognition floods through my body, and my pulse quickens.

Lucinda Rhyner. The wife of Damian Rhyner stands at the end of the platform with an amused grin. The same silky white dress clings to her lean frame, and the same golden necklace traces down her shimmering neck.

"Oh fuck..." I mutter.

I turn to Desson, who is shaking his head and breathing heavily. The floor trembles. Something large and inhuman steps off the platform. Its roar fills the room, echoing in my skull. Glowing red eyes sit above a large jaw of glistening, spiked teeth. Standing taller than an Ogre, dark metal covers its massive artificial body. Light bends and refracts off the beast. Sharp ridges run along its angular head that trail down to a long neck of glistening square scales. A tail whips in motion, smacking against the wall and creating a cloud of dust.

A paralyzing sensation consumes me as if molten lead replaced my blood and hardened, keeping me in place. I stare in wide-eyed fear at the metal beast I saw all those years ago. The same monster that tore apart a whole squad of officers. The four-legged beast resembles a wingless dragon pulled straight from old fantasy books. The only difference is that this is real and before me.

The ground vibrates again as it takes another step closer, its metal claws scraping against the concrete floor. It lowers its head next to Lucida and tilts its face, staring at me. A long, split tongue flicks out of its jaw and shrivels back into its mouth.

"I was wondering when I would be seeing you again," Lucinda says.

What am I still doing here? We need to call for backup! I spin toward Desson, who is turned in my direction. He is clutching onto something in one of his palms. Shoulders slumped, he licks his lips before his eyes flick to meet mine.

"I'm sorry, Harkones," he says.

My brows furrow while I shake my head. "What are you talking about? Let's go!"

Desson's hand snaps forward before I can react. A heartbeat later, an EWEB spreads around my being and constricts like a vacuum-sealed bag. My body goes stiff. Electricity ripples through me. It feels as if a hundred knives are simultaneously slicing through every inch of my skin. I tumble sideways, hitting the ground and biting my tongue. I try to scream at Desson, but only garbled words come out. My muscles spasm. Pain courses through me. Grinding my teeth, I peel open one eye, looking up at Desson as anger, confusion, and fear swirl through me.

"I need the money, Harkones," Desson says. He shakes his head with a reluctant sigh. "I'm not getting any younger."

I manage a rough growl. This can't be right. We were about to finish this! Why is this happening? I should be home right now.

Desson's gaze rises to Lucinda. "It is done. I did what you asked and brought him here. Now pay me what you owe."

Convulsing on the ground, I try to pinpoint where I went wrong. How did I end up here? I can't leave Raena and Zinny with nothing.

Desson steps forward toward the platform, out of my line of sight. I feel the ground shudder as the beast takes another step.

I close my eyes and try to think through the pain. What should I do? What can I do?

27

Actions

Blood coats my tongue. No matter how hard I strain, my body does not stop convulsing. My senses go in and out of focus. I twist and roll to my other side, putting Desson back in my field of vision. The four-legged beast looms at Lucinda's side, its brutal eyes studying Desson's approach. The electricity pouring into me hurts like hell, but I know it's not set to a lethal voltage. I need to get out of here but how can I with my arms pinned to my sides? My fingers can move, but I can't reach my weapons. Gritting my teeth, I curse under my breath.

Are Sicarius and Pandemon working together, or are they one and the same? Lucinda, a Pandemon member or maybe even leader, is married to an executive member of Sicarius. How far do her fingers reach into the company? How much of what Damian does is guided by Lucinda's hand? I need to get out of here.

"Did you not hear me? I did what you asked. Now I want my money!" Desson shouts.

Through one squinted eye, I see Lucinda tilt her head and trace her murderous eyes up and down Desson. "Oh, indeed you did, Detective, and you will be rewarded."

The sound of heavy footsteps emanates from behind a row of containers. Lucinda swivels her head in the direction of whatever is approaching. "There you are. We owe our friend a debt," she says while nodding in Desson's direction. "Do you mind helping him kneel to receive his reward?" The orange-glowing eyes of the Ogre come into view with his ax clutched between his hands. The Ogre nods, staring at Lucinda, and steps in Desson's direction.

The old detective takes a small step back and raises his hands. "Wait! What are you doing? We have a deal! I did as you asked, just like before."

Lucinda runs her tongue along her teeth. She smacks her lips and stares at Desson, shaking her head. The crimson curls of her hair bounce. "You did help, and I appreciate that, Detective. Without you, the authorities would have been involved earlier, but as you can see..." She flicks her eyes in my direction. "Things have taken a turn."

Desson takes a step back, reaching for his belt. The Ogre does not falter, and steps closer. Panic courses through Desson's eyes. An instant later, the crackle of electricity sounds. I squint at a bright blue light unfurling from the old man's grip. The coil straightens to a rod, electricity pulsing through each vertebra.

"What are you doing? Stop where you are!" Desson yells. He pulls out his Z4 and fires a blinding blast of blue energy. The Ogre bolts out of the way, the energy rippling through the air, and crashes into the side of a cargo container. Now, within striking distance, Desson takes another step back from the beast. He lunges with the hyper coil, the rod going slack as his hand whips back and forward. The mockery of a man moves with calculated precision, sidestepping the pulsing coil, and slashes his ax in a rounded arc, slicing clean through Desson's legs below the knee. The coil drops from his grip, and he crumples to the ground, letting out a deep howl of pain.

My breath catches. A horrible sinking sensation eats at my stomach.

Desson grunts and stretches his arm, reaching for the fallen coil. Before he can grab it, the Ogre kicks it and sends the grip skittering away. The detective shouts while raising his Z4, pointing at the looming thug. In a flash, the Ogre grips the detective's wrist and twists. The sudden snap of bone echoes across the floor. Desson howls again in pain. The modified man looks down with an expressionless stare and stomps on the Z4, smashing it into pieces.

Seeing Desson splayed on the ground, I feel powerless. There is nothing I can do. He gasps in agony while blood flows from his wounds. The Ogre walks back toward Lucinda and stands as stiff as a statue behind her. Lucinda takes a few delicate steps forward and stares down with a grim line across her mouth. Her lips curl upward as if she is amused.

"If only my idiot son didn't steal what was not his. If only my intellectually challenged husband didn't call the police. If only, if only." Lucinda's gaze darts in my direction. Her eyes go inert, no longer glowing. Grief spreads across her face. She starts sniffling. "If only, Detective," she says in a sad tone, mimicking when I first met her earlier today. Her face suddenly morphs into a venomous stare, her eyes blazing orange again. "If only you listened to my warning, we wouldn't be in this mess, but the world isn't built on ifs and onlys. It's built on actions."

The ground rumbles as the beast steps closer to Lucinda, its tongue flicking out.

"I act in the best interest of this business. For our stakeholders, our clients, our customers, our members. For a business to thrive, sacrifices must be made..." Lucinda stares down at Desson with pity in her eyes. "Some people may have died from our product. I'm not denying that, but that's what early adopters are for. We learned a great deal from version one of Oblivion. Less than four percent defective." She smirks and shakes her head. "Only a small fraction of the limitless potential of Oblivion!"

She steps to the side and glances at the beast. It takes another step forward, closer to Desson. A deep hum sounds as its chest starts expanding. The hum gradually becomes louder. A dim, deep red starts glowing from its underbelly.

"Why?" Desson coughs.

"You demand too much for someone who is no longer necessary."

The hum builds further like the rumbling of an approaching storm.

"Wait!" Desson shouts while holding out his hand. "I can still help! I can be of use! I have connections!"

A red beam of devastating energy bursts from the beast's mouth. Desson screams, but it's too late. The beam slams into the upper half of the fallen man, incinerating flesh to nothing in the blink of an eye, leaving a gaping hole in the floor. What's left of Desson's charred body drops to the ground with a thud.

"I have connections as well..." Lucinda sighs and flicks her eyes to me.

My mind reels as I stare at Desson's remaining husk. Bile threatens to escape my stomach. The beast lets out another inhuman roar, echoing throughout the floor. It flicks out its tongue and extends its neck to Lucinda.

"Fuck..." I grunt again while struggling to move, electricity still coursing through me. I need to focus. I need to think. What can I do?

"Detective Harkones..." Lucinda says. She stands over me and leans down. "I'll grant you that you are resilient. You have proven to be resourceful, and I am intrigued by how unrelenting you are. Not only do you not listen to my warning, but you take it a step further and kill my people, my associates."

Her golden necklace spills out from the low cut of her dress and dangles in the air above me. A wingless dragon pendant gleams on her necklace. It's been in front of me this entire time, hidden behind a layer of fabric.

"I was fond of Bronk and Sabine, but maybe I found someone to take their place."

What the hell is this woman talking about? It's hard to think. I grit my teeth and try to concentrate while stretching my fingers. I can get out of here if I can just get to my weapons.

She gracefully steps back. "Your friend may no longer be needed, but I can always use someone who is capable. Let's see if you remain resilient."

The ground trembles. I hear a low hum.

I grind my teeth and squeeze my eyes closed. I'm stuck in this web, electricity running through me, and I can't reach for my weapons. Wait a second... The web! Maybe I can break free if I can deactivate or disable the emitter.

Bending my knees as much as the web allows, I slam my feet down while thrusting my hips up. My exoskeleton amplifies my motion, making me hop a foot off the ground. My lower back slams back against the ground, with my head following an instant later. I let out a grunt of pain, still trapped in the web.

The hum of the beast nears its peak, its chest no longer expanding.

I scream, bending my knees again and hammering down my feet. My body bounces off the ground and lands with a loud crunch. The web unfurls, and the electricity coursing through me ceases to be. Panting, I open my eyes and stare into the red-glowing jaws of the metal beast. Bending to a sitting position, I raise my hands, and fling them down in balled fists. My hands smack the ground, lifting me just enough to pull my feet under and leave me standing. I dash out of the way, and a second later, a torrent of energy unleashes from the beast, disintegrating the ground where I was a heartbeat ago. I keep running despite my lungs protesting every breath.

"Ah, you have a gift," Lucinda yells.

The ground trembles again. Another building hum sounds behind me. I rip out my Z4 and flick the dial to the PUSH setting. I twist on my heels, pointing the barrel toward the beast, and slam the trigger back. A blast emits from the barrel straight toward the creature's body, pushing it back a couple of feet. The humming stops, and the dim red glow of its chest dies down. A guttural shriek unleashes from the beast that resonates through the warehouse floor.

"Oh shit..." I mutter under my breath.

The dragon charges toward me, the ground trembling like an earthquake. I snap a hand toward my belt, pull out an EWEB, and hurl it with an overhand throw.

I hold my breath and pray to whichever god will listen. The EWEB starts to unfurl, electricity coursing through it, creating an ethereal blue glow while it sings through the air. The beast abruptly stops and explodes in motion, whipping its tail out. On impact, the central emitter of the EWEB shatters. A latticework of artificial threads falls helplessly to the ground, no longer constricting or coursing with energy.

A shiver runs down my spine. I twist on my heels and lunge for the door, grabbing for the handle. I fling it up, pull the door, and bolt into the stairwell while holding my breath. With my cheeks puffed out, I sprint up the first flight of stairs and glance back. The head of the beast smashes through the doorway, unleashing a bone-shattering roar that bounces around the narrow stairwell. The head retreats, with its claws raking through the doorway, tearing at the floor. This is my chance to get out. Move, Sol, move now!

I run. My legs burn with every step. The exoskeleton is the only thing allowing me to keep my momentum. Strapping my mask over my face, I take deep, panting breaths. I glance at my suit's power level. Four percent battery remaining. I need to move. My heart pounds. Rushing up the stairs, I pull up my holo grid and tap the display. I almost stumble while clicking the call button under Coleson's name. The dial tone rings. He doesn't pick up. I can only hope the drone is still outside, waiting for us to make a quick escape.

The rooftop door comes into view and is only one flight ahead. Loud pops like gunfire sound from outside the door. Goddamn, what the hell now? I hope Coleson is alright and pray the drone is still in the air. I approach the door, throw up the handle, and push. It swings open.

The sky is on fire.

Explosions sound in all directions. Chrome birds spiral all around me. I twist my head toward the source of the gunfire and grin. My relief is quickly replaced with a grim line of worry. The NCPD drone is zipping through the air and firing off rounds of bullets at the attacking Pandemon birds. There's too many for Coleson to keep up. My stomach drops as the birds speed through the air and slowly peck at the drone. Coleson maneuvers the drone in random directions, firing off more rounds and taking down a couple of birds. A flock of five comes from behind the drone while closing their wings, becoming something that resembles large silver bullets.

"Coleson!" I scream while running onto the roof. I'm too late. The birds careen through the drone, ripping it into shreds of metal.

My heart twists as I see what's left of my salvation plummet toward the city. The ground of the rooftop shakes, sending a tremor through my bones. Rhythmic thumping sounds from below the edge of the building. A heartbeat later, a claw rises into view and slams down onto the roof. The head of the dragon lifts in the air, its other claw pounding the ground, spewing dust from beneath. It shrieks an inhuman roar into the night sky while chrome birds zip through the air.

A shudder runs through my body. I'm at a loss. There is no escape. I have failed, and I am not going home.

Blinking rapidly, I try to hold back the wave of regret threatening to consume me. A tear runs down my cheek. I will not be able to read that book to Zinny. I will not be able to pay for her schooling, her future. I will not be able to kiss or embrace Raena again. I failed them. I am a burnout, after all.

I stare at the rooftop surface and sigh while my body aches. I might not stand any chance against this creature, but I'm still breathing. I will not just lean my neck out. The least I can do is try.

My gaze lifts toward the charging dragon, each of its steps creating a shockwave of vibration. I dig my heel into the ground and unholster my hyper coil. The familiar weight rests in my hand as it thrums to life, crackling with energy. I clutch my Z4 in my other hand and point it straight ahead, thumbing the dial to the BLST setting. Holding my ground, I aim and squeeze the trigger. A low hum emits from the weapon's core that quickly builds to a sharp snap like a lightning bolt and jolts my arm back. A blue blast of energy unleashes from the barrel with a hissing screech toward the rushing beast.

The creature jumps at an impossible height over the blast of energy and crashes back to the rooftop, one of its legs smashing through the concrete into the building below. It rips its leg out of the hole and careens forward. Plumes of dust disperse with each step.

Words get caught in my dry throat. I pace right. My foot taps against something, making me take a downward glance. My brows rise, looking down ten stories to the ground. I focus on a large mound of jumbled trash, spilling into the street from the Swamp. A knot forms in my stomach. I dart my head from the ground to the beast. I holster my Z4 and grit my teeth while quickly stepping back. Adrenaline courses through my veins, staring at the sprawling city beyond.

"Oh fuck me..."

Charging forward, I gather momentum while clutching my hyper coil. I push off the ledge, launching into the open air. I feel weightless until gravity starts pulling me down. Howling wind whips at my face. I glance behind my shoulder and see the beast leap off the building after me. Snapping my head forward, the pile of decay rushes up to meet me. A throaty scream escapes my lips. My feet strike the mound with a wet crunch. A jolt of pain lances through my feet and up my spine. Rolling uncontrollably, I bounce off sharp and mushy objects.

I skid to a stop on hard pavement. A brown sludge coats half of my mask. Everything hurts. I struggle to breathe. My vision is blurry and spinning while I stare toward the sky. Something glints in the air and I squint to make sense of it. My senses return, and my eyes go wide. The dragon quickly takes up my entire field of vision like a falling comet. Something blue tugs at my peripheral vision. I twist my head right and realize I'm still clenching my hyper coil.

The ground explodes as the dragon lands on all fours directly above me. Through a plume of dust and debris, I make out the intricate detail of the metalwork on each panel of the beast's underbelly. It takes a few steps back, a deep hum emanating from its throat. A tongue unfurls from its opening jaws that display rows of sharp, deadly teeth.

Jumping to my feet, I whip the hyper coil at one of its legs. I grit my teeth while the coil wraps around the thick chrome plating. I thumb the dial to constrict, holding on to the grip with a tight fist. Metal begins to screech. Abruptly, I'm lifted off my feet and thrown in the air by the dragon flinging its body back. I lose the grip of my hyper coil and fall back toward the ground. Smacking the pavement, the air I have left escapes my lungs. I snap open my eyes and notice a crack on my mask that is spread from side to side.

The hum of the dragon fills my ears, reaching a crescendo. I cough while dragging myself to my feet, holding my Z4 in one hand. The dragon's glowing red mouth looms ahead. Its chest expanded, ready to set loose a wave of destruction. With my heart hammering against my chest, I take short gasps of air, my body trembling.

In one quick motion, the dragon's head rears back, and a violent red beam of energy streaks toward me. I thumb the dial of the hand cannon and fire while screaming. The dragon's beam courses forward, coating everything in its path in a wash of deep crimson light. My beam of blue energy rushes to meet it, the two forces colliding with an earth-shattering crack, sending a residual wave of energy in all directions. I fall back, my head smacking the pavement. A deafening ring sounds in my ears. Tremors run through the ground beneath me, shooting vibrations through my bones.

The beast is moving closer, and all I can do is cough and groan.

I crack open one eye, holding my hand cannon in front of me. The BLST setting is at thirty percent, slowly charging. Deep humming sounds again and I see the red glow within the plume of dust about ten feet away. Still on the ground, I narrow my eyes at the holographic display on the side of the Z4. Thirty-five percent. Shit!

I stare at the dial on the gun's grip and switch the setting. The metal dragon releases another beam of destruction that twists the dust around it in a vortex as it speeds forward. Baring my teeth, I aim at the ground and pull the trigger back.

A rush of transparent blue energy domes around me. The red beam smacks against the protective layer and fires back in the direction it came. The dragon whips its head to avoid the blow, a heartbeat too late. The beam slashes into its extended neck, tearing metal apart. The beast shrieks like a dying animal in pain. It stumbles, trying to reorient itself. Half its neck falls forward, hanging by a thread of metal. It cries out while its head swings like a pendulum. I climb to my feet and sprint toward the beast with what energy I have left, my lungs and legs on fire. Clenching my jaw, I grab hold of its metal skull and heave. The head chomps down between my grip. I wrench it free from its body with a hard snap. I stare down at the dragon's head between my palms and breathe slowly. Its red eyes dim to black.

A chime sounds and my skeleton powers down. The head suddenly becomes as heavy as a boulder, causing me to drop it to the ground. The clamps around my suit rapidly pop off. I collapse to the pavement with nothing to support me. I take a deep breath and exhale.

Straining, I rise to my feet and stumble toward my hyper coil, grabbing it off the ground. I let out a long sigh and lift my gaze. On top of the warehouse roof and below the chrome birds still zipping through the air, I make out the shape of two figures. The glint of something large and sharp stands out. I squint my eyes and shake my head, focusing on the orange glow of four eyes peering down. Turning on my heels, I limp away toward the city.

I swear I hear clapping.

28

Decisions

Fatigue washes over me. Every movement feels like I'm pushing against a wall. With my remaining energy, I hobble toward my cruiser, glancing over my shoulder. I expect to hear sirens heading in my direction but it's silent besides the buzz of the city. I round a corner of an alleyway and lean against a wall, resting my head on the cool surface. I take deep breaths, trying to settle my burning lungs.

Where is my backup? I look around and above me and chew my lip. Wouldn't Coleson call this in? He should have requested assistance the moment he saw the birds fly out of that cage. Unease eats at my already throbbing stomach. I wince, raising my holo grid. The screen doesn't materialize. Repeatedly twisting my wrist, I try to bring up the display, but nothing shows. I roll my eyes, seeing that it's cracked on one side of the device. Most likely from my fall or being thrown around like a rag doll. I must have smacked it against the ground.

"Shit..." I mutter. This is my only means of calling in for backup, at least on me right now. I can use the cruiser's internal computer to call this in, but... I need to get there. I suck in another deep breath of air through my nose and close my eyes.

My mind drifts.

Oblivion, Pandemon, Sicarius... It's all connected. The warm, gentle smile of an old man enters my mind. "Desson..." I snarl. "Where the hell did that come from? Desson offering to help with Mirk and getting a location out of him. Desson pointing out the bird in the sky. He's been prodding me forward this entire time and I didn't see it. Why would he turn his back on me? On the force? All for what? For money? For modifications?

Rubbing my forehead, I think of all I've done today. All I've done for more credits. All this shit I go through just to get by and provide a better future for Zinny.

I push off the wall with a grunt and hobble forward. Looking behind, I expect to see the Ogre stomping toward me, but he doesn't appear. At least not yet.

Emerging out of an alleyway, I stare up toward the upper levels of a parking tower. More fucking stairs. I need to hurry up and get this over with. Reluctantly, I make my way to the exterior stairwell and wince with each step. My fingers grip the handrail, using it as leverage to pull myself forward while the muscles in my legs start to twitch.

"Almost there..." I whisper through raspy breaths.

Relief floods me upon finally reaching the seventh floor. I peer across the level and see the cruiser sitting as if Desson and I just left it. I approach the vehicle, looking for any signs of tampering. Circling the cruiser, I don't see anything that is outwardly glaring. Satisfied, I step to the door that automatically opens upward. I stagger inside and slump into a chair. The cruiser door closes with a soft hiss, and filtered air flows into the cabin. I unclasp my mask and rest it on my lap between my palms. I trace one finger along the crack on the outer layer before strapping it to my belt.

I clear my throat while holding my ribs. "Call Lieutenant Amix."

"Calling Lieutenant Lacet Amix," internal speakers ring out in a modulated voice.

Gritting my teeth, I rub my stiff legs, waiting for the call to be answered.

A chime sounds, and a second later, Amix's face materializes in the center of my cabin from her shoulders up. She is still wearing her blue NCPD formal wear, her hair tightly pulled back, and her blue eyes still pierce into me under furrowed brows. It looks like she hasn't stepped foot out of her office. Does she have a life outside the station walls?

"Lieutenant, did you hear from Coleson?" I ask. "We found a Pandemon supply hub. Desson was working with Pand—"

"Harkones..." she says. "You are to leave this case alone, go home, and return to the station in the morning."

I sink into my chair. My jaw hangs open, and I rapidly blink.

"Head home?" I exclaim. "Sicarius is working with Pandemon on a new drug! They could be after me right now!" I shake my head in disbelief. "Ma'am, I'm telling you: we need a team out here *pronto*. We can take out this whole operation before they have time to mobilize and scatter."

"Harkones, you don't understand. There's been a development."

"What do you mean? What happened?"

245

An uneasy silence hangs between us. My head, my ribs, my whole body aches. This isn't how it's supposed to go. We should be acting right now. I rub my temples.

"Lieutenant, why are we not acting on this? Sicarius Pharmaceuticals is manufacturing a drug that is killing people. Pandemon is working with them. How can you ask me to stand down?"

Amix gives me a cold stare. "Do you know where NCPD funding comes from? How you get paid?"

I lean back and stare in disbelief. "What?" I exclaim. "Funding? From taxes on the city, sales, properties... but what does this have to do with anything?"

"Not just taxes," Amix says while propping her elbows on her desk. "Donations, Harkones. Donations to the NCPD come from multiple parties within and out of Nox City. Donors who want to help keep the streets of this city safe. Donors who want to keep businesses operational." She rests her chin on her knuckles and raises her brow. "Do you want to guess who one of our largest donors is?"

A chill runs up my spine. I move one hand through the back of my hair and lower my gaze. I didn't dredge in the muck of Pandemon for nothing. I didn't just almost die for nothing!

"I don't give a fuck about donors. Oblivion is here!" I snap, darting my eyes back to Amix. "I have proof, and we have an opportunity to take Pandemon down a notch. Right here, right now!"

"You should care, Harkones. Donors are the reason we are able to give bonuses..." Amix sighs. "I have been given explicit instructions to offer you a bonus for today's work and for you to move on to other assignm—"

"Hush money?" I blurt. "You expect me just to move on? Desson is dead! More people are going to die from this new drug, and Sicarius is involved!"

My veins start to bulge while gripping tighter to my armrest. Mirk's words from earlier echo in my brain, "*corrupt cop.*" Hush money. Donors. Corporations paying to keep the streets safe... It's bullshit!

I glare at Amix's eyes. "You told me about the spike in brain trauma cases. Well, here's your goddamn answer!"

"Eighty thousand credits will be deposited in your account this morning."

Eighty thousand credits? My brain whirls, and my heart skips a beat. That's at least five months of consistent level five or six cases being closed out. This will more than get me out of the hole with Zinny's school and pay off QuikCred. I pinch the bridge of my nose and close my eyes.

"Who? Just tell me, who gave you instructions?" I mutter, already knowing the answer.

Amix's demeanor shifts to be slightly more relaxed as her shoulders drop. She knows she has my attention. "That does not matter. What matters is that you go home and file your reports in the morning."

I scoff and roll my eyes. File my reports and call it an ordinary day? Is she really telling me to sweep this all under the rug and just move on? People are dying, and this is just the beginning! I chew on my lip. Eighty thousand credits, though... It's what I wanted. Closing out the Benji Davis case and opening a new one dealing with Oblivion that would lead to a huge payday. The hole in my pocket would be stitched up, at least for a little while. I won't have to be *reminded* again about my loan balance. Zinny won't be ripped out of school. She can continue learning in a safe environment. She can have a future above these grime-filled streets.

"Why did you have me check out the brain trauma cases in the first place if they all point back to Oblivion?"

Amix leans forward in her chair as a flat line forms across her mouth. "I did not know that Oblivion was relevant to these cases. As I said, there has been a new development. New information has come to light." She lowers her head, her eyes still peering into me. "With Desson gone, can I count on you?"

Sicarius, Pandemon, or both, somebody above Amix is pulling strings. Strings that dangle with credits held out in front of me. Credits that I need. I lick my dry lips while I think about what I should do. If I accept this money, I'll be under someone else's thumb, but... how would that be different from how things already are?

Zinny's face comes to the forefront of my mind, a huge smile spread from ear to ear. She is all I can think about. It's her. Making sure she is safe. Trying my hardest to keep her smiling and happy. Desperate for her to have a life more fulfilling than mine. All I do is do for her and Raena. Both of them deserve more. More than what I can offer right now. I'm trying, and that's all I can do.

If I go down this path, it needs to be worth it.

"Harkones, I need an answer. Can I count on you?"

I take a deep breath and slowly exhale, dragging the moment out.

"Double it," I blurt out. "Then you can count on me."

She stays silent for what feels like hours. "That's not how this works."

"It's how it works for me." My eyes flick back toward Amix. "Terminate the call." Amix's surprised face flickers out.

"Call terminated," the cruiser announces.

"Take me home," I say in a tired voice. I slump back into my chair and stare out the roof window. The propulsion units kick to life, and a gentle tremor runs through the cruiser. It lightly jerks and begins its ascent. A deep feeling of worry forms in the pit of my stomach. Am I making the right decision? Did I just put myself in an early grave?

My fingers drum the sides of my skull, the exact spot where Oblivion is used. A drug manufactured by one of the largest corporations in the city. Pandemon goons pushing it out to the masses. People accepting it, wanting a new way to escape.

So many questions still remain unanswered. What are the repercussions of continual use? Is it addictive? Why are the chips frying people's brains and putting them in catatonic states? Can I let more people die knowing the cause?

Benji Davis's expressionless face surfaces in my mind. It's where all this shit started. Chasing Mirk under the suspicion of him installing defective modies. A low-level-three case morphing into a beast trying to incinerate me to ash.

"Mirk..." I say in a low grumble. What the hell am I going to do with him now? He irks the shit out of me, but Benji somehow got a hold of Oblivion. Most likely, a defective chip. I chew on my lip, thinking. What will Amix have me do once it's known that his implanted modies were legit?

"New voice message from Lieutenant Lacet Amix," the cabin speakers announce.

I take a deep breath and roll my neck. "Play it."

"Your terms will be met." She pauses before continuing. "I expect to see you here in the morning. A new case waits in your inbox."

A chill runs down my spine. 160,000 credits. More money than I've ever seen at one time. Dirty money. Is this the right path? Being bought out? How else am I supposed to win and get ahead? How am I supposed to ensure the safety of my family? What is the alternative?

I stare out the window. Lights blur and meld together. My eyes come into focus as the cruiser plows through a stack of steam, tinged blue from the city below. Out of the fog, the shape of a familiar tower pulls my eyes. Elexor. The home of a Pandemon leader hiding in plain sight. I'm reminded of the hushed conversation I couldn't make out when I visited the Rhyner residence through the view caster. It wouldn't hurt to see what the commotion was.

Using hand controls on the grip of my chair, I navigate menus on my display until I pull up Tito's case file. Clicking into the file, I scan a list of recordings from the numerous view casters placed throughout the home. I won't have a three-dimensional view of the home, but that shouldn't matter. I double-click on the first recording file. A view of the Rhyner residence materializes on the display. It looks like the same spot where I arrived when I visited earlier. I arrow through the files until I find myself in the living room, where I think the source of the noise came from. Fast forwarding a few minutes, Lucinda Rhyner pops into view. I jerk my hand and pause the video. Her eyes stare daggers toward Damian, sitting on the couch with his head between his legs. I resume the playback at normal speed and squint, trying to hear their exchange.

Lucinda licks her lips and stands above Damian. "You imbecile..." she says in a hushed, angry voice. "How could you let this happen? How could you be so—" Her eyes snap straight toward me. My heart jumps until I remember this is just a recording. She is only staring at the view caster device. Her eyes flick toward the home entrance and then back to Damian.

"Act. Your. Part." Lucinda says with malice dripping from her voice. Damian moves to stand and wipes at his eyes. His gaze shifts toward Lucinda. Tendrils of fear swirl behind his eyes. His demeanor then suddenly shifts into a confident and defiant stance. A moment later, my avatar steps into view.

I close the recording and exit out of the menus. Shutting my eyes, I slump back on the headrest. It was right in front of me this entire time. I didn't think to check Lucinda's record when I took the assignment. How did I just gloss over that?

Sinking further into my chair, a flood of thoughts pours into my brain. Raena, Zinny, Amix, Lucinda, the fucking dragon. My body aches, and I stink like shit. It feels like my brain is on fire.

I close my eyes and breathe. In and out.

The outline of a door comes into view through my unfocused vision. I shake my head and blink, staring at it. This is my apartment door. I glance at the number above the frame to confirm. It's my door. I was so lost in thought that my tired body just went through the motions. I don't even know what time it is. All I know is that it's late. Very late. Some would even call it morning. I take a deep breath and move my hand toward the panel on the side of the door. Waving my hand, the scanner flickers to life. A second later, the panel displays, "Welcome home, Sol." The door pops open. I head inside the small breezeway and silently close the door behind me.

I open the second door, attempting to be quiet and not wake Raena or Zinny. It clicks as the latch recedes. Pushing it forward, I see our worn couch directly ahead. Something is stirring on the cushions. I squint, trying to make it out while inching my hands to my sides.

A blanket folds over, and Zinny's head pops out from under. "Daddy?"

Zinny kicks the blanket off of her and climbs over Raena to the ground. She yells, "Daddy! You're home!" Her five-year-old legs rush in my direction. She grabs hold of my pant leg, squeezing with all her strength.

Unclasping my mask, I look down at her upturned face, her green eyes sparkling with joy. Her messy hair sticks out in wild curls while she bounces on the balls of her feet.

"Hey baby girl, I'm sorry I'm late." I bend down and wrap my arms around her, squeezing back. "I hope you can forgive me," I say, with a warm smile.

Raena stumbles out of the blankets onto her feet and stretches her back. She walks in our direction and leans against the kitchen counter, crossing her arms. A wry grin forms, curling her lips. She stares at the two of us, shaking her head.

"It's okay, Daddy. I didn't take a sneak peek!" Zinny says while bobbing her eyes between me and Raena. "Mommy said to wait, so that's what I did!"

"Did she now?" I say in an amused tone, looking toward Raena with an apologetic expression. "We'll read that book tonight after school, okay? I double pinky promise." I hold my pinky fingers together. Zinny wraps hers around mine.

I am home.

The weight of today slides off my shoulders, falling into oblivion.

THANK YOU

Thank you so much for reading Falling Into Oblivion, my debut novel! It means the world that you took time out of your day, week, or month to read this story. I can't wait to explore more of Nox City and for you to see what comes next for Sol. To stay up to date with me and my work, be sure to follow me on social media or subscribe to my YouTube channel, BiblioTheory. You can also sign up for my mailing list at www.bibliotheory.com.

Before you go, please leave a review on Amazon, Goodreads, or wherever you review books. Even though many hands have helped create this book, being a self-published author is a one-man operation, and your review will go a long way in helping get this story out to more readers.

Aaron
July 2024

Acknowledgements

I always thought writing a book was a pipe dream. Something that would always be an unattainable idea in the back of my mind.

In the past couple of years, I have come across and met with several self-published authors who have helped change my mind. All I had to do was try.

If you have been following my BookTube journey, you will know that I started interviewing indie authors around December 2023. I didn't realize it then, but I was slowly chipping away at the invisible walls holding me back from attempting to write my own story.

Now, we're here, and my story is in your hands. I have a whole new perspective on what writing a book actually means. So much goes into writing a book. Way more than I ever thought. One of the most important things I learned and took away from this journey was the importance of building a support system during the writing process of this story. Without the help of others, I can only imagine this story would be a lot different.

First, I wanted to thank my wife for her support and ability to always listen to my incessant rambling about this story. I can't tell you the amount of times I talked her ear off about the idea, the writing process, the plot, and so many other things about this book. I love you and can't thank you enough. Also, I wanted to apologize now because the wheels are turning in my head, and you know what that means.

To my parents for their support and excitement in reading my story. I only hope this story isn't too vulgar.

To my friends who encourage and support me with whatever path I go down.

To my beta readers who didn't hold anything back in their critique and impressions of this story. You guys inspire me and continually encourage me to continue pushing forward. Thank you to Jon, E.J., Josh, Scott, and Boe.

To my editor, Sarah, for being incredibly attentive and detailed on what works and doesn't work within my story. You have helped create the best version of my book. Also, I have to thank Dom for diving into this book with a fine-tooth comb, searching for any tiny details or typos that fell through the cracks.

Lastly, thank you, dear reader, for taking the time to read this story. You took a chance on a brand-new author, and I can't thank you enough. I can only hope to provide more great stories for your enjoyment.

About the Author

Aaron M. Payne has long been a fan of all things science fiction and fantasy, especially books! He loves reading so much that he created a YouTube channel called BiblioTheory to discuss his passion and talk books.

He currently lives in Lakeland, Florida, with his wife, daughter, and two fluffy dogs.

@bibliotheory | www.bibliotheory.com | BiblioTheory on YouTube

Made in the USA
Columbia, SC
01 November 2024

63ab61ad-d159-447f-9535-537b0aed4ef3R01